The Masters
of Silence

BY THE SAME AUTHOR

The Gardens of the Apocalypse + *The Seven Rings of Rhea* (translated by Brian Stableford)

The Masters
of Silence
and
They Came
From the Dark

by
Richard Bessière

translated by
Michael Shreve

A Black Coat Press Book

ISBN 978-1-61227-297-9. First Printing. July 2014. Published by Black Coat Press, an imprint of Hollywood Comics.com, LLC, P.O. Box 17270, Encino, CA 91416. All rights reserved. Except for review purposes, no part of this book may be reproduced or transmitted in any form or by any means, electronic or mechanical, including photocopying, recording, or by any information storage and retrieval system, without permission in writing from the publisher. The stories and characters depicted in this novel are entirely fictional. Printed in the United States of America.

TABLE OF CONTENTS

Introduction 7
THE MASTERS OF SILENCE.....................................21
THEY CAME FROM THE DARK............................147

Introduction
Richard Bessière: Maestro of Delirium

"From the moment the needle is pushed into my skin I stay lying on my back, not moving, observing the gradual fading of my physical sensations. On the fundamental level of 'consciousness' there suddenly opens up, opens wide, the arcana of my memories and details layered upon details with terrifying sharpness and precision. So, I close my eyes and the film of recent events starts rolling, like being inside a giant kaleidoscope, with the strange sensation of melting away in a whirlwind of colors and movements.

"This is how it began. With a giant statue in the middle of a big rectangle of light..."

"This is how it began."

Henri Richard Bessière's *Les Maîtres du Silence* (translated here as *The Masters of Silence*) opens like a psychedelic artifact of the 1970s, post-Albert Hofmann, post-Aldous Huxley, post-Timothy Leary, perhaps even post-Carlos Castaneda.

The first character we meet even talks like Leary or one of his acolytes, as caring an acid-trip guide as any neophyte could have hoped for in the '60s or early '70s ("Gently... Make a little effort... We're on the way...we're on the way... Free yourself... Free yourself..."). You'll forgive me if I'm immediately projecting onto this character the face of Bruce Dern,

Peter Fonda's "guide" in Roger Corman's 1967 movie *The Trip*, or my personal first-time trip guide from my college days.

But it isn't an artifact of the 1970s. It is a brainchild of the 1960s.

As a child of the '60s myself—born in 1955, my personal arc as a reader/viewer/listener indelibly shaped by the psychedelic era before I'd ever dropped acid or sampled my first foul-tasting mushroom or peyote button—I can't help but respond to the cues, even when I'm not looking for them.

But when they're there, they're *there*, as is the case with *The Masters of Silence*.

It's a real trip, as we used to say.

Each generation has its cues, particularly in science fiction. By the time the casual contemporary 21st century reader arrives at Bessière's reference to "*the second level*" ("Make a little effort, Valerie, we're entering the second level"), one might be forgiven for responding to nonexistent video game cues and references, which simply aren't there, save perhaps as prescient teasers. And yes, they arguably are present: "Nothing remains but the screen, empty, covered with a spectral glow..." But 21st century owes much of its gaming terminology to old hippies and vintage television, after all.

So yes, let's go the second level, shall we?

But first things first... let's address the first level, if you will.

Black Coat Press has already covered Bessière's biography in the foreword to their first reprint volume, translated by Brian Stableford, which offered *Les Sept Anneaux de* Rhéa (translated as *The Seven Rings of*

Rhea, 1962) and *Les Jardins de l'Apocalypse* (translated as *The Gardens of the Apocalypse*, 1963) between two covers in English.[1]

As noted therein, Henri Richard Bessière was born August 20, 1923, to a show-business family. The war changed the family fortunes, redirecting young Henri Richard into music as an agent and composer—but this was before family friend Francis Richard became "one of the collaborators of Armand de Caro, founder of the then-fledgling popular publisher Fleuve Noir."

With the launch of Fleuve Noir's *Anticipation* imprint—"science fiction" wasn't a marketable genre moniker in France as yet—editor Francis Richard tapped Henri, who just happened to have "an unpublished manuscript that told of a great, epic journey of exploration through the Solar System."

Thus, Henri's career as a novelist was launched in 1951 with the trilogy *Les Conquérants de l'Universe* (*The Conquerors of the Universe*), *À l'Assaut du Ciel* (*To Assault the Sky*) and *Retour du Météore* (*Return of the Meteor*), published under the name F. Richard-Bessière.

As noted in the previous Black Coat Press volume, "As Bessière became increasingly successful, the 'F.' was dropped in 1965 in favor of the hyphenated 'Richard-Bessière,' and then the hyphen was, in turn, dropped in 1980, in favor of the more accurate 'Richard Bessière.' "

Got that? Good.

The Seven Rings of Rhea and *The Gardens of the Apocalypse* followed Bessière's darker late '50s sf novels with their own original fusion of horror and sf. As

---

[1] ISBN 978-1-935558-68-2.

noted in the previous Black Coat volume, *The Seven Rings of Rhea* was "...the most reprinted of the author's novels in France," and thus arguably an ideal entry point for English readers new to the author, embracing "all his favorite themes, from his concerns about the nature of evil and the fundamental duality of the universe to the exploration of a nightmarish world which seems truly alive." What better way to begin?

Darker still was *The Gardens of the Apocalypse,* "a reworked and far more elaborate version of his earlier novel, *Légion Alpha* (1961), present[ing] another grim view of a post-cataclysmic Earth where survivors—or, more accurately, their descendants—try to reconquer their planet." The monstrous beings inhabiting Bessière's titular metaphoric "gardens" were terrible indeed: "demonic visions, worthy of Hieronymus Bosch, of new forms of life, transgressing the fundamental barriers between plants and animal."

Which brings us to the *second level,* and the book now in hand, which opens with *The Masters of Silence*.

As I say, this novel is a real trip. Yes, LSD and "LSD-based substances" most certainly play a role here, but that's only the beginning.

Instead of a Dr. Albert Hofman—the first man to synthesize, and indeed the father of, LSD: lysergic acid diethyl amide—Al Hubbard, the so-called Johnny Appleseed of LSD, or Dr. Timothy Leary and Dr. Richard Alpert, the founders of the Harvard Psilocybin Project, who were fired from Harvard University and became advocates of psychedelic drug use: "turn on, tune in, drop out", Bessière casts one Professor Gregory Watson in the role of experimental guru, a scientist whose "psychophysiological work" has proven so "very disturbing" to the authorities. With his pulp sf roots proudly showing, Bessière incorporates mad science into his twist on Hofmann, Hubbard, Alpert, and Leary's realm, complete with white-garbed nurses and scientists, a devastated laboratory, and an inexplicable device that triggers a catastrophe. The flavor of *Weird Tales* and *Fantastic* and 1940s and 1950s horror movies lingers, but this was—and remains—pretty heady stuff for its day.

Our nominal hero, Robert Milland, is the utterly American everyman tripper, so to speak, interrogated upon his re-entry by a quartet of scientists intent upon investigating whatever-the-hell-it-is Watson was up to. "Was" is the operative word: again, I can't help but respond to the cues and clues.

Was Watson a fictional construct Bessière fabricated from the real-life case history of rocket pioneer and occultist Jack Parsons, killed in a mysterious lab explosion in June of 1952? Absolutely; even a demolished lab is central to Bessière's setup herein. Just as Parsons was survived by his occultist/artist wife Marjorie Cameron—who Parsons considered his "Elemental Woman"—Bessière works the surviving Mrs. Watson, Valerie, into his often cruel narrative schemes, "floating between fiction and reality," albeit along a more traditional heroine lines—her rescue, after all, initially drives the narrative.

Despite assurances at the outset that "the marital relations of the Watsons [was] completely normal, despite their age difference," Bessière adapted the rumored/reported experimentation real-world husband-and-wife Parsons and Cameron indulged in with ritual magick—to sire a *homunculi*, according to some accounts!—into Watson having "experimented on

11

Valerie."

Whatever Watson and his wife were up to, it involved something other than normal marital relations, though penetration was involved: "a degree of psychological penetration beyond everything we can imagine in the field of depth psychology," it is said at one point. What were they up to?

"Watson went too far with Valerie," we're told, "and in probing the chambers of her soul he triggered a shock."

Poor Valerie.

Ah, I'll leave the rest for you discover in the novel itself.

But it began, I believe, when Bessière first heard or read about Jack Parsons and his death in a laboratory explosion.

What was he up to?

"This is how it began."

Furthermore, Watson was both mirroring and anticipating the work of real-world scientist Dr. John C. Lilly, and playwright Paddy Chayefsky's fictional spin on Lilly's career for his 1978 screenplay and novel *Altered States*, filmed by Ken Russell in 1980. By the end of the 1960s, Lilly's use of psychedelics, sensory-depravation chambers, and cartography of interior head space became even more influential—and infamous—than his famed dolphin intelligence research.

Thus, Watson seems to me a fusion of Parsons, Leary, and Lilly in more ways than I care to enumerate here. I'd argue the case further, but I'll not hold you hostage with details about either Parsons or Lilly—look them up, and draw your own conclusions.

Whatever the inspiration, Bessière makes the

mysterious Watson's mind-bending explorations of inner space the catalyst for all that follows. Bessière's scientists, Professor Greysson, pharmacologist Aymes, and psychiatrists Lindsay and Dayton, are struggling to keep up, and our hero Milland—a former GM worker and practicing progressive electrical engineer, who requires a cigarette before making a decision—is out of his depth, to say the least, cast "body and soul into a weird and totally incomprehensible adventure."

As you soon shall be, too.

First published in 1965, *The Masters of Silence* was also another of Bessière's invasion-from-space novels— or, to be more precise, from a space, somewhere "out there," a lineage that began with his *S.O.S. Terre (S.O.S. Earth)* in 1955. As noted earlier, when Bessière began to incorporate more horrific strains into his science fiction novels, starting with *Escale chez les Vivants (Stop-Over Among the Living*, 1960) and *Légion Alpha* (1961), he fashioned a more distinctively persona and originall blend, ahead of its times.

Bessière's sf/horror novels remain unique and unusual today. *The Masters of Silence* resonates with echoes of H.P. Lovecraft, without being Lovecraftian in the usual sense. It is as Jungian as it is Lovecraftian, but neither term is accurate, given the often intense sweep and action of the novel. The echoes are clear, particularly those of Lovecraft's short story *"From Beyond"* (written in 1920, first published in 1934)—forbidding experiments, an electronic device that resonates with and links to some unseen realm, that link becoming a doorway, a lab in ruins—and more: women as portals to other dimensions, other beings, the Other. Listen, the echoes are herein: "Do you mean the new dimension that you refused to accept?"

Still, those are only echoes.

Bessière was very much of his time.

So, yes, *The Masters of Silence* emerged from the promise and dread of '60s psychedelia. The novel positively revels in hallucinogenic visions, attuned to the counterculture that was sweeping through France, Europe, and North America, though Bessière spoke the language of pulp sf.

But wait, there's more.

There are ripples and memories of everything, from Jack London, H.P. Lovecraft, Robert E. Howard, Carl Jung, and M.C. Escher to flashes and foreshadows of Carlos Castaneda, Stephen King, and movies like William Castle/Edmund Morris's *Project X* (1968)[2], the afore-mentioned *Altered States* (1980), Joseph Ruben/Chuck Russell/David Loughery's *Dreamscape* (1984), Wes Craven's *A Nightmare on Elm Street* (1984) and its franchise(s), Tarsem Singh/Mark Protosevich's *The Cell* (2000), Christopher Nolan's *Inception* (2010), which really incorporated the video game 'levels' as an aspect of dream logic: new dreaming paradigms and platforms for the first full generation of video-gamers-as-audience, and TV series from *The Outer Limits* (1963-65) to *Fringe* (2008-2013), among others. They all owe a vast debt to literary sf precursors like Bessière's *The Masters of Silence*, truth to tell.

I'll be blunt: whenever two characters lie down to link their dreams to rescue one another and/or their

---

[2] based on L.P. Davies' *The Artificial Man*, 1965, and *Psychogeist*, 1966; Davies was an immediate contemporary of Bessière writing at-times-parallel-themed sf and espionage novels.

world, Bessière's template is being applied. The linking of dreamers and dreams, and what that process might unleash, is now everywhere in the pop culture. It is a sub genre onto itself, and Bessière was among its founding pioneers in sf/horror.

Despite the slow-rising pop *tsunami* that followed—the plethora of dreams, dreamers, and adventures, all imitations—knowing or unknowing—of Bessière's novel, this still is a marvelous, breathless reading experience.

In its ripest delirium *Masters of Silence* remains trippy stuff:

"Stone toads move around the base, crawling up the purple tunic, in and out of the folds and pleats, slipping up the bronze skirt to reach the blouse and disappear in the architectural twists and turns of a proudly aggressive chest.

"A strange sun shines its red rays over this source of nightmares through the serrated gaps of a distant wall.

"Everything is coming to life, little by little. The circus clown with starry eyes wriggles inside his bottle. His head rolls from right to left and left to right like a giraffe sticking out of a glass barrel at the end of a long reptilian neck.

"A repulsive monkey hangs from the pendulum of a gigantic clock that slices through the air like a steel blade. As it swings through the air its long hands snatch up the naked children encircling the weird machine whose face is nothing but a round, gaping mouth of blackness. And one by one the children disappear inside the clock, swallowed up by the insatiable mouth, swept away by the flow of time.

"The statue has lost its face and I feel as if I am the

one refusing to see it. The face is that of an angel or a demon whose distant smile is that of Helen of Troy ordering the high towers of Ilium to burn..."

"This is how it began."

Then comes the accident, another death—the unfortunate Miss Foyle—and the terrible "dark goo... [oozing] out of every fleshy shred," and the overwhelming stench of it...

"It must have got into the room... but I wonder how..."

Oh.

I've already revealed too much.

The less you know going in, the better.

Rest assured Bessière will take you places you've not been before, though others have been there since.

"In a matter of seconds I realize that I am cut off from the exterior world. The walls collapse on me and I am swallowed up. I feel like I am plunging headlong into a world of darkness... Beyond time and space... Beyond the boundaries of my body...

"I dive inside..."

Shhhhhhh.

You hear that?

No?

How could you hear what can't be heard?

Hearing and not hearing are central to this novel, as the title promises.

Here, let me whisper this to you:

Being of sound mind and body won't serve his purposes or your needs—though sound itself will, as you shall see, and hear, and not hear, for yourself.

Again, I've already said too much.

"Watch out, Milland, you're entering the second

16

level!"

The "*second level*" of this volume is Bessière's *Cette Lueur Qui Venait des Ténèbres* (*That Light Which Came from the Dark*, translated here as *They Came from the Dark*, 1967), another child of the 1960s.

The novel is presented as the private journal of yet another electrical-engineer-as-hero, William Ashby by name, scribed during what was in America "The Summer of Love," circa 1967—but Ashby is far from Height Ashbury. He's in Swinging London, where things were really happening at the time, and London was the heart of the British youth countercultural scenes: music, fashion, art, theater, the Beatles, *Blow-Up*, etc.

Alas, Ashby is just out of prison; he's missed all that. Anything that was swinging about London passed him by. Instead, just out of the gates, he finds himself being watched by an odd man in a bowler hat, "a funny little chap, only five feet tall looking grimy in his yellowish gray skin," who is soon offering Ashby a one-time-only job opportunity. This "once in a lifetime opportunity" requires Ashby to make a nighttime appearance at the *Time Club*, "a smoky cellar. A real dive, all shadows and lights, stinking of alcohol and tobacco. Garbled mutterings… Shifting forms… and soft music coming out of some hidden stereo speakers…"

This nightclub-where-no-nightclub-should-be in Putney Commons is a doorway, too, like many things in the Bessière universe. In short order, Ashby finds himself with a blonde, golden-eyed woman who happens to be an artist and seems to know Ashby, and has evidence to prove it. Enter Captain Zachariah, with the promised offer for a year of "honest, steady work" on a ship about to leave harbor.

But this is the *Time Club*, and nothing is what it seems.

British folklore, fantasy, and science fiction is peppered with such London portals, from H.G. Wells to Neil Gaiman—his *Neverwhere*, the BBC serial and the novel, comes to mind—and J.K. Rowling, as is French genre fiction. Jean Ray, a.k.a. Raymundus Joannes de Kremer, alone put the conceit to ample use time and time again.

Bessière primes pumps that seem familiar enough at first, only to derail expectations—Ashby's and our own—again and again. Just as *The Masters of Silence* eventually unveils uncanny entities with deadly designs on our reality, *They Came from the Dark* harbors its own malignant parasites with an appetite for shanghaiing whatever or whomever they need—and I do mean "appetite."

Burke and Hare were pikers by compare, and besides, they were just two men, not an entire species of body snatchers...

There I go again.

As with *The Masters of Silence*, I've already said too much.

The less you know going in, the better.

Accept the somewhat foul-tasting scotch Captain Zachariah has just purchased for you from the bar, and drink up. You'll need that drink, trust me.

Every sip is a yes.

Are you ready?

Yes?

Good.

Maybe you think you're ready...

"Yes, maybe... But things keep unfolding clearly

and precisely… So, let's see where the story goes…"
    This is how it begins.

Stephen R. Bissette
Mountains of Madness, VT
April 2014

LES MAITRES DU SILENCE

RICHARD BESSIÈRE

FLEUVE NOIR

ANTICIPATION

THE MASTERS OF SILENCE

PART ONE

CHAPTER I

From the moment the needle is pushed into my skin I stay lying on my back, not moving, observing the gradual fading of my physical sensations. On the fundamental level of "consciousness" there suddenly opens up, opens wide, the arcana of my memories and details layered upon details with terrifying sharpness and precision. So, I close my eyes and the film of recent events starts rolling, like being inside a giant kaleidoscope, with the strange sensation of melting away in a whirlwind of colors and movements.

This is how it began. With a giant statue in the middle of a big rectangle of light.

Stone toads move around the base, crawling up the purple tunic, in and out of the folds and pleats, slipping up the bronze skirt to reach the blouse and disappear in the architectural twists and turns of a proudly aggressive chest.

A strange sun shines its red rays over this source of nightmares through the serrated gaps of a distant wall.

Everything is coming to life, little by little. The circus clown with starry eyes wriggles inside his bottle. His head rolls from right to left and left to right like a giraffe sticking out of a glass barrel at the end of a long reptilian neck.

A repulsive monkey hangs from the pendulum of a gigantic clock that slices through the air like a steel blade. As it swings through the air its long hands snatch up the naked children encircling the weird machine whose face is nothing but a round, gaping mouth of blackness. And one by one the children disappear inside the clock, swallowed up by the insatiable mouth, swept away by the flow of time.

The statue has lost its face and I feel as if I am the one refusing to see it. The face is that of an angel or a demon whose distant smile is that of Helen of Troy ordering the high towers of Ilium to burn.

"Make a little effort, Valerie, we're entering the second level."

"I'm afraid… Oh!... Greg… Please… Stop, I can't take anymore…"

"Simple depressive reaction… It's nothing."

"I don't want to, Greg. I don't want to…"

"Gently… Make a little effort… We're on the way, Valerie, we're on the way…"

The light dances and vibrates like in the heart of summer.

Big, black flies buzz around the infernal ballet, others plunge into the black, gangrenous stone.

Invisible hands throw sand that plugs up the deep openings so that cries for help rise from of the huge steel bars that flood into the rectangle of light.

"No, Valerie… No, not that… Free yourself… Free yourself…"

"I can't. I don't want to…"

"Remove that bar…"

"Greg!"

The gate collapses on a deserted square. And from the crenellated wall greedy fingers dig out the sand plugging the cracks. Long, monstrous fingers, with gold and emerald rings, scratching the walls gnawed away by saltpeter, enlarging the openings that become grottoes, caves exhaling dying gasps.

A black flame shines in the dark and it looks like in the icy fire a road appears, narrow, leading to a tunnel open onto the infinite. A round mouth, slightly agape as if for a kiss.

"Greg… no… It's not possible… I don't want to…"

"We're reaching the third level…"

"Greg…"

The mouth gets bigger, becomes huge, ready to swallow the emptiness and dark, embracing and menacing, like some monstrously vast sea of flesh.

"Greg…"

All of a sudden, the gate slams shut, locked up tight with a huge chain and padlock… The stone wall springs up from the darkness… The colors fade, blur and disappear… Nothing remains but the screen, empty, covered with a spectral glow.

"Cut!"

And Professor Greysson's finger pushes a button and the normal light once again shines in the "viewer."

CHAPTER II

The rest appears to me with unbelievable clarity through the veil of my memories, as I gradually sink into the nebulous void. The film continues.

I hear Greysson's voice saying to me, "Well, Mr. Milland, what's your conclusion?"

I am surprised by the question. I nod my head, embarrassed. "I'm not a psychiatrist. Not even a bad psychologist, but..."

"But?"

"But they seem pretty obvious Freudian symbols, especially in the interpretation of... well, of this voluntary confinement of Valerie Watson where the symbolism is in the clown bottle, the glass barrel, the clock orifice, the wall, the gate and the chain. In my opinion it's her unconscious refusal to pursue this stupid dream."

"It's not a dream, Mr. Milland." And he hastens to add, "Not a normal dream! It's the cenesthesic reactions of the unconscious that interests us since Gregory Watson's daring experiment is very disturbing to us. Can you swear on your honor that Professor Watson never confided in you at all about his psychophysiological work?"

Like the clown in the bottle I shake my head from right to left and left to right.

All four of them are here in front of me, examining me with obvious interest. I can describe them each in turn:

First, Professor Anthony Greysson, the director of the psychophysiological center of Boston. He is tall, thin and bald, his skull in the shape of a dome. He is a dynamic psychologist with a great reputation. Big horn-rimmed glasses sit on his slightly hooked nose.

Next to him I see Ludovic Aymes, a respected pharmacologist. The small, nervous man who cannot stop playing with his skinny fingers, continually cracking his knuckles. His skin is dark and his beady eyes expose his constant alertness.

As for Fred Lindsay and Herbert Dayton they are both world famous psychiatrists. For many long years they have been friends with Gregory Watson and they are like two inscrutable beings, keeping their comments to a strict minimum; two men of science who are methodical and reserved. The more I watch them the more I think they look like two big, articulated puppets.

The four men come and go in and out of Watson's house where they have lived for the past three days. That is where I found them an hour ago when I rang at the gate bringing a personal invitation from Professor Watson. I explained everything to them very briefly.

My name is Robert Milland. I am American and I have worked in Melbourne at a center for electronics for many years, that is since I quit General Motors. I never knew Gregory Watson, nor Adam nor Eve, and when I received his invitation by way of Graham Whiley, I could not have been more surprised.

I had been chosen, apparently, out of a list of 200 technicians to assist Professor Watson in his work in the field of electronics. That is all I could say about it, except that I was motivated to accept by the princely sum offered for my work.

Unfortunately I arrived too late, with the feeling of throwing myself body and soul into a weird and totally incomprehensible adventure. At least it was like this until now, given the scanty revelations that they gave me and which had completely devastated me.

Mrs. Watson had killed her husband during a fit of insanity and they had found her a few hours later in the laboratory, a wreck, completely unconscious, curled up, lost in some inner dream, escaping the consequences of her action as well as grim reality.

But now Greysson has decided to start everything over from scratch. The man disturbs me though I cannot say why.

"Let's see where we're at," he tells me. "We're going to need your services, Mr. Milland. As long as you know the whole situation. Mrs. Watson has not been charged and the police are blaming her actions on pure insanity. Furthermore, the information we've got about the marital relations of the Watsons is totally normal, despite their age difference. We also have a complete report on Valerie Watson."

Greysson opens a file and scans a typed page. He speaks with the solemnity of a judge. "Age, 32. IQ, 135. No mental defects. Emotional sensitivity a little higher than average. Only a slight systolic heart murmur, unquestionably functional. No schizophrenic problems and the constant report of her…"

He will not read further. He closes the file and nods. "But this report dates back before Professor Watson experimented on Valerie, so it doesn't matter anymore. You've seen the encephaloscopy report and noticed the appearance of certain Freudian reflexes due to the regressive reactions of her nervous character. Watson went too far with Valerie, there's no question about it, and in probing the chambers of her soul he triggered a shock. He's the one responsible for it."

He stops talking to let Lindsay finish the presentation. "However, one thing is certain and Watson hinted at it to us the day before his death. He had made an extraordinary discovery that could destroy everything we know in the field of depth psychology. Our only hope of finding this important discovery is to somehow break through the defenses of this morbid state in which Valerie continues to shut herself away. And that's why we're here."

"Where is Valerie Watson?"

Ludovic Aymes points to the floor above us. "In an experimental room. We're trying to use the reanimation methods used by Watson himself and with his own machines. A few days from now, if we fail, we'll resort to other methods."

I take a deep breath to hide my confusion. Because none of this explains why Professor Watson invited me here.

After I mention this Herbert Dayton shakes out of his indifference. He starts fidgeting in his chair and suddenly looks human. In his opinion, it is very simple: Watson needed a highly specialized technician to build an electronic device before moving on to new experiments.

I accept the idea because it is sound, logical and rational. But why did he have to search so far afield? Why all this mystery, all these precautions, all this discreet overkill by this man? This is the question that crosses my mind but that I prefer to keep silent in order not to complicate matters further because right now I am getting drawn in. And I do not really know why.

This affair is becoming more and more fascinating to me as Greysson places his hand on a big machine the size and shape of a chest on the wall. Above it is a rectangular, plastic screen, slightly curved on either end. It is the encephaloscopy unit designed and built by Gregory Watson. It is used to record the auditory and visual stimulations of the most hidden circuits of the memory.

"A dream recorder, in a way?" My question makes him smile.

"Much more than that, Mr. Milland," Lindsay corrects me in a calm voice. A dream, properly speaking, is located in the first level of subconscious functions. It provides man with a release as well as fulfilling a certain psychological need for escape. But the second level is connected with the cenesthesic sensations in the cortex, which is completely foreign to our conscious mind. It's the unknown and mystifying region whose seat is in the parietal convolutions that Watson was exploring with this machine. In other words, a new dimension."

"I don't think I really understand."

Greysson shrugged his shoulders. "It doesn't matter," he said. "Anyway, We don't put much faith in Watson's theory, which is a little hazy in our opinion. In truth, according to the information that Watson was willing to give us, his work was focused on the time sacrificed to sleep every day. He thought that with the right method, two hours a night was enough for an average person to recharge his batteries, so to speak. The elimination of repressive dreams and certain cultural barriers, without any mental constraints, can help empty the mind, thus allowing the mind-body entity to realize its full potential. This prospect offers humanity two important possibilities. First to eliminate the dead time devoted to sleep and then to allow every individual to replace these neutral periods with some activity. In a word, to take full advantage of life during the time we have here on earth. Quite a tempting project, isn't it?"

I nodded in agreement. "Of course, this is the secret you're hoping to get out of Mrs. Watson?"

"We think so. Although there's certainly a lot to do to get such results. Mrs. Watson's psychological accident confirms our fears, but we're ready to pursue the work of our colleague and review the formulae that we found in his files. They concern the 'psychedelics' used in the experiment."

"Do you mean hallucinogenic drugs?"

"Not exactly. The LSD[3]-based substances used by Watson are brain accelerators that aim to modify the states of consciousness. Unfortunately, the phenomenon in the brain depends on the potential of redox or oxidation-reduction, and we fear that the product used by Watson might be harmful over time, causing lesions in Valerie's brain due to this reduction of oxygen consumption. This, in our opinion, would account for her homicidal madness, purely accidental though it might be."

At that instant a red light blinks on a board and Greysson cuts short his explanations. He waves me after him and says, "Come on."

I follow him. We leave the research room to the other professors, who dive back into their dusty files. I do not like these people. It is funny, I think they are weird, creepy, with little human about them. They are like characters in a dream, bland, insipid, insignificant. Everything is mechanical and rigid. Too severe. I feel like...

Yes, of course, the injection! That soft couch... that feeling of floating in the void...

---

[3] Lysergic Acid Diethylamide, derived from ergot, a grain fungus that grows on rye.

I sink into the dream little by little... Maybe that is what distorts my judgment in a reversal of values... Yes, maybe... But things keep unfolding clearly and precisely... So, let's see where the story goes...

I see us walking inside the house. Greysson and I pass through a tastefully decorated hall... We climb the stairs to the second floor on a wooden staircase covered with a thick, wool carpet. A landing. In the back, several doors.

I see two nurses walking down the hallway. One of them comes to meet Greysson, holds out a white smock. He puts it on and takes me into a round room, perfectly round; its walls are painted white.

Strange machines hum quietly in the obscurity. The room is deadly silent except for this. While Greysson prepares a hypodermic needle, my gaze falls upon the relaxing couch. Motionless, dead still under the white sheet, I see the most gorgeous, the most ravishing creature that exists in the world. Only a little paleness dulls the radiance of her face whose features are of the rarest purity... a doll's face, angelic and supernatural, that belongs only to dreams.

Here is one of them, the face of Valerie Watson!

CHAPTER III

Professor Greysson pulls the needle out of her vein, puts the syringe away and turns to me. He points to Valerie with a wearied gesture. Me, I cannot stop looking at her.

"I'm really afraid that all our efforts will be useless if she keeps herself hidden away."

"What would happen in that case?"

"The more she avoids reality, the more disinterested she becomes and she'll end up escaping the real for good. It'll mean insanity, the asylum and death."

"But there has to be a way to bring her out of this kind of coma."

Greysson smiles at my ignorance and naiveté. "The brain is a well protected fortress and the subconscious will is its strongest weapon of defense. It'd be easier to grind down a rock with a sponge. We're fighting against her will, Mr. Milland… because she's dreaming, there's no question. We continue to see certain physiological effects due to the variations in the endocrine glands, the relaxation of all her muscles recorded by electromyography and the curve of cenesthesic sensations…"

I tear myself away from his psychodynamic jargon to look at Valerie more carefully. She seems to be floating between fiction and reality, with her long, black hair, her long, slender hands, her delicately curved lips and her large eyes, closed, shut tight on the unknown.

She is barely breathing, but the slow, regular movement of her chest is the only sign of life there is in the body of this ancient goddess, who fascinates and paralyzes me. She makes a strange impression on me that I cannot analyze or define... I watch her for a long time...

Greysson's voice pulls me out of my reverie, brings me abruptly back to reality. Reality? What is real in what Greysson is showing me?

I see a big, black hole in a small, plastic screen that is attached to the head of the bed. It is like I am looking into a well, a bottomless pit. The Freudian symbol goes on and on inside Valerie's dream behind a thick bulwark of darkness, emptiness and nothingness.

"Even her dream eludes us," Greysson adds as he turns off the encephaloscope. "There you go, Mr. Milland. Now you know as much as we do."

But I still have more surprises in store and I notice the sudden interest that Greysson takes in me. He leads me out of the room and we go back downstairs. He heads down to the end of the hallway and opens a thick, heavy, metal door. I follow him down a small, stone, spiral stairway that leads us into the basement and we enter a huge laboratory that is in complete disarray. Objects are lying on the floor, bare wires stick out of the walls and the gutted machines bare witness to the sad spectacle of their mutilation. All this is the work of Valerie!

Greysson points to where Professor Watson's body was found half-burned. The frayed high-tension plug that came in contact with poor Watson is still hanging a few inches above the ground to remind us of the tragedy.

Greysson explains to me, "All these machines here were built by our colleague, Professor Watson. In spite of all the damage, some of them can still be identified. The rest, the ones that are unexplainable and beyond our understanding, will very soon be examined by a team of specialists. Come over here."

He shows me a small, ebonite box against the wall standing on two stout legs and bearing the marks of Valerie's destructive frenzy.

"This one is particularly troublesome. Its inner workings defy all reason. Everyone who has studied it resorts to pure guesswork as to its purpose. A washing machine or simple television, even if it were half-destroyed, wouldn't fool anyone, but this is different... It's like we're faced with a machine designed by a Martian."

I appreciate his humor, which lightens up the usual gravity of his words a little, and I cannot help smiling. "It's that bad?"

"I'd like you to take a look at it."

"I'm no Martian."

He smiles back at me, but impatiently repeats, "You're not a psychiatrist, you're not a psychologist and you don't come from Mars. I agree with all this, but you are an electrical engineer. Besides, you had Watson's trust in coming here. I think you're the perfect person to uncover the mystery of this device. In any case, nothing is preventing you from trying."

I lift the cover of the ebonite box and peer inside at the complex network of wires, coils and transformers all jumbled together. Of course at first sight it means nothing and I scratch my head in confusion. "I'll need a few things to restart the..."

"Everything you'll need is in the closet in the back there. Call me if you need anything else."

It is clear, simple and unambiguous. In other words, "Get to work immediately. This is your job, not ours."

After two hours I am starting to give up hope.

With admirable patience I screwed in and rescrewed the main parts of the mysterious machine, then connected and reconnected the circuits. I try to join the circuits together in an order that seems logical to me. I undo it and start over, again and again, by trial and error, mindful of the results. I feel like I am tackling a job that is beyond not only my skills but also beyond logic and rationality.

Finally, two, then three lights start flashing inside the box and this small satisfaction galvanizes my energy.

At one point I have to interrupt my work to swallow the dinner that I preferred to be brought to me in the lab. The others in the house do not make the most cheerful company and a gnawing apprehension makes me dread any contact with these men who are constantly coming and going, reminding me of machines devoid of any human sentiment. I cannot help making this comparison with the nature of psychiatrists, normally pretty introverted people who see life only through a series of symbols and conditioned reactions.

I get back to my work when night has already fallen, trying to control my growing jumpiness. There is nothing more exhausting and more demoralizing than continuing a job you do not understand. I do not like what I am doing. No, not at all!

Armed with my soldering iron I attack a network of wires that had short-circuited and fused. I separate them one by one and group them kind of randomly. Wanting to verify that the lights are still working, I flip a switch. This time they all turn on and start blinking in a non-stop dance of lights, rods start vibrating in their frames and the coils spin in slow motion.

Well, this is interesting! I cannot help smiling, but my smile soon hardens into an expression of fear and worry when I get clumsy and drop a screwdriver on the tile floor. *The tool falling on the hard floor makes no sound!*

Intrigued, I pick up the screwdriver and after a pause I repeat the experiment. Once again the instrument crashes to the floor in complete and all-encompassing silence. Good God, what's happening? I suddenly feel like I am in the middle of an empty space, without sound, as if the world around me has ceased to exist.

Overcoming the fear that is gnawing at my stomach, I look at the strange machine and try to scream. Horror! No sound comes out of my mouth! This is not possible!

My fingers tremble as they grab the switch, but I cannot flip, as hard as I try. It is stuck. I pick up the screwdriver and start to panic when all of a sudden I see the heavy steel door swing open to reveal Greysson and Aymes. I see them but I do not hear them. They are waving their arms and running towards me and I can read the questions on their mute lips. We have a conversation between deaf people in which only gestures and hand signals mean anything.

I point to the machine and make a funny face at the same time. "It's coming from this... Don't be afraid... It'll only take a minute..."

I stick the head of the screwdriver into a slot and poke around at the screw threads. It finally unsticks and the switch flips back on the dial to zero.

"...damn machine? What happened, Mr. Milland?"

Greysson's voice rattles me, but the inhuman shrieks coming from the upper floors freezes the blood in my veins. It is a terrible, agonizing scream that stirs up the echoes in the sleeping house like some nightmarish cry.

Greysson turns around, pale and waxen. "Now what the…"

He is the first to rush off. I am right behind him, scrambling up the stone stairs, with a horrible fear hot on my heels, almost out of control. Our mad dash continues without a word being said and when we reach the first floor the screaming stops. We run into Professors Dayton and Lindsay who have just run out of the research room.

"It's coming from upstairs," Lindsay tells us. "Quick!"

So we bound up the stairs where a panicking nurse is waiting for us and just as we reach the landing we find out who was producing the harrowing screams. I see Miss Foyle, the head nurse, lying on her back in a ludicrous position, her face deformed by fright. Her bulging eyes stare violently at us and her mouth is still twisted by her scream.

I figure it is too late at the same time that Greysson leans over her and says softly, "She's dead. Her heart gave out."

The door to the room where Valerie is lying is wide open. I am already headed through, guided by some obscure anxiety, but I am quickly reassured. Valerie is still dreaming, unconcerned and unfazed by the drama that just played out.

And it is just as I turn around that I notice the weird black streaks around the bed, seeping into the tiles. The marks continue onto the landing where they suddenly disappear, only a few feet away from the body of Miss Foyle.

I call Greysson over, horrified by what I have stumbled upon. "Look… Look!"

Then I realize that I am standing in the blackish goo that stains the floor outside of Valerie's room. Everyone comes over, intrigued by the strange and baffling phenomenon. Wherever the black trail has gone, the tiles have lost their color. It is like a blurry image engraved on a sensitive plate.

"Good God," Dayton murmurs, "where did that come from?"

"Come see this!" Aymes' voice follows. The pharmacologist points to the corner of the wall next to Miss Foyle's body. What I see makes me nauseous. The entire surface of the wall is splattered with some slimy substance that looks like pieces of flesh, as if a living creature was blown up by a grenade in the middle of the landing. Dark goo oozes out of every fleshy shred, trickling down the white wall in a thin streak.

It is awful. The smell especially is disgusting. I think I have never breathed anything so foul, so vile and the gooey stuff on the bottom of my shoes makes me want to vomit. Then I realize that everyone has run into Valerie's room.

I look at the trail. There are even traces on the sheets and on the metal bars of the bed. Yuck! What a horrible thing!

The nurse who is still following us around starts to look frail. We figure that she is on the verge of a nervous breakdown. Greysson puts his arm around her and leads her to the stairs. "Okay," he orders, "go downstairs. Don't stay here. We'll call you if we need you."

He speaks off the cuff, not really knowing what he is saying, stunned and devastated by the unbelievable scene we have just discovered and which we are utterly unable to explain.

Greysson mumbles to himself, "It must have got into the room... but I wonder how..."

"What are you talking about, Anthony?" Dayton sounds annoyed.

"Well, uh, about... about this thing..."

"The experiment room is completely shut off from the outside. For heaven's sake, Anthony, don't get carried away by your imagination. I'm sure there's a perfectly reasonable explanation for all this."

Unfortunately his tone is far from convincing, but Greysson nods his head. It looks to me like he has pulled himself together all of a sudden and recovered his self-confidence. "Well, then, Herbert, I'm all ears."

It is my turn to step forward. "You know, I, too, would be curious to hear your explanations." I point to the sheet with its disgusting brown stains in the shape of rings, but that are, at least, still there after the gooey liquid has disappeared. It was transformed into a thin, shiny film before our dazzled eyes, crumbled, flaked off and turned to dust. On the tile as well the sludge melted away like magic.

Aymes' voice coming from the landing is tinged with utter amazement. We hear him shout, "Look at this! Hey, come here! You've got to see this!"

The lumps on the walls have vanished. There is not a trace. It is unbelievable. Even the smell has gone.

All that is left is Miss Foyle, crumpled in the corner with her terrible secret that we will never know. Only her bulging eyes testify to the final, ghastly vision that she saw.

A reasonable explanation, Dayton said. Poor guy!

CHAPTER IV

This morning they came to take away the body of Miss Foyle. The second nurse ran away during the night and we have not seen her since. The situation is obviously too much for her health, her salary and her faith. I applaud her because I should probably follow the poor girl's example and leave Greysson and his puppets to clear up this frightening, nefarious mystery.

I was convinced at the start—These people here are playing with fire, like a sorcerer's apprentice, going up against unknown forces and opening forbidden doors. But is it really for the good of humanity? Or simply to satisfy their individual curiosity beyond the rules and principles imposed upon man since Genesis?

I do not know. The fact is that I, too, was sucked into the whirlwind and now I can no longer back away without the risk of sinking into an obsessive fear that would haunt me for the rest of my life. This is why accepted and why I continue to flounder in this absurd and insane dream.

But let's go back and look at the events as they occurred. Maybe it will help me understand.

We had just got back to the laboratory in the basement when Greysson started the discussion.

"We could not all have been victims of our imagination. The symptoms of a collective hallucination usually show up with evidence of the syndrome…"

"Let's stick to the facts," Dayton jumped in.

"You mentioned a reasonable explanation, didn't you?"

"Listen, Anthony…"

"For heaven's sake, stop bickering, will you," the deep, mechanical voice of Aymes intervened. "The only explanation I can find is this: the phenomenon of materialization coincided with the period of silence that we experienced and that the machine being examined by Mr. Milland apparently caused."

"It did," I agreed, pointing to the metal box.

"So, what do you think this machine was really used for?"

"It's a noise guzzler, a sound destroyer, a sonic annihilator. Call it what you will."

"Mr. Milland…"

"You were talking about a reasonable explanation. That's the only logical explanation I can come up with. I repeat that this machine was designed and built to destroy sound waves. I mean all those frequencies that the human ear can capture, from 20 cycles per second up to 20,000 cycles per second. Now, it's possible that its effect extends into the infrasounds and ultrasounds, but for the moment I don't know."

Silence. I continued, "Anyway, I don't see what relation there could be between this silence-making machine and the… well, the appearance of…"

I could not find the words to express myself, but they understood me perfectly. They, too, seemed apprehensive about using terms that could break the bounds of logic and rationality. But what kind of logic or rationality was there in the mysterious apparition that had gone back to the void leaving only its dark and indelible prints behind?

And yet two facts coincided in time, even though we could not find the least evidence of cause and effect. But Greysson, who was pacing up and down the laboratory, was the first to give up the idea of concurrence by trying to consider the phenomena separately instead of together. The materialization phenomenon seemed to occupy all this thoughts and I have to admit that he had good reason.

"A dream spilling over into reality," he surmised. "Yes, that's it... there can be no other explanation."

"What do you mean?"

His face had taken on a muddy hue. He looked to me like he was terrified by his own words. "With Valerie, Watson had reached a degree of psychological penetration beyond everything we can imagine in the field of depth psychology."

"Do you mean the new dimension that you refused to accept?" I asked, staring into his eyes.

He nodded and sighed. "Let's accept it, even just for the sake of the most reasonable argument possible. Let's accept the existence of this unknown dimension. Let's imagine a kind of parallel world that coexists with our own through the network of the unconscious."

"That's absurd," Dayton spoke up.

"Herbert, please, let him continue," Aymes pleaded, cracking his knuckles.

"Damn it all to hell! A psychological phenomenon cannot in any way enter our material universe!"

Greysson got angry. "What do you know about it, Herbert? You know only the limitations of an object in space that obey only the physical-chemical rules of Cartesian philosophy, but a unified vision of things has turned many conceptions on their head since Heisenberg. Do we know how certain particles, which we find in space, can come from a parallel universe and cross the boundaries that we ascribe to the physical universe? No, but we accept the fact. In the field of the unconscious, we're still very ignorant, but nothing is keeping us from thinking that we are facing an aspect of the unified field that eludes present-day science."

Dayton stood up like a fighting cock. "And monsters could burst through the unconscious to enter reality, as solid as you and I! That's insane! It's the most ridiculous nonsense I've ever heard!"

"One minute!" I put my hand on the switch of the sonic annihilator, cutting short the tirade of this stubborn mule Dayton. "I'm asking you for a minute. Supposing that there is a connection between the two phenomena, do you want us to redo the experiment?"

Dayton swung around. He was pale. He sprang at me, tearing me away from the machine. "Don't do it!" he yelled. "For the love of God, don't do it!"

There was a moment of silence in which all we heard was the cracking of Aymes' knuckles.

I could not help smiling. "And yet you seemed so sure of yourself…"

"It's not your decision to make, Mr. Milland. It's beyond your expertise."

"And, unfortunately, yours. The heart of the matter lies in Mrs. Watson, I believe. She alone knows the truth. Trust me, we should concentrate our efforts on her before its too late."

"Everything we're tried so far is just barely legal."

"So I suppose that there are other means that we haven't tried yet?"

"That's for the forensic investigators to decide."

"And when the decision is made, Mrs. Watson will be ready for the rubber room," Greysson raised his voice. "No, I think Mr. Milland is right. The decision lies with us before the specialists mess up our work."

"What do you have in mind, Anthony?"

"I think I have an idea."

Greysson looked at me hard and searchingly, which made me kind of dizzy. No one dared to speak and I felt terribly worried, wondering what was expected of me.

Finally Greysson shrugged his shoulders and said to me, "Mr. Milland, the situation is about to turn sour. I think we're going to have to act quickly if we want to avoid the worst. Will you help us one last time?"

"What else can I do?"

"Just bring Valerie Watson back to reality."

"How in God's name can I do that?"

"By joining her in her dream."

"In her dream?"

"If you manage to break through her mental barriers, I'm sure you can try to convince her, to reason with her."

"I don't understand what you're saying."

"I think the experiment is feasible."

"How's that?"

"We put you into an artificial sleep and we tune your subconscious personality to Mrs. Watson's, meaning that you will be completely free of all inhibiting sensations, physical and otherwise that might affect your psyche from external stimuli. Tuned in to the resilience harmonics of Valerie Watson's neural network, you can get in touch with her, all the while keeping your own personality, of course."

But of course! What else could I expect! A shiver ran down my spine. I was literally stunned by what Greysson was saying. "But… really… why chose me? I don't know Mrs. Watson and I know nothing about your…"

"Time is short and I need my colleagues to see this experiment through."

I nodded my head, feeling uncomfortable. The whirlwind was still spiraling down. This time I was trapped for good. I asked, "What are the risks?"

"I'll be frank with you, Mr. Milland. This is the first experiment of its kind that has been attempted. Practically speaking, there is no risk if you follow all the orders you're given during the 'trip'. Anyway, we will be watching you carefully during the whole experiment. At the first sign of trouble, the slightest psychological danger, we'll bring you back."

"How long will it take, in your opinion?"

"It could be only a few hours, but it could also last for days. If you fail or decide to give up, you just have to tell us. We'll bring you back that very second." He stared at me intently. "Well, Mr. Milland, what's your decision?"

"Give me a cigarette first, will you?"

I humbly admit that I did not know what to say and I was as uncertain as I had ever been in my life. The four doctors started an animated discussion in front of me, like I was not even there, but I did not listen to them, I was lost in my own thoughts, all suffused with the image of Valerie.

I was battling with myself, torn between two contrary forces that were fighting for my decision. One was fear that shrieked its dreadful warnings, commanding me to flee and leave all of this behind... The other aroused my desire and my curiosity to finally meet this dreamlike creature under whose spell I had involuntarily fallen. I realized, without being able to do anything about it, that I was fascinated by the image of Valerie and of course that was what made up my mind.

I turned to the doctor and asked softly, "When should I leave?"

Greysson put his hand on my shoulder in a kindly, fatherly gesture. "I believe the sooner the better. Let's go."

That is how the series of tests that Greysson deemed necessary began, with the association of ideas, the stripping down of my whole brain, its emotional capacity, its strengths and weaknesses.

A second bed has been set up next to Valerie's in the experiment room and I see the four doctors bustling about in the dim light like shadows in a nightmare, preparing the phases of the operation with expert precision.

They work without talking, without wasting any time, until Greysson lets me know that everything is ready for "the big leap." I lie down on the bed and Lindsay puts the helmet full of electrodes on my head, checking all the connections on Valerie's one last time. I see hands fiddling with the machines, lights blinking and a soft hum fills the silence in the room.

I know that the crucial time has come when Greysson walks up to me with a syringe full of a yellowish liquid. "Ready, Mr. Milland?" he asks.

"Ready!"

"Take Mrs. Watson's hand."

I do as he says and my fingers wrap around her warm, soft, satiny hand. A strange sensation suddenly washes over me at the moment when Aymes seals our union with a copper bracelet packed with wires. But it lasts only a split second, only until the needle digs into my upper arm. Then a torrent of fire rushes through my body, charges through my veins, my arteries, my heart and brain...

In a matter of seconds I realize that I am cut off from the exterior world. The walls collapse on me and I am swallowed up. I feel like I am plunging headlong into a world of darkness... Beyond time and space... Beyond the boundaries of my body...

I dive inside...

PART TWO

CHAPTER I

...of a bottomless void. A big, black hole in the shape of a cyclone grows bigger and bigger and wraps me up in its whirling motion.

Now the whirlwind has disappeared and I am fully aware. I continue drifting through a weird, colored universe of wondrously bright, abstract images.

In my dream the fiction is bound to reality and my memories of the real world persist with extraordinary clearness. I feel free, rid of my cares and worries as if I have become able to resolve all the problems of the world.

On the first level of consciousness, I suddenly discover the relic-images that are buried in the depths of my neurons and that rise up in the mysterious universe of my memory.

I am floating above a blue lake, glistening with light, where all the stars of the night are reflected. A stone bridge arches over and leads me to a tiny island beaten by the sunny waves. Its colors meld with the gigantic rainbow that dips into the infinite sea. It's Capri!

I swing down through the cracks in a chain of clouds to find a garden in the rain. Brooklyn! I see the stone bench from my shy, 16-year old encounters. I am a child running to the Junior High gate, a soldier jumping into the sky for the first time, a man behind the wheel of a car speeding down a long, smooth highway. A road sign: Melbourne, 28 miles!

I bow before the statue of Lincoln and I kiss, incidentally, Beatrice's lips. I see myself in Nancy's limpid eyes. My hand is held captive in the wild waves of her silvery hair.

"Hamburger, three cents." The silver ball lights up the red and green cones. "Tilt!" Red, green, "Tilt!"

Whistles on the corner... Kepi... *Black entrance...* Metro entrance... "Direction: Pantin... Place d'Italie..." *Black entrance...* tunnel... *black entrance...* darkness... *black entrance...* nothingness.

"Watch out, Milland, you're entering the second level!"

"Everything's okay."

"We're keeping the resilience quotient... Right! You see clearly?"

"Sure."

"Now you're free of your audio-visual memories... We breaking the mnemonic chain... Relax... Concentrate on the tunnel..."

"It's pulling me in."

"Let yourself go... Whatever you do, don't fight it..."

"Here we go, I'm inside... I don't see anything anymore... The wind blowing here is ice-cold."

"Transmit more slowly... We're not reading you here very well... Take a little break."

"I'm freezing... I feel like I'm stuck in a piece of ice... What's going on?"

"It's nothing. A simple reflex in reaction to the lowering of your temperature. Your heartbeat is syncing with Mrs. Watson's. It'll pass."

"What did you say, Greysson? It's hard to hear..."

"Milland... Re... Hello?... Mil... spond... What's hap... ning?"

I get nothing more. Nothing but the patterns in the dark melting into the bridging of the selective circuits.

And I keep going deeper inside the big, black hole, into the icy cold that stabs my souls like a steel blade. All of a sudden the drop speeds up, dizzying, alarming. Balls of light that look like distant stars appear, with pale, blurry haloes. Strange constellations, weird shapes and colors, lighting up the darkness of the abyss. They look like candle flames caught in ice.

Very cautiously I start to resist the motion sensations of the false continuum surrounding me, clinging desperately to Greysson's instructions.

What, really, could have happened? Why this silence, this break in the psychic connection?

I rein in the fear that is pervading me... I repress it... No... relax... patience... wait... hope...

Fear is my only enemy. What an awful thought, but I have to fight... fight... It's me or *It*...

I am floating in this dream world when an exit suddenly appears, where a bright light is shining, shimmering like the surface of an infinite lake.

And I see. I see the black, glistening shape lying on the surface of the lake. A fantastic being, out of all proportion, but apparently human. The creature looks like it is sleeping. It is sleeping, I know it... I feel it... I divine it... It sleeps.

It sleeps, but I do not see its face because the gigantic creature has its back turned to me. Its feet are awash in the murky mud of a distant shore.

Just then a star in the darkened sky wobbles and falls into the depths of the lake. A second... A third... The lake around the sleeping man swallows the stars and devours their light. In the sky, one by one, the stars go out like carnival lanterns. The myth of the fall climaxes in this symbol stamped with its terrible mystery.

"Milland!"

In a flash everything disappears: the abyss, the darkness, the stars, the lake and the sleeping man.

"Milland!"

A giant wave casts me onto a deserted shore where all the colors of the universe are gathered.

"Hello! Greysson... God almighty, what's happening?"

"It's nothing. A bad contact in the circuits. It's fixed."

"I was starting to lose hope."

"We completely lost contact. Where were you?"

"It doesn't matter. I stuck it out, but..."

"Whatever you do, don't panic. Everything's going great."

The cold feeling has gone. I am still clear-headed and my confidence is back. "Okay. Everything is going fine."

"You've reached the second level."

"I don't see anything... except colors. Curves and broken lines... they're turning every which way."

"We're registering it. You're now hooked up to Mrs. Watson's harmonics for good. Watch out for the final leap... it might be tough... Concentrate all your energy..."

I understand exactly what he means. Now it is the unknown, the forbidden zone. Where no man has ever probed except for Watson. I start to feel the vague, mysterious attraction of Valerie's mind.

"Are you ready, Milland?"

"Ready."

"Let's go!"

New concentration. New effort. New dive.

All of a sudden everything looks like a sphere glimmering with an almost unbearable brightness. I feel like I have reached something both sublime and super-human, a mystical illumination and absolute contemplation. Also the feeling of opening a door onto the mystery of an obscure night where, in my head, the source of an anti-cosmos bursts forth in all its spiritual horror!

An excruciating pain just when I cross the last mental barrier... Greysson's voice harassing me... A torrent of fire pours into the central sulcus of my brain. My head is blown to smithereens. I scream when I drop like a cannonball down a well.

A split second of floating and I am on hard ground. My hands touch the smooth, cold surface... I turn over... I sit up... surrounded by darkness.

I scream and shout, "Mrs. Watson!"

CHAPTER II

Little by little my dread melts away; the fear and pain disappear. I stand up as best I can until my fingers clutch the rough surface of what seems to be a wall. But no, it is not possible, it is only a dream wall... An illusion of a wall, a ghost of a wall. Any yet it is a wall! A wall as real as my body. It is hard and solid... It is...

I sit back down to catch my breath as around me the darkness dissipates. A pale twilight now shines in the unknown region where I have just made contact. I wait a few seconds for my eyes to get used to the obscurity, for my senses to wake up, listening to the silence. That is when a faint noise makes me shudder.

It comes from barely a few yards away, just at the corner of the wall. A dark form, curled up, becomes visible in the shadows and I suppose that it is real... dreadfully human. Its eyes shine like agate and stare at me with a mixture of horror, curiosity and worry.

"Mrs. Watson..."

In the blink of an eye I see her face. In a heartbeat her frail outline appears, with a halo of pale light fluttering around her like silk.

"Mrs. Watson..."

It is strange. Now I feel like I am waking up from a long nightmare, leaving the dream behind for reality. And yet it is a dream here in this dark hole where I pant and huff like a damned soul.

It is in the dream that I mumble again, "Mrs. Watson, answer, please..."

"Who are you?"

"Don't be afraid, I won't hurt you."

"Who are you?"

I answer simply, "My name's Robert Milland. We're tuned to the same harmonics. I've come to meet you in your dream."

"What do you want from me?"

There is fear and a great deal of worry in her voice. Her voice that is, however, not a voice, but just a concept.

"I've come to help you, Mrs. Watson."

"I don't need your help."

"Listen to me. You have to listen to me."

"Stop! Don't come any closer!"

A singular horror darkens the radiance of her face. I stop two feet away from her, trying to reassure her the best I can. I tell her about Greysson and our project, about all my efforts, about the danger lying in wait if she remains stubborn, but it is no use. I feel like I have run into an insurmountable barrier.

She speaks plainly, "You have no right. Leave this world and leave me alone."

"I will do nothing of the kind. I have to make you see reason, to bring you back with me."

"What are you getting out of this, Mr. Milland?"

I hesitate again to tell her the truth. This awful truth that lies behind my expedition. No, let's try to start over from the beginning.

"Why did you kill your husband?"

She starts scratching the wall with her nails and shaking her head with disgust. "Be quiet... For pity's sake, be quiet..."

"There was a reason. What was it? You can remember. Now you can remember."

"Be quiet! I can't take it anymore."

"Free yourself once and for all, damn it!"

"Can't you see that you're torturing me? Can't you see that?"

"It'll get worse very soon… If you keep on, you'll be lost… lost…"

"Leave me alone! For the love of God, leave me alone…"

"Insanity is waiting for you, Mrs. Watson. You're afraid of it, but you stay closed up in yourself trying to escape your memories. Hiding away in your unconscious keeps you struggling with remorse. Your brain is sick and denies responsibility. The world terrifies you but you voluntarily subject yourself to this enslaving repression. These walls are nothing but the partitions of your embittered mind. Am I wrong?"

"My God, let me die!"

Gasping, she looks at me with her wide, bewildered eyes and seems on the point of having a fit.

"Make an effort, I beg you…"

"But you don't understand that I just can't?"

"Come on, calm down. I'm going to help you…"

Her refusal has a *sound* of decrepitude, of eternal old age in contradiction to the angelic, almost childlike beauty of this captivating creature.

I am about to call out for Greysson. But I change my mind. Anyway, it is out of his control. I have to manage on my own. But to convince Valerie, to bring her back to her senses seems terribly hard to me.

I let a little time pass. One second or an eternity, maybe. I look up searching for the opening of the hole. The steep walls are lost in the darkness. The hole is like a box thrown into an abyss and trying to imagine what exists beyond these nightmarish walls chills me to the bone. And yet I must find a solution. It is absolutely necessary.

I turn to Valerie. "Why did you say that?"

"What did I say?"

"You said you couldn't recover from your fall."

"That's right. It's all too much for me now."

"Where are we?"

"How should I know?"

I point to the top of the box. In the patch of dark emptiness I think I see big, pale clouds prowling around with maddening slowness. A ray of moonlight pours its silvery dust through the narrow opening and shines its icy glow on us.

"So, what universe did you create outside of these walls?"

"I don't know. Oh, please! Wake yourself up, Mr. Milland!"

"This world is real, isn't it?"

"It is... or at least it was... when... Oh, I don't know, I don't know anymore..."

Her voice has turned nice, almost friendly, and in the silvery dust I have the feeling that her entire being is rotting away. Then all of a sudden she stares at me with tiny, hard eyes full of skepticism.

"I can't... Don't ask why... There's nothing you can do for me."

"Let me just try... Look!" My hands, feeling along the surface of the walls, bump into an iron ring. A few inches above it I find two, deeply embedded, metal spikes whose purpose totally escapes me. Damn, now I wonder where the dream stops and reality begins?

And this body that I cart around (as material to me as the one I left in the experiment room), what is it?

I chase away these thoughts to concentrate solely on the iron spikes. And I have an idea. I'm going to climb up first, I decide. Once we are out of this hole, we can start talking again.

I grab on and pull myself up into the darkness as best I can, balancing my movements, supporting myself on the iron bars. I hold out my hand to Valerie, who hesitates. "Come on, do what I say."

I pull her up, help her as much as I can, and we start climbing toward the narrow opening. A gust of air lashes my face and while Valerie does her best to climb, I try to lift up what seems to be a huge and heavy, terribly heavy slab. I brace myself and push as hard as I can, but I have to do it several times. With every thrust, the loose slab nudges a little, gradually letting a slice of sky break through the ominous clouds. But I have to take breaks to catch my breath as I feel the blood pulsing in my head.

Dead silence hangs overhead while the icy wind blowing through the opening smells like it is sweeping along all the stench of the world built up for centuries.

With boundless patience I force the slab until I finally get it pushed off. I pull myself up and over the edge, then I lean over, grab Valerie's hand and pull her up next to me. She helps as much as she can and falls onto the ledge, pale and out of breath. When I stand up to look around, I feel dizzy and struck by overwhelming terror.

In the shadows of the cypresses, crosses and crypts, I suddenly discover the dreadful reality of this nightmare world. A cemetery!

CHAPTER III

Valerie tears herself away from me and runs. I throw myself at her, stretching out my arms without thinking. Jumping off the tomb we had just climbed out of, she runs down a row, knocking over a cross, which falls with a sinister sound.

"Valerie!"

The feeling of my own powerlessness overwhelms me when I see her stumble on the soft ground. I hear her cry out. I see her lose her balance and I rush forward just in time to stop her from falling head over heels.

"What got into you? Are you crazy?"

"Leave me alone... Leave me alone..."

She looks at me, her face smudged with tears, her eyes stretched out in a weird way, gawking. Crazy, yes, this woman is crazy!

And while I hold her in my firm grip, I point to the gloomy scene before us. "So, wipe this out of your memory! Make all this horror disappear! You have no right to lock me up in your madness... You have no right..."

She looks like she is trying hard to gather her thoughts and express them. "It's not me... It's not me," she groans. "It belongs to this world... You don't understand anything, do you? Oh, God! I can't take it anymore... I can't..."

Her sentence ends in a kind of wheezing. My entire body is shaken with nausea. This time it is too much for me and I concentrate on calling Greysson, but in the mess of my subconscious my efforts are useless. I cannot reach him.

A dreadful anxiety infects me amidst the persistent silence. A crushing fear hits me and I cut myself loose in total, mental confusion.

But really, what is happening?

All of a sudden in the sepulchral silence I hear strange music in the distance. Something haunting, thumping, moving from major to minor. "Listen!"

I drag Valerie to the edge of the pathway between two tall trees that are whining in the wind. With a trembling hand she points to the end of the path and whispers, "It's coming from over there."

The music is awful, chilling, harsh... It is like the sound of a harmonium playing softly, whose weird, grinding chords fly off into the cold, darkened space. Something unknown, unimaginable, carried to the limits of harmony and human music. An invisible musician is playing in the abandoned cemetery and the mystery of the unseen presence shakes me out of my stupor and awakens my curiosity.

Valerie does as I ask and follows me. We walk down the deserted path, guided by this Ariadne's thread as it unwinds through the maze of dark pathways, this music from beyond the grave.

All of a sudden I stop to look at the stony ground. Instinctively I pull Valerie close to me, overcome by an invincible horror when I recognize the monstrous stains found in the Watson's house during that infamous night before my departure. The ghastly muck is spread out in front of us in a long, black trail leading to the absurd and impossible concert. The ground is completely soaked with it and catches the moonlight in the gooey stuff that sparkles in places like a colony of glistening worms.

But I cannot ask Valerie about it. She is nothing but a staggering creature whom I am dragging around aimlessly and who follows me like a blind woman. And then rounding the next turn in the path I run into a strange building standing in the glowing fog. At the same time the haunting melody becomes clearer, louder, reaching its climax in a wild crescendo. I look hard and clutch Valerie's hand in mine.

It looks like a chapel. Through the smoky, shadowy patches of fog I see the roof covered with moss and yellow cataracts; the walls seep greenish silt; the small windows have square, multi-colored panes; clumps of colorful flowers sit at the foot of the wall in beds of black roses that invade a red brick overhang.

The peaceful place echoes with the call of crickets and the distant croaking of a frog and then the music calms down like a mysterious and irresistible invitation.

Valerie and I, as if mesmerized, are seduced by the weird enchantment. We walk up to the door left ajar, push open the sculpted oak and enter... My God, it is as harsh and shocking as a jet of cold water in face.

The inside of the chapel is full of people. Men and women, all the human creatures are surrounding an altar. No one is moving. They stand there, rigid, motionless, like statues, holding long candles that burn slowly in their tight fists. No one turns around to look when we enter. Not one of these creatures seems to care that we are there.

Near the altar I finally see who is making the demonic music. Or at least the hands because only the hands are visible in the shadows of the spectral glow from the candelabra. The long, bony fingers, with gold and emerald rings, remind me of the ones that were scratching the saltpeter walls in the recording of Valerie's dream, focusing the Freudian symbolism. It is weird. These same fingers are running over the keys of the harmonium like spider legs weaving its web.

And the music swells... swells... beyond the walls and the universe.

In front of the altar I notice two empty seats, kind of like prayer desks furnished with red velvet cushions. It is Valerie now who leads me, unthinkingly, down the aisle and I have the vague impression that the seats are reserved for us. I walk, I move forward, but the fear that has not left me is once again screaming its ominous warning.

No... Robert... No, not this...

The human shadow beats its hands wildly in the shade of the altar, which seems to swell with the rhythm of the music. Then the black marble starts to glimmer as if it were smeared with the black drool that haunts me and hounds me with its ghostly persecution.

No... No, Robert... Don't go near it... Don't go near it...

This screaming in my head like a panic storm.

All of a sudden I tear myself away form Valerie's grip, from the cursed altar and the alien music. The fingers freeze on an agonizing note when I turn around. I feel the weight of all the eyes staring intensely at me... But no, they are only blind, dead eyes with no expression.

Everything is false and absurd. At this moment I realize the whole, frightening comedy of it. These creatures are not human. They are just wax figures, museum pieces, frozen in eternal poses.

In the heavy, suffocating silence I look at the dozens of pale, shriveled up faces, cracked and furrowed. Then suddenly they start melting in the candle flames, their features turn slack and soft, almost coming alive in strange and revolting expressions that makes my hair stand on end. The wax melts... melts... and soon they are nothing but ghastly wounds, vile tumors bubbling and sizzling in the yellow flames.

"Valerie!"

I realize that Valerie has disappeared and I am alone in the middle of the cursed chapel. In a fit of mad rage I run for the exit, but the door is closed and locked from the outside. I run back, knocking over some of the dolls that smash and crumble to the ground.

"Valerie!"

Stumbling through the warm, soft wax, stepping over the nightmarish mannequins, I head for the windows, but they all have grills of unbreakable iron. I catch sight of a door to the left of the altar and run for it. It opens. I jump through and fall back on it, slamming it shut with a muffled thud.

CHAPTER IV

Time passes. I passed out. Maybe it stopped what was happening?

It is also possible that it has no meaning whatsoever in this apparently senseless universe where I continue to struggle beyond all logic. And why doesn't Greysson contact me? What could have happened? Are they going to leave me here, abandon me, too, in this unknown world?

I know that insanity is beyond fear, more terrible than death. For God's sake, can there be anything more terrible and more frightening than death?

And Valerie? What has become of her? Why did she run away? Why her sudden, baffling disappearance? What role is she playing in this adventure where she seems to be the key?

I struggle with an alternative. Come on, let's try to be reasonable. In the first place, let's accept Greysson's idea, meaning the existence of a parallel world that coexists with our own through the network of the unconscious. And let's suppose as well that this world could spill over into our. Then Valerie would be like an instrument of this phenomenon. A kind of door that opens onto this inscrutable universe. Yes, that makes sense. Exactly how it works, I have no idea. It is obviously beyond my comprehension and yet I can accept it in principle.

But is Valerie aware of her role in this connection or not? This is where I stumble and understand nothing. Is her escape from the outside world voluntary? Should this imprisoning withdrawal into a grave be considered a symbol of remorse? Is all this a figment of her imagination, a creation of her psyche or is it the work of the real masters of this illusive world? And for what purpose? Is it, in fact, reality or trickery? Who is behind all this?

Who? What?

So many questions that will obviously remain without answers and the problem becomes more complicated because Valerie is gone. But I have to find her at any cost.

I gather my strength, my composure and my courage. Then I look in front of me at a long, stone staircase that leads deep down into the ground. This must be the way that she took. I step down the narrow, vaulted passage, listening closely, all my senses on alert. Still the same, mysterious silence.

I continue to descend but stop after a while to rest a little. Before me the stairs plunge down, down, down into the absurd world.

However, they have to lead somewhere. Unraveling the absurd with logic is a challenge and I quickly grow anxious when I realize that the stairs are endless.

It's an endless staircase that goes down forever into the infinite.

I see the danger of this blind, crazy journey and turn around. I would rather face the traps of the cursed chapel. But I do not get twenty steps when a terrible foreboding makes me turn back.

Good God! What's happening?

Behind me the stairs have disappeared as if they were sucked into nothingness, a nothingness that is swallowing the steps under my feet, little by little, as I progress. I have the feeling that the whole staircase *descends* into nothingness. Me, I stop moving. All my strength, on the other hand, is focused on keeping me on this border between the material and immaterial. It is like I am trying to go up a down escalator in a department store! My crazy march is like a hamster in a wheel.

My God, how long will I be able to hold out? Hounded by fear and horror I try as hard as I can to escape from the infernal cycle and I manage to climb up a few steps... a few more steps...

But in looking up this endless, imaginary staircase I suddenly lose my balance and fall headlong up the stairs. I say "headlong up" because my climbing had abruptly changed into a fall, thus breaking the directional field of gravity. Now the stairs are no longer going up. They are going down! I have lost all sense of direction and I have no idea where I am.

Using my feet and legs I manage to stand up, climb the other way and after a dozen steps I find the "connection" again. It is a neutral step, going both ways at once. Beyond it the steps become anti-steps and I have to correct myself and turn 90 degrees to feel like I am "going down" this same straight staircase that even so has two different directions: that which goes up and that which goes down.

It is bewildering. Bewildering because the two directions both end up nowhere. The trap goes on with the symbol of the infinite grafted onto the unknown.

They are trying to make me crazy, obviously. Losing one's balance is the first step into the valley of madness. If I don't react, I'm lost... and I know it. But what can I do? What can I do, Lord?

Oh, Greysson... Greysson... Why don't you answer? Where are you? What happened?

My voice echoes and the nothingness around the dream stairs suddenly materializes. A spectacular landscape appears. Huge, gigantic... A park... A forest... Flat, stiff, petrified in the shade of contrasting hues. It is a two dimensional landscape that resembles a giant painting with its subtle colors intensified in an abstract and subjective play.

A blind force pulls and pushes me at the same time. A violent, irresistible force that makes me stretch out my arms when I am catapulted into the marvelous scenery. I shoot forward like a bullet and rip through the canvas. The sound of a bell pounds my ears; the world wheels in a concert of vibrations; and the wave of fire, glittering with sparks, vanishes before my dazed eyes.

A lie there, stretched out on the ground, for a minute, not moving, breathing hard... A light breeze shakes the tall, green trees of a forest in spring... I let the tender grass caress my face.

I stand up, turn and look around. The sight behind me is terrifying. A monstrous hole separates the two scenes like a bridge spanning from nowhere to the real. From the ground up to the sky the landscape is *ripped apart.*

CHAPTER V

I tear myself away from the frightening vision to face the pseudo-reality. I move forward at random, walking into the huge park between the massive, imposing tree trunks, trampling the thick grass under my feet, which feels like a soft carpet. Silence is everywhere. It does no good to listen carefully, not a sound can be heard.

A distant sun shines above me in the hazy sky, pouring down a hard, clear light that contrasts with the shadows of the forest and brightens the colors of the landscape. And these colors seem to come from a palette that does not belong to Nature. They are too intense or too pale, with the emerald green of the streams, the dark pink of the paths, the blue hills and silver branches overhead. It is as if the very essence of the painting were rising up from some unthinkable source of light. But the huge painting comes to life, is alive, extending beyond its proportions.

I keep walking under the foliage, getting my eyes used to the half-light, but soon I realize that I am not alone. Someone is following me… or something.

It is hard to say since it is only a shadow. A kind of nebulous, dark brown thing clinging to my feet, with vaguely human contours but a head that is just a round ball without eyes or a nose or a mouth. It imitates everything I do, stops when I stop, walks when I walk, runs when I run.

What is this blind, docile creature that follows me around like some dreary, beaten dog?

I dive behind two big trees, trying to get ahead of it, but it does me absolutely no good. The shadow is still tagging along as if I were the center of its world.

"What is going on?" I ask aloud, "What do you want from me? Who are you? Answer me!"

I get no answer. Just complete stillness from the shadow, which looks like it is studying my reflexes, my behavior, my way of moving.

Based on human criteria it is hard to grant any intelligence to this strange creature. Does it even understand me? I pick up a rock, but my threatening gesture has no effect. The rock flies and disappears inside its smoky body, but it still does not flinch.

I feel myself starting to get nervous and angry in the face of this failure that once again proves the powerlessness I am wallowing in. This creature is unbearable. It reminds me of the one playing the harmonium in the cursed chapel. Except the hands here have only the dark and hazy semblance of human hands.

I jump quickly behind a hill and roll over to face my pursuer, but now its reflexes are faster. The synchronicity is almost perfect. The shadow is before me, waiting peacefully.

Damn, I think I've got it. This creature is just a relay. Nothing but a semi-material projection of another being that stays invisible or imperceptible to my human senses. Moreover, the shape was rough at the start. Now its outline is almost perfectly human and in it I see my own figure. Like the image of my body if it were lit up by a powerful beam of light and thrown on a screen.

The study goes on, there is no doubt about it. They are studying me in body and soul and so quickly and so effectively that I see the danger in the terrifying form of an entity that can suck me up entirely and leave me just a ragdoll, a bag of bones, a giant cocoon, an empty, motionless corpse. And then would they abandon me here in this phony Ruysdaël nightmare? But who is controlling all this?

Who? What?

Alas, everything I try to imagine about these beings who haunt this world correspond to nothing. It is beyond human imagining.

I stand up straight, slowly, trying not to think about anything. However, the idea of attacking this creature is nagging me. I can only attack by surprise if somehow…

But I reject the idea. Right away! Instantly!

Then I act on instinct, without thinking, using my reflexes rather than reflection. I dive to the side, clumsily, wildly, stumbling behind a tree trunk and in a flash I know that my uncoordinated movements have confused my adversary. I wait a second and lurch for the shadow, which I throw into an awkward position.

I feel like I am sinking into a mass of cold, empty space that stinks of sulfur and ether. I swing wildly inside the energized network, breaking the lines of perceptible energy that kind of branch out inside the vapory mass.

It is a frightening, dreamlike battle that fills me with disgust and horror. I strike and swing, slice up and down inside the mother mass until the short-circuits fritter away the energy in a harmless spurt of golden sparks.

When I come around, sick and nauseous, I see the energy network of the relay-creature breaking up into small, round, droplets that roll away over the ground and disappear without a trace. The battle is over. I breathe deeply and look around, then I choose to run without a moment's delay, stopping only to catch my breath every once in a while.

But it is to be expected that the masters of this world are not going to leave it there. The destruction of the relay-creature must have registered somewhere.

I keep running... blindly, wearily, with this ever-present fear that won't leave me.

I finally reach what seems to me to be the edge of this strange and incomprehensible forest, but I stop short before the infinite space in front of me, all of a sudden, filled with noise and movement.

In the middle of the vast clearing fairground stalls stand in the rural warmth. I see wheels of fortune with their big numbers spinning... spinning... Trap shooting... Balls dancing on jets of water... small, light, round, white balls spinning... spinning... And even a carousel and its wooden horses with their flowing manes that go round... and round... and round... to the sound of a barrel organ.

I walk timidly, scrutinizing the deserted fairgrounds, and suddenly I think I recognize Valerie's silhouette drifting through the stalls. Unconsciously I rush forward, reach the first row of stalls, stop to look around, rush off and stop again, each time seeing the image of Valerie appear and vanish as if by magic.

A studded wheel of fortune stops turning. 8... number 8... And off it goes again!

Four aces spin on their clay supports and the pipes accompany their endless rounds.

Farther along a roulette wheel clicks away with its silver ball, which jumps from one slot to another. Here, there, back again. 10! Number 10! And off it goes again!

God, how my head is spinning! It is Valerie's image that whirls around the stalls, on the numbered wheel, on the never-ending carousel.

Valerie!

I catch sight of her silhouette on a wooden horse and move forward, drunk on the perpetual motion.

"Valerie!"

In a single bound I leap forward, grab a brass pole and pull myself up. Valerie flees into the infernal circle, sliding, slight and snake-like, between the wooden horses going up and down.

"Valerie!'

Spinning round, I try to spot her amid the horses that prance to the endless rhythm, but her image dissolves, dilutes in the movement.

And then an arm of energy springs out of the control box inside the ride. The jointed arm stretches out to me, but in a mad dash I escape the greedy hand's grip. The arm grows longer and chases me around the platform. The index finger is pointing to the floor. Instinctively I jump between two feisty Pegasus with cruel and menacing wooden smiles.

And right then I realize that the edge of the platform is just a series of numbers. Like the wheel of fortune! And I have just jumped on number 5.

The arm of power retracts and disappears, swallowed up by the box and the grinding organ while I watch the carousel slow down. And I understand, beyond fear and reason, the Machiavellian purpose of this monstrous game.

A huge mouth, out of all proportion, which resembles Valerie's, with delicately curved lips, has just appeared in the ground around the carousel. The mouth stretches and smiles at me. Then all of a sudden it opens wide like a hungry beast. I see it get bigger and rounder at every spin, little by little as the carousel slows down.

Yes, I understand… I understand what is waiting for me if the number 5 stops in front of the voracious mouth.

I want to jump off and flee this horror, but it is impossible… Impossible because an invisible barrier blocks my every effort. So, I calculate; I watch; I try to foresee the fatal number… No, not 5… The 8… No, watch out… Quick, the 9…

Like the silver ball on the roulette wheel I jump from one number to another. I have suddenly become the ball of chance in this chilling suspense.

The 7… The 1… The 4… And the 8 wins the round. Missed by only one slot. My God, is it possible?

The mouth grins and disappears into the grassy carpet as I jump off the platform that has stopped and let down its energy barrier. I run, shouting my terror, into the fairground, which is just another trap laid out by the masters of this world.

But here in the midst of my flight, Valerie appears. Like me she is running, panicking, into the deserted clearing. When I reach out to grab her we roll on the ground, exhausted, overwhelmed, blending our breath, our anguish and our madness!

CHAPTER VI

When I open my eyes Valerie is still here in front of me, lying on the soft grass, her eyes staring up at the cloudy sky. The fairgrounds have disappeared. There is nothing around us but infinite space fanned by a light breeze. No sound... Nothing... As if all the silence of the universe were gathered up in the heart of this clearing.

Valerie finally looks at me with her big, clear eyes that reflex the dark shores of an ocean of sorrow. Her chest rises and falls to the rhythm of her breath and the heat from her body makes me unspeakably dizzy. We are beyond words, conventions, rules and principles. Outside of time, space, human contingencies, whatever is or is not. Beyond Life... Beyond Death!

We are just two beings lost in the vortex of madness.

"All this is horrible, isn't it?" she whispers.

"Why did you run away from me? Why?"

"I was also trying to run away from myself, but I couldn't do it."

"If you had only tried to understand..."

"You can't do anything for me, Robert. You can do nothing... Nothing! You've seen what they can do! I belong to them for eternity. It's too late now."

I sit up next to her without taking my eyes off her. "What if we start from scratch? What if you accept my help a little? Maybe we can..."

"Why did I kill my husband, right?"

A dim smile crossed her lips and her eyes went back to the hazy sky.

She murmured, "I had become Greg's instrument. Nothing more than a tool, a probe to visit the unconscious, this unknown dimension that he had discovered in the depths of himself. But Greg had a very weak emotional quotient. He needed someone with a more receptive, more flexible psychological nature and who could give themselves wholly to the hypnogogic effects. It's because I have this that Greg made me his one and only experimental subject. It was awful. Awful because Greg's work was the work of a madman."

She looked away from cloudy sky and straight at me.

"And every day he dragged me farther into this madness that I was scared of, but that I became a prisoner of little by little. You can't know, Robert... you can't know. The worst thing is that I didn't kill him in a fit of insanity. That's a lie. That's what everyone believes, but I swear to you that it's a lie. It's just the opposite, in a burst of clarity, that I did what I did... because I had to do it. I had to!"

Tears flowed like an ocean of sorrow had suddenly broken the dams in her. I let her weep out her terrible secret, leaning over her like a vigilant psychoanalyst, drinking in her words.

"For some time Greg was working on a kind of electronic machine that he said could destroy all sound waves. At first I thought it was some revolutionary process in his field of research. Greg was trying to reduce the amount of sleep by getting rid of the sounds from the sleeper's body. I thought it could only improve the process psychophysiological regeneration. But I was wrong and he himself told me the truth. A man or a group of men could rule the world if they built a machine able to wipe out all sound waves on the surface of the Earth.

Everything was ready and he had even sought the help of a technician. The man could not know anything about the real project, of course, but Greg was sure he could convince him later and rally him to his cause. That's when he tested the machine in front of me and I knew that he wasn't bluffing and that nothing could stop him. I also knew that it was impossible for me to escape and warn humanity about the crime being planned. That's why I destroyed the machine and killed him."

She stops talking. Her face is flooded with tears.

I nod. "I'm the man Gregory Watson sent for."

"From Melbourne?"

"Yes, Melbourne."

"So, it was you."

"Unfortunately, the machine was only partially destroyed. I fixed it… It works fine."

"My God!"

She jumps up but I calm her down with a soft hand and a soft voice. "There's one thing I don't understand. That bothers me. Was Gregory Watson good enough at electronics to build such a complicated machine?"

"No, certainly not."

"Then how did he do it?"

"I don't know."

"But really…"

She shrugs. "He said he got the idea in his sleep."

"That's weird."

"He quoted the example of Niels Bohr digging up most of his quantum theory from his dreams… Tartini's Devil's Trill Sonata composed in dreams… and Kekulé's revelations about benzene, also during his sleep."

74

"Niels Bohr was a physicist, Tartini a musician and Kekulé a chemist. But what did Watson know about electronics?"

In the silence that follows, I decide to avoid the awkward subject. There is another that is bothering me. To find out the *real* reason that compelled Valerie to hide away in this world of nightmare.

Certainly there is the conscious remorse behind it, materialized with the mental creations of her subconscious. We start from here. Then everything gets confused, completely baffling because Valerie does not seem to me to have built the reality of this unknown dimension by her repression. For her this was just a psychological sanctuary that might allow her to escape from the reality of things.

Okay, but a conscious hideaway or a repressive hideaway due to a dependence on "psychedelic" drugs? That is still the question I ask myself. But when I talk to her about the invisible creatures chasing us and attacking us since we climbed out of the grave, she is seized by an agonizing terror.

She admits that she is the prisoner of this strange world and her voice sounds the same as in the throes of madness. A return to normal life is something impossible for her from now on, too much for her strength and willpower. But am I not in the same boat? Haven't all my ties with the outside world also been cut? And yet I think I could find the strength and the willpower if I really wanted to.

I do not know. It is like a vague feeling I have deep down inside me. In all, thinking logically, I am just transplanted onto Valerie's unconscious network. She is something else... And so?

Therefore, I am forced to return to my original idea. Unconsciously Valerie is the agent of the materialization that I witnessed before I left. But I have to be careful in planting this idea in her head. Otherwise...

I prefer to broach the subject that seems important to me. "But there must be a normal way to make contact with these creatures," I say softly.

"It's impossible. They've got us and there's nothing we can do about it."

"Because we've never tried. We've done nothing but endure their psychic attacks."

"Robert, try to understand. We're in a universe that is totally foreign to human senses. Everything we see or hear is a trap or a trick. The rest, the essence of this strange world, is inaccessible to us. For the mouse that nibbles on our cheese, the cheese exists; it accepts it as it is, but can it understand the nature of the cheese and the whole process necessary to make it? The spider weaves its web in the corner of the ceiling, but what concept does it have of a ceiling? And the mosquito, is it conscious at all of the man it's just stung?"

"Because they have no reason. But us, Valerie, we're different. We can communicate intelligently with any intelligent creature."

She sighs and struggles with her own powerlessness. "It would spell our end, our ruin... our death."

"And if the fate of all humanity rests in our hands, Valerie?"

"Why do you say that?"

I am on the verge of admitting the truth to her, of telling her about the danger I imagine and that I vaguely glimpse... But no, I still need all of Valerie's faculties, her courage and whatever stamina and nerves she has left. And anyway, what proof can I give her? Nothing meshes in this damn story.

The only option I have, as I told her, is to contact these creatures and try to find out what they have in mind for us. Then, maybe, I will understand.

I catch Valerie staring at me, like she was trying to search my soul and read my thoughts. I see her turn pale at my decision. And at this moment I feel as if I have known her forever, as if we have lived alone, just the two of us, since the beginning of Time.

I look at her stretched out on the soft grass, which dries up and turns yellow before my eyes. Well, this is weird! It is like the springtime has just abruptly turned to autumn. But no, all the colors are disappearing. The sky above us is the color of lead and the forest has turned black and white, like a huge cartoon drawn with charcoal.

Nothing but black... white... gray... The world around us is dissolving, fusing into these three hues.

"Robert..."

In a fit of excitement, I lean over and take Valerie in my arms. I kiss her wildly, mindlessly.

And the world tips over, spins round and collapses...

CHAPTER VII

Valerie is gone. She dissolved with the rest of the world. My arms wail in the void and dark. An inky night surrounds me. I am floating in an absurd nothingness. I try to move, but none of my movements make any sense.

Where am I? This time I am determined to keep calm and cool-headed, not to give in to panic but to try to analyze coldly everything that happens. I need all my power to confront this new trap because I figure it is new attempt by the mysterious creatures to test my reflexes and my human capacity.

The wait drags on in this neutral time where I hold onto the image of Valerie and the taste of her lips.

Then all of a sudden a bright light shoots out of the darkness. It is like a blinding spotlight aimed at me. In the perpendicular beam springing out of the void, a game of chess appears, with its pawns and pieces all lined up. Two hands emerge from the dark and stop in front of me at the edge of the board. Two bony hands with long fingers wearing gold and emerald rings.

The index finger points at the line of white pawns. "You can start, Mr. Milland."

The voice from nowhere sounds cold and impersonal. My invisible adversary is mingled with the dark void he seems to be part of. Only his pseudo-human hands are visible in the dazzling light that shines on the chessboard. The voice explains the rules.

I ask, "What are the stakes?"

"Your life, Mr. Milland."

"I'm only a mediocre player."

A cruel laugh rises in the void, sneering and insulting. "On the contrary, you are very good… A remarkable player."

The trick has no effect. The creature probed my intellect, searched my memory.

It hastens to add, "The chances are equal."

"To be equal the stakes have to be reciprocal."

"They are, in a way, seeing that I want your life."

"Wouldn't it be simpler for you to get it another way?"

"Certainly, but I'm giving you a chance to win and myself a chance to lose. Your life will be of no interest to me if I lose. Well, Mr. Milland, it's your move."

I move a knight forward and the attack is launched straightaway. Strange concept nevertheless to stake a man's life when it would take almost nothing… maybe a simple gesture on the creature's behalf…

The fourth move captures my knight and puts my rook in danger.

"Are all the solutions to your problems defined by combinations of calculation and chance?"

I think I hit the target because the voice responds, "All."

"So if I understand rightly, the decision is imposed by the game. Winning or losing decides the event."

"These are not the rules of the universe, Mr. Milland. Sorry about your rook… Your attack, however, was wonderful. Coming back to your question, we consider the game in all its forms, like an interpolation of chance in the universal game, because chance does not exist. Chance is just the result of an infinite sum of conditions and underlying events. To create it through a game seems to us the only reason for a justifiable struggle against the game of the universe. To win or lose one's life in a game of chess also means the obligatory acceptance of one's errors."

"What chance do you give my fellow men? To gamble their lives on a simple game of chess?"

I swipe his knight and focus my attack on his queen. Silence.

"The possibility of fighting against us, of winning or losing scientifically, considering the terms of perturbation and the factors of probability."

"But why? What do you want?"

"To conquer your universe... your dimension. To impose our principles, our rules. It is a universal law, nothing shocking. All it takes is finding a way to reach your universe. And we have found it. Fate will decide."

I am scared by so much cynicism. For these creatures, the conquest of humanity and of our universe is just a game! Just a simple game with its own rules and tactics limited only by the intelligence and cleverness of the players. Exactly like on a chessboard.

My knight counter-attacks, but the persistent battle on the black and white squares makes me feel like I am gambling my soul against the devil.

My thought travels to the creature who, in the midst of his defense, seems to appreciate the symbol. "God and Satan are also formidable adversaries, Mr. Milland, in their eternal conflict. Like us, someday, one of them must lose."

"And in your opinion what will happen?"

"A check and a mate will decide the celestial throne."

"What do you make of the omnipotence of God?"

An icy laugh rattles through the darkness. "An omnipotence that seems to me very compromised before the devil's cunning. The very existence of the devil contradicts this all-powerfulness. No, you see, I don't agree. They, too, are of equal strength as they face off in the game of Good versus Evil. And humanity is nothing more than the stakes of the game."

The laugh becomes even more cynical, more monstrous. "Don't let that stop us from playing, Mr. Milland. If the game is the eternal symbol of virtue and vice, we cannot give it up. We are not built in the image of our creators, are we?"

His reasoning repulses me, but I appreciate his knowledge of the game, his subtle attacks, his mastery and his ingenuity. The invisible being seems well versed in all the finer points of the game. At the end of a blitz offensive, one of his pseudo-hands suddenly swipes up three more pawns and I feel a cold sweat dripping down my spine.

It is the loss of my soul that is played out in these last turns, but I also see the fate of my fellow men in the victory of these demonic creatures. As a result, and this is the cruelest thing, I also imagine God playing against Satan at a celestial chessboard defying the laws of space and time. Like me and this alien creature, I see them sitting across from each other, waffling from hope to despair as the pieces come and go, attack and counter-attack.

Yes, it is possible... A match that can end in Satan's victory and in the reversal of values. I picture God losing his Light and sinking into eternal damnation.

Oh, no, it is impossible... impossible... This is too frightening. The idea is just a trick, a ploy sent out by the extra-terrestrial creature to frustrate my mind and divert the focus I need to confront him.

I forget about the images, I deny them, I reject them, to devote my full concentration to the last possible attacks. Then, all of a sudden, I see a way out. I bait my rival to divert his attention. The attack is just the start of a chain reaction whose result I am trying to hide by a new move that will make me look clumsy and bungling. The being giggles. I do not think he has seen the trap.

"You are really playing worse and worse, Mr. Milland. I think your life is hanging by a thread. A very thin thread. Please, I'll give you time to think."

I give up another pawn, just to build his confidence, and then finally launch the decisive attack. I open a path to his king!

I hear a kind of quiet gasp, the expression of profound surprise. His defense is fast and hard, but too late. I have destroyed all but some feeble defenses. He is cornered.

His bony hand sweeps away the pieces and pushes back the chessboard when I announce, "Check and mate!"

A bad sport? No, I do not think he is. I am at his mercy. He only has to wave his hand to destroy me, but for this being the decisions of the game are the only ones he knows. His own are secondary, dependent on those imposed by the game, whatever they are!

He says calmly, "You are free. Bravo, Mr. Milland. You won this time."

"Does that mean we will see each other again?"

"Of course... but later."

I nod. "I have one more question to ask you."

It's about Valerie, of course, but the creature pulls his hands back from the chessboard. The pawns and other pieces have already vanished like magic.

"I'm sorry but we've told you everything we can."

"And yet you allow your most formidable enemy to go free..."

"Because you know our intentions? Because you suspect the way that will lead us to your fellow men? Because you can warn humanity against the danger threatening them?"

The same cynical, monstrous laugh breaks out, with a hint of irony. It is the final answer the alien creature gives me as he returns to nothingness with the chessboard and the bright light from the invisible source.

I plunge into the dark, floating in the fog of an endless void where time means nothing. Then all of a sudden I come out fully awake inside a big round room.

Completely round.

The circular wall surrounding me has no opening. The wall is of metal, glowing with a dim, hazy light, curving around a ceiling as smooth and bare as the interior of this strange cabin.

The sudden awareness that I face no danger here compels me to try once again to contact my own world. I call Greysson. I voice answers me, penetrating into my subconscious. The cerebral flux quickly tunes into my selective circuits.

"Okay, Milland, we're getting you out. Lie down… Relax…"

I do as he says. I am washed over by a wave of hope, but I still think of Valerie. Maybe…

"Don't worry about anything," the impersonal voice responds. "Let's deal with you first, Mr. Milland."

"But what happened? Why didn't you an…"

"Lie down… Relax… Watch it… We're starting to bring you back…"

There is no need to insist. I obey the will that is directing me. The wall starts spinning and becomes a thin circle of light that starts spinning faster and faster. I close my eyes, feeling dizzy, unable to move at all... to think at all...

Time races... Time flies... in the dream universe streaming by in reverse.

The "resurfacing" is devastating, suffocating. I feel like all the atoms in my body are exploding and scattering in a burst of sparks.

And then the dizziness fades. The wave throws me onto the shore of consciousness inside my body, my real body of flesh and blood, and an intense heat spreads quickly throughout my organism.

My head is heavy, my eyelids burn... I lift my head up and look around. I am lying on a soft, comfortable bed... in the middle of a dimly lit room. The circular wall surrounding me is of metal. I am in the middle of a big...

PART THREE

CHAPTER I

… round room.

Completely round.

Nausea mounts. God, how sick I feel!

But where am I? I do not recognize the experiment room in Watson's house. This place is foreign, totally unfamiliar… and the most frightening thing is that this room is like… Oh, my eyes! My head! I can barely make out the figures moving around me.

"Greysson!"

The white forms dance across the veil of fever. I feel a hand on my forehead… I see another holding out a bowl to me. I drink and swallow and close my eyes on the muddle of my last sensations, the incoherent intrusion of vague impressions.

And in a flash! The only… the only memory I have of the return trip. Again that man lying on the shimmering surface of an infinite lake. That gigantic being who keeps turning his back to me and who seems to be sleeping while the lake around him swallows the stars. Always the same vision of coming and going… that I attribute to an obsession or to some Freudian symbol of my unconscious that escapes my understanding.

"How do you feel, Mr. Milland?"

The voice jolts me back to reality and after a few fruitless efforts, I finally manage to open my eyes. The fever is lifted; I breathe more easily; my muscles are less stiff. It's funny, I do not know this person standing over me. His bearded face looks like an old patriarch. Next to him are two doctors wearing white coats and caps and plastic gloves. But I still do not see Greysson, Aymes, Dayton or Lindsay.

"Who are you?"

"I'm Professor Sullivan," the bearded man answers. "Don't worry about anything. Everything went just fine. Drink some more. You have to eliminate all the toxins in your body. Go on, drink."

I obey. Something is troubling me. Valerie's body is not here in the round room and when I ask about it, Dr. Sullivan nods his head and says, "We'll talk about that later. For the moment you need to rest. Your brain suffered a rather violent shock. Don't shake it up for no good reason."

"I have to talk to you... You have to listen to me..."

"Later. Later."

"It's very serious, please... I have to..."

"Come now, come now, calm down."

All my efforts are in vain. On Sullivan's order I am put on a gurney and rolled out of the circular room into a small chamber with painted walls under the watchful eye of a young nurse. I get a new drink and take a new plunge, but this time into a deep, restful sleep without dreams, where I lose all concept of things and myself...

CHAPTER II

The young nurse waits for me to put on my clean, disinfected clothes that they brought to me when I woke up. The others are soaked with sweat and the stench of pharmaceuticals. I leave them with no regrets.

"This way, Mr. Milland."

The door opens onto a brightly lit hallway. It looks like the inside of a hospital or a research center, which are always built on the same design. Rooms, hallways, elevators, spotless walls and polished floors. In Melbourne it was exactly...

"No, not there... Over here."

I had almost run into a transparent panel. For a moment I just stand there, not moving, stunned. Inside the room I have just found Valerie lying on her relaxation bed. There is no mistake, it is really her or at least her body because she is still, apparently, stuck in her unconscious, withdrawn into herself, completely absent and closed to the outside world, to the room where the men in white coats are bustling around.

The endoscopic memories that bind us come back into my mind, vibrant but only momentary because the nurse's hand grabs my shoulder.

"Come, Mr. Milland. Please come."

I do not understand anything that is happening to me. I let myself be guided to the end of a long hallway and when a door opens and I enter a big, airy office, I immediately recognize Professors Greysson and Aymes along with Dr. Sullivan. Their smiles look frozen, stamped with worry and distress.

Greysson walks up to me, holding out his hand. "We're very glad to see you again, Milland. I hope you're feeling better. Everything is okay, isn't it?"

He quickly shows me to a chair as I see Sullivan turn on a tape recorder. Slowly the reels start spinning on their axes.

I look at Greysson. "What I have to tell you is very serious, but first I have a few questions to ask. Where are we?"

"In Dr. Sullivan's psychiatric clinic outside of Boston."

"Why am I here?"

"By order of the forensic investigators. We couldn't continue the experiment at Watson's. Don't worry, the transfer was made under excellent conditions. Moreover, everything had to be set up to watch over the psycho-physiological consequences you might suffer on your return. We can keep a close eye on you here."

"But I feel totally normal…"

"We don't doubt that in the least, Milland. By and large, the preliminary tests are pretty encouraging."

"Why do you say 'by and large'?"

Sullivan answers, "You suffered a nervous shock. There are still a few scars to get rid of on the conscious level, but with a little time everything will be all right, I assure you."

It is strange. I have never felt healthier in body or mind. All this talk bewilders me. I look at Aymes, who has stopped cracking his knuckles and is concentrating on a coin that he is flipping in his hand.

I turn back to Greysson. "Now it's time for me to open your eyes. Do you know that this world really exists, Greysson?"

"The fifth dimension?"

"The one you talked about, yes. You followed all the phases of the trip on the encephaloscope, I suppose?"

"Only some because there were blackouts. I have to tell you that we had a really hard time keeping in touch with you.

"Wait a second. How long did my trip last?"

"Eight days."

I look at him gawking and gaping. Eight days! I can hardly believe it. But time does not much matter; it is secondary.

I speak in the same tone. "Listen to me, Greysson. What you fear is about to come to pass on a grand scale. We're on the eve of an invasion launched by these abominable creatures who live in the fifth dimension. And nothing will stop them, I assure you. It's the world of the unconscious that is spilling over into the reality that we call OUR reality. What happened in the Watson's house on the night of my departure was just a trial run, a test, if you will. But now they know the way."

"What way?"

"Valerie Watson, of course!"

"Poor Valerie," Aymes sighed, continuing his game of heads and tails. "What next?"

"Then there's the sonic annihilator, the sound swallower."

"Better and better. Keep going."

I feel a sudden weakness from my head down to my toes. What is happening here? I say, "The two phenomena are connected. I have learned the strategy of 'the silent ones'."

"The silent ones?" Sullivan repeats, staring at me with curiosity.

"Yes, that's what I call them because they can only live in silence. Do you understand now?"

Greysson nods his head, deep in thought. Aymes fidgets with his flipping coin. "This is very interesting. Tell us everything you're thinking, Milland."

"I've thought long and hard about the problem and I believe I've found a solution. These beings are allergic to sound waves. The slightest noise can destroy them in the same way that an explosion shatters windows here with us. Of course this is just a comparison because for these creatures it's much worse. Their molecular architecture breaks apart and dissolves in contact with sound waves. Just like what happened when I turned off the sonic annihilator. Remember? Therefore, for their invasion to be successful, they had to find a way to wipe sounds off the face of the Earth. Seeing a way open in Valerie Watson, they used her to influence the mind of Gregory Watson, who then built the sound swallower by order of 'the silent ones'. Believe me, these beings know human psychology better than we know ourselves. They simply used Watson by letting him believe that he was the master of his own will. And Watson, in his madness, dreamed only of ruling the world for himself. I beg you, we have to destroy this machine."

Their heads move... the reels keep spinning...

Greysson clears his throat. "Don't you think you're exaggerating a little, Milland?"

"What?! How can you ask that? Come on, you must have recorded my contact with Valerie. She told me everything about the machine. You saw this world the same as I. It exists. The traps I fought against were real. The beings, too, were real. So?"

"Unfortunately, that's a subject we've discussed a lot," Sullivan responds, "and we've come up with our own conclusion."

"I'd love to hear it."

"Okay. The cenesthesic reactions of your subconscious under the influence of psychedelic drugs wove the web of this universe by calling upon the memories stored in your neurons. At the moment everything is mixed up, deformed and turned into a nightmare. Yes, it's only a nightmare… You *lived through* a nightmare. Do you understand?"

"But that's impossible!"

"Why?"

"There's Valerie. Valerie is still a prisoner of 'the silent ones'. She's the one they're using."

"Anyone can tell you that there's no hope of saving her. All we can do is maintain her heartbeat with empirical methods, but we're not fooling ourselves. You, too, failed, Milland, and it's too bad because now it's over for her."

I sit there debating with myself because I see how completely their minds are made up. Something must have happened that I cannot put my finger on. Still, I give it another shot.

"Greysson, there really were those marks… those black traces… the remains of flesh. That thing cost Miss Foyle her life."

He looked at me, shaking his head. "I'm going to disappoint you again, Milland, because there's something you don't know and we don't know either. The autopsy revealed that Miss Foyle had a heart lesion. Any loud noise or a good fright as a result of nervous tension could have done her in. That's what the coroner concluded. As for the traces you talk about, well, I have to agree with Professor Aymes. We were all victims of a kind of collective hallucination."

"A hallucination?"

"Yes. You know the house was chock full of drugs and you can't breathe in such intoxicating stuff without suffering the effects. Eight times out of ten such kinds of hallucination are contagious."

I suddenly feel like he is trying to convince me in any way possible, even by exaggerating whatever truth lay behind his words.

"As for the sonic annihilator, hold on tight, Mr. Milland…"

"Oh, please, let's go! I'm ready for anything now!"

"Well, we tried it out four or five times already, but in front of an investigative committee sent by the government. We couldn't take responsibility for such an important secret, you understand?"

"And what happened?"

"Nothing. We destroyed all sounds within a 100 yards and that's all." He smiles when he says, "No manifestation from the beyond!"

I have been watching Dr. Sullivan for a minute. He is hunched over his desk and playing with some matches. He had used a pencil to draw a horizontal line on a piece sheet of paper and was entertaining himself by seeing how many passages it would take for an uneven number of broken matches to cross it. I know the game. It is the river crossing puzzle where a boat has to transport cannibals and missionaries to the other shore without ever having more cannibals than missionaries together. The trick is to work backwards and keep them equal. First you have to…

I tear myself away from this idiotic game and look at Greysson. "What happened to the machine?"

"It made a lot of noise," he joked. "First of all in the FBI. They are trying to figure out how Watson could have pulled off such a stunt. But it doesn't matter. The main thing is that thanks to him our country is now in possession of a powerful weapon that is turning all the strategies of the Rand Corporation[4] upside down."

I turn pale. "I... I don't understand."

"But it's very simple. All they have to do is make a stronger annihilator and wipe out sound in a range that in one second can deprive the enemy of all telecommunications, meaning radios and telephones. The army will become deaf and dumb as it watches its country be destroyed."

I jump out of my chair. *The same tactic!* Lord! So, they have no idea that it is the same tactic as the one dreamed up by "the masters of silence" to destroy all of humanity? Don't they understand?

I try to be convincing when I say, "Greysson, for heaven's sake, listen to me or else we're lost for good. Please try to understand. It's all a trap... The day you decide to..."

He cuts me off, "Milland, you know very well that we have no intention of using this weapon against any country in the world. But we're not safe from war either."

"That's not what I mean."

"You don't understand anything. This machine is a weapon of war."

"That's what's bothering me..."

"And we have no right to destroy it. Look, try to understand our side of it. If we want to keep peace in the world this machine becomes one more ace in the hole for us."

"Greysson, do you realize what you're saying?"

---

[4] Research and Development: An American organization of operational research.

But he just shrugs. "Anything that wins the day is worth it. Believe me, war itself is just a game."

I stare at him, horrified. Instinctively I turn to Aymes who is still concentrating on his game of heads and tails. Then I look at Sullivan playing with his broken matches. My God, what are they doing?

In a split second I realize the drama playing out around me. The game! No doubt about it, the passion of the game is now rooted in their minds. The contagion is on the march and this thought freezes my blood. I figure that the subversive attack was launched exactly like at Watson's house, through Valerie's psychological channel and with the formidable telehypnotic powers of "the silent ones" that can subjugate a human being without him knowing.

Yes, the truth flashes before my eyes in all its horror.

And how many people have been turned into blind and oblivious playthings of the dreadful creatures from the fifth dimension? I think of all those people who are at this moment working around the machine, this demonic instrument that will sooner or later cause the fall of humanity.

"Hey, Milland, what's wrong?"

Greysson's voice is like a cold shower. I gawk at him, unable to find the words to convince him, to convince all of them... but do the words even exist?

"Greysson, you're infected. Your thoughts are not your own. You're all contaminated by the telehypnotic powers of our enemy. For the love of God, look at what you're doing, look deep down inside yourselves. I'm begging you, make an effort."

Sullivan sits up straight, visibly irritated. "Come on, that's enough, Mr. Milland. You're tired. You need rest."

"I was appealing to your understanding, not your anger, which doesn't hold water here."

"That's crazy. And what exactly are you insinuating? Are you maybe trying to influence our subconscious?"

I confirm, "Absolutely. So you'll end up thinking the same thoughts as anyone else. Yes, that's it. So you'll end up doing what they want you to do."

"Please, stop your ranting. We've had enough."

In a fatherly gesture, Greysson puts his hand on my shoulder. "Come on, Milland, our friend Sullivan is right. You're tired. I suggest you get a little rest and we can talk about this again later. Okay?"

I react immediately. "No, there's no point. I won't stay here one second longer. Too bad, but I'll manage on my own…"

Sullivan stares hard at me. "I'm sorry, but it's still too early for you to leave the clinic. For now, we cannot let you go free. I really regret having to tell you this, Milland."

A door opens and two nurses enter the office. I know that from now on anything I might attempt around Greysson and his clinic is useless. Hopelessly useless!

CHAPTER III

24 hours of solitude in a rubber room has got the better of the little will and courage I had left. From time to time a nurse enters the room to bring me sparkling colored drinks that they force me to drink with much kindness and persuasion. I willingly undergo an encephalograph test and I even answer a series of ridiculous questions. They think I am crazy and it is obvious that everything I say is turned against me... Of course, they cannot understand. *They can no longer understand.*

Meanwhile, between the Pacific and the Atlantic men are secretly busy working on the most monstrous machine that men have ever known. How much longer before they finish their huge "sound swallower"? That is the question I keep asking in my solitude and impotence.

They are bringing me once again to the testing room, passing through corridors. I try to draw a rough map of the place in my head, but my hopes are frustrated, if not dashed. This clinic is worse than a prison. It is like Fort Knox with its magnetic doors, its impenetrable locks and all its personnel whose vigilance is equal to the GIs watching over the state treasure.

And it is weird to talk about GIs, but I did see some making rounds outside the clinic. No, I was not mistaken. I saw them clearly through a window. There was even an electric fence around the building. Yes, it is weird, especially since I have never heard of psychiatric clinics or even insane asylums with such a high level of security.

So why all this protection and all these precautions? Are they really so scared of me escaping? Maybe they are afraid that I will tell the secret of the "sound swallower"?

Idiots! Yes, of course, in their eyes this is the sensible, the most persuasive reason. They accept it because they force them to accept it. Whereas in reality… Yes, in reality, there is another reason. But they are unaware of it because theirs is insidiously dictated by "the masters of silence."

In short, I am the only one who knows the truth. And I am a huge risk in the game. I am the disruptive element, the probability factor in their concept of chance.

And now I understand the ironic laughter of the chess player. By letting me go free, he knew perfectly well that those who were about to welcome me back were already on their side and any interference by me would hit a brick wall. Yes, so far, everything has played out according to the rules.

When I fall sleep, overwhelmed and exhausted, the despair that drowns me turns into dark, despicable laughter. Always tainted with the same irony.

CHAPTER IV

This morning I found myself once again lying on the soft ground, panting and grunting like a frightened animal. What happened to me is unthinkable, staggering, mind-boggling. I have Valerie again!

But how? I hesitate, again, to believe it. And yet everything played out as predicted and expected. Now it is our turn to play! Oh, always this word I hate to use, but I can find no other.

It happened during my sleep. Just like that, suddenly! Valerie's voice pervaded my subconscious with such force that I could not resist. It was like some desperate appeal rising from the abyss of my soul.

"Robert, let yourself be guided... Don't resist... Let me do it... Robert, it's me, Valerie... Don't be afraid... You have to know something... Robert, I found... I found..."

All of a sudden I was diving into the depths of the void like a dizzying fall inside an elevator whose cables had snapped. An uncontrollable fall that brought me into a neutral space devoid of forms and colors.

I saw Valerie right away, holding out her arms to me at the bottom of a huge chasm that my reason and the memory refused to picture correctly. She was there, still as alive, still as real as the last time we met. Still as human...

"Thank God! You're here!"

"Valerie, how did this happen? How did you..."

"It wasn't easy, but I managed to locate you." She smiled weakly to convince me. "I kept the trace of your own harmonics. But let's forget about that, okay? What I have to tell you is very important."

"Where are we?"

"No need to fear. We're in a neutral space on the second level. Do you know that I almost woke up today?"

Her smile grew in the face of my astonishment. "I said almost. Come on, quick, let's not waste time. I have to explain. I managed to create a mental barrier against the assault of hypnotic waves that are holding me prisoner. I had already done this unconsciously during one of Watson's time experiments, but it was so fast that I had no memory of it. I don't know how, but it came rushing back. And I have to tell you that after you left I tried to act. I…"

She shrugged. "Well, it's not important. When I came up to the surface, I understood right away what was happening. Everyone around me was talking. They were talking about you mostly. Of course, they weren't wary at all… Oh, Robert, it's horrible! They don't even realize that they're the unwilling accomplices of a impending doom."

"I know, Valerie, I know, but what can I do? The clinic is surrounded. There's no escape. And in the meantime…"

She cut me off, "There's a solution, Robert."

"What do you mean?"

"We can talk safely here. No one can hear us. So listen up. It's not a sure method, of course, but let's accept Greysson's first idea. I heard them laughing about it."

"The unconscious spilling over into reality?"

"You understood perfectly. Yes, Robert, now I know."

"But where are you going with all this?"

"That's why I called you back here. It's very simple. In this "bodiless" state we're in right now, I think we're on the same harmonics as the creatures living in this dimension. Are you following me?"

"Yes, go on."

"So, if it's possible for these creatures to leave their universe and enter ours by taking on a material form, there's no reason why we can't do the same."

"Hold on. You're forgetting that we already have a physical body. To get back to our dimensions, we must undergo a process of 'reimbodiment'."

"The normal process for waking up normally, okay, but if we aim our return at some target, if we can integrate into our universe in our current 'bodiless' state and wake ourselves up all of a sudden, what would happen?"

I furrowed my brow. "Valerie, come on, that's impossible! We can't exist in two forms in the same continuum."

"That's true and you just said it. There will be a fusion of the two bodies automatically. But logically the one with our mind and soul should prevail over the one left behind in the clinic. Exactly as will happen when these fiendish creatures launch their attack. They will integrate some predetermined space. So, we have to do it first. I think it's our only chance of getting away from Greysson and the clinic."

I liked Valerie's idea and could imagine that the game was far from over. It was a hard but logical idea, if accepted, for the inhabitants of the fifth dimension—the possibility of invading our world by using, basically, the same process. But the experience was not so simple because we had to take into account certain mechanical laws binding energy masses and our "reintegration" could not be left to chance.

The transmission of a mass reduced to the state of energy must be determined in accordance with a fifth dimensional concept resulting from the space-time and entropic coordinates of the place we would choose as a target. Only our minds could locate the place and determine its coordinates with maximum precision. Otherwise, we would risk crushing into some solid or even integrating in a molecular fusion with catastrophic effects.

But Valerie had already resolved the problem thanks to her knowledge and experience. The main thing was to define all the coordinates and stay masters of our will. Then everything should play out at "the speed of thought," meaning at absolute speed, our physical bodies in the clinic serving as "the way out," to keep Valerie's image. Our complete recovery would then happen at the end of our projection.

"Where have you chosen?" I asked anxiously.

She appeared to think about it for a few seconds. "First of all we have to choose a place familiar to both of us. There's no point in us being separated because when they notice we're gone, they'll start looking for us immediately. So, I think we ought to take certain precautions."

For her, the ideal place was Watson's house or at least the grounds around it. The day I arrived I got a pretty clear picture of the place and the space-time coordinates between Dr. Sullivan's clinic and the house were specified by Valerie. We agreed to land on the lawn across from the house's front door.

Valerie's hand gripped mine. "Ready, Robert?"

I suddenly had a weird feeling of fear and dread. What was going to be the result of this experiment that I was the first man to attempt?

But I shook myself and nodded. "Ready, Valerie."

"Pay attention, think of nothing, free yourself. Concentrate only on the directional vector."

I closed my eyes. Her hand suddenly became burning hot. I, too, felt a strange sensation of heat wash over me from head to toe.

The rest is too vague, too blurry, too abrupt for me to piece together with any precision. It is as if I were racing inside a dazzling light... feeling like I was vomiting on my relaxation bed. The ray of light whipped through space. My head hit the ground, I spit, I gagged and turned over still unable to realize what had happened.

I regained my sense of reality only when I saw Valerie crawling towards me on the grass. We sat there for a minute, hugging each other, unable to do anything at all.

She stood up first and pulled me after her, figuring it would be better to hide in the house where we could think about what to do now and in the immediate future because we had to act quickly.

They had sealed up all the doors, so we got into the house through the laundry room. Once inside, Valerie sighed and smiled at me.

"This is surely the last place they'll come looking for us."

I smiled back at her.

"I have to admit that we couldn't dream of a better hiding place."

But I was also thinking of what Greysson and the others would think of our mysterious disappearance.

I burst out laughing. God, how good it felt to laugh like that!

CHAPTER V

Now we can consider our situation calmly. I agree with what Valerie tells me.

"I know of only one solution. Alert Washington as soon as possible."

"It won't be easy to convince them."

"We'll explain it to them. Everything from A to Z. But first I'll see Captain Lewis of the FBI. He's an old friend of the family and will trust me. Besides, we'll be safe with him. Now we just have to find a way of getting in touch with him right away."

Of course there is the Bentley in the garage, but when we go there we find the tank empty. Not a single drop of gas. Valerie groans as she remembers a leak in the tank that was never fixed. Watson had put it on the back burner because before his death he never left his room, so to speak, obsessed as he was by his work and numerous experiments.

Valerie gets upset. "Well, that's all we need! Especially since the train stations and airports must be watched. Don't even think of it, we'll be spotted in a second. No, we have to find our own way out of this. We can travel by night. Right now I'm going to try to find the gas."

"And the leak?"

I crawl under the tank and see the small hole in the metal. I confirm, "Nothing serious. With some chewing gum and tape it should hold out."

I open the trunk and grab the jerry can. "Where's the closest station?"

"Don't you think you should wait for nightfall?"

"No. And for two reasons. First because every second counts. Second because they couldn't have broadcast our descriptions yet. In an hour or two it'll be harder, so we should take advantage of the little time we have left."

"Yes, you're right. There's a Shell station two miles from here on the edge of town. It's the closest. I don't know any others…"

"Two miles? Hmm… well, I'm going to try."

Valerie opens the garage door, gives me a sign of encouragement, one last look full of confidence and I am off on the sunny highway, walking fast with my jerry can in hand. The heat is stifling. My shirt sticks to my skin and beads of sweat start streaming down my face. Traffic becomes heavier the closer I get to the outskirts of Boston, but I keep a steady pace on the side of the road, all my senses wide awake. I put on some dark sunglasses and pull my big, canvas hat down.

Finally I get there. I see the gas station with its snack bar and hot dog stand. When I approach the attendant in his blue coveralls, he starts talking straight off about the heat. "Damn heat! Can you believe this weather? Must be some funny storm getting ready to break."

"Yeah, no two ways around it."

He looks at me with a little smile. "You broke down?"

"Yes."

"I hope you're not too far."

"No just around the bend."

"What kind of ride you in?"

"A Bentley."

"Doesn't surprise me. Those boats suck up too much. Take my advice and stick a gas pump in your trunk."

Still the same old jokes I have heard a hundred times. I bend down to grab the jerry can, but a little too fast and my glasses fall off and shatter on the ground. When I finish and want to pay, I notice the attendant staring at me with interest, if not with anxiety.

I feel doubt surge up in me. Boy, they lost no time. Our descriptions have already been sent out. I curse to myself and get ready to leave, but the man grabs my arm, trying to seem friendly.

"Wait a minute," he says, "I'll find someone to take you back. Come over here... This heat's no good..." He tries to lead me inside the station, but I spot the trap immediately.

Forcing myself to stay calm, I say, "No thanks, there's no need. I'll manage on my own."

"Hey, just wait one minute."

I turn my head to the sound of engines and see two motorcycle cops pulling in to get gas. Obviously, destiny wants to give me a hard time. The attendant is all ready to rush off to them, but I swing the jerry can into his stomach and he slumps over while the surprised policemen jump off their bikes.

I take off, a little panicky, running haphazardly, and I hear them behind me. Without turning to look I dive between two cars, cross the street and manage to get a little head start, but they have seen me and their sirens wail. The two motorcycles are on the street. I race down another street, running as fast as I can. I turn around and see the two men on their bikes. They are not giving up. They spotted me in the crowd on the sidewalk as they were weaving between the cars.

I am off again, on a blind run, turn to the right at an intersection and skirt along a big wall that never ends. No doorway or opening where I can jump in. On the other side of the street is an empty lot. If I dash over there, I would be found immediately. Like a hunted animal I stop, out of breath. It is too late anyway. The two motorcycle cops have just turned at the intersection and they spot me in a heartbeat.

I take off again, hounded by fear, and in my mad dash I end up in front of an open gate which I lunge through, without thinking, onto the gravel of a long, straight path bordered by trees that look like votive candles. On both sides are nothing but crosses, chapels, gravestones and mausoleums… Good God, a cemetery!

The sky suddenly darkens as drab, stormy clouds swoop down on the silent, deserted necropolis, but I can see the forms of the policemen, like two nightmare shades, walking slowly between the graves.

This time it is the end for me. Cornered like a rat.

"Milland, give up! We're not going to hurt you for Christ's sake!"

The voice cracks the sepulchral silence. Too hard and urgent to result from a friendly thought.

The fools! If only they could understand!

I do not even try to analyze my state of mind. I am full of anger and bitterness and I decide to fight it out until my last breath. I sneak between the graves and crawl deeper into the macabre pandemonium, watching the policemen approach, although more hesitant now that they have lost my trail.

But what am I to do? What should I do?

And all of a sudden when I turn down another row, I stop short, fascinated by what I discover. My body is soaked in cold sweat when I recognize the grave in front of me. It is unbelievable. Like it popped up out of nowhere, out of the ghastly nightmare I lived through with

Valerie. Yes, it is the same one. I recognize it. Valerie's desperate refuge... where... Oh, God... my head... my head...

And the marble headstone that catches my eye... with its finely graven letters: "Here lies Gregory Watson."

CHAPTER VI

"Milland, for the last time, give up!"

A black form has just emerged from behind a chapel and I see it heading for me. By instinct I dive, rolling between two abandoned graves. But what's the use? What am I hoping for? Sooner or later they will end up getting me. I have no chance of escape.

And all this for lack of...

I resume my crazy flight through the cemetery, but soon find myself cornered against the surrounding wall. I hear stomping footsteps and I know that this time they have me.

Everything happens very quickly, as if the scene unfolded with extraordinary violence and rapidity. And I can do nothing but suffer it.

It is the world around me that pushes me up to the wall and forces me to climb it, grappling the worn and broken stones. In a fit of desperate energy I reach the top and jump over just as two loud curses ring out.

Then there is a street drowned in the drab, stormy atmosphere that swallows my footsteps all the way up to the corner where a squad car sits with its engine idling. Hiding behind a big moving truck parked at the curb I notice the wide open door of a building. I run into the dimly lit entrance and I am struck by the smell of old paper and the sweet, cool air of a church.

There are two open doors in the silence, the darkness, the fragrance and freshness. Over all is the sound of a blaring siren and the threat of the outside world that grows and grinds on me. The huge room welcomes me with its nightmare of shadows and frozen silhouettes.

They, too… like Watson's grave… have risen out of the dream and the horror.

The wax figures!

They are here but this time with their royal outfits, their blond wigs and their crinoline gowns. A face grimaces in the background. A doll's face I see hunched over a harmonium. The waxen hands poised over the dusty keyboard have the same long, bony fingers… the fingers of… Oh, no, it is not possible… Not those fingers… No, no, not this!

And then… and then a shadow moves, slipping behind the harmonium. I watch it in horror, frozen like the statues around me.

"We're closing, sir, the visit is over."

I watch the shadow creep toward me and I make out an old man wearing a cap with a leather visor.

"Good thing I came by," he said kindly. "I'm about to close the museum."

I try to smile at him. "I… I was dawdling. Please excuse me."

"No harm done, my boy. But it's time and I have to close."

"Yes, of course. I'm going."

"No, come over here. You can go out the back door. The other is already locked, see? Come on, follow me." He is as blind as a mole. His little eyes sparkle behind the big glasses.

Of course this is more luck. More luck like the police car that had cleared the intersection when I escaped the cemetery. The storm has blown away. The sun is back out, chasing off the last clouds, but the heat is still unbearable. I run off.

Unfortunately my hopes are quickly dashed because the threat comes charging back to the sound of a barrel organ with the police surrounding the area.

I hurry my steps in triple time, inspired by the organ grinder and the wheezy waltz. To the sound of natural flats I enter the fairgrounds amongst the crowds, the stands and the noise. I float like a castaway on the human tide, tossed about by the ebb and flow of the crowd, swept up in the whirling throng.

Balls, clay pipes, numbered wheels that roll and spin and grind.

"Number 8!"

"Number 4!"

"Number 12!"

And round it goes... And on and on it goes... The nightmare, still the same, I haven't left... I'll never leave!

I have had enough, enough, oh, yes! Enough!

Good God! What's happening? These shadows that are lunging through the crowd, sliding in my wake... these dark robes... these...

I leap excitedly onto a turning merry-go-round, hanging onto the mane of a wooden horse.

"Hey, you there! Hey!"

The voice sounds like it is coming out of the round mouth of the barrel organ... One, two, three... One two, three... One, two, three... The waltz... The waltz... The smiles and the manes, all the rollicking in perpetual motion.

"No, but come on, can't you pay attention? You're crazy..."

Stunned, I look at the man whom I have just run into. A fat, round guy who pushes me off, swearing, "This guy is completely nuts!"

The crowd is gone… The waltz is stopped. There is nothing but the road spinning and the sun shining.

Tires screech on the pavement and another voice says, "Hey there, what's got into you? You trying to kill yourself or what?"

I notice the truck in front of me… the bare chest leaning out the door, the bald head glistening like an egg.

"Hey, what's up, pal, come on?"

He looks like a good guy, a family guy. I imagine him with a herd of kids around him, worrying more about his beefsteak than about political intrigues. I do not know why I am thinking about all this.

He opens the door and waves to me. "Come on, climb in, it'll clear your head."

The wheels spin and we leave town. He asks me no questions. I hear nothing but his humming and grumbling about the heat. He does not care about anything else. Me and the world included!

And that is when the truck stops and the man's voice snaps me back to reality.

"I'm not going any farther. Well, I hope things get better for you, okay?"

I nod, get out and return his friendly wave. A few minutes later I am alone on the side of the road. On the horizon I watch the sun setting over the roofs of Boston.

CHAPTER VII

I ponder the situation and regain my confidence and courage.

I am more and more tortured by thirst. I look around until I spot a house. It is a small, simple looking cottage built in the middle of a field. I also see a telephone wire leading to the house. Of course my first thought is to call Valerie, but I hesitate, weighing the risks, and I finally make up my mind.

I enter the yard where there is a well. I walk cautiously as I approach it. The yard is empty. No one is in the vicinity. I am surrounded by silence. I cannot resist. I hook the pail to the chain, drop it down the well and pull it back up. I drink heartily, dunking my head in the fresh and refreshing water.

When I turn around, a little old lady is watching me with surprise. She is wearing a black dress decorated with a white lace collar. She does not look scared in the least. Just astonished at my presence.

I point to the pail. "Sorry, but I was so thirsty…"

She gives me an age-old smile and says, "The Lord's water knows no master."

"You're very kind, madam."

"And you must be weary, my boy, no?"

"Indeed I am."

The strangest thing is that she seems delighted by my presence. Happy and almost overexcited, she turns toward the front door where a second little old lady pops up. They look so much alike, down to their outmoded fashion, you could call them twins.

"Hortense! Come quick! The Lord has sent him…
He came…"

The second little old lady crosses the yard and scurries over to me. "Praise the Lord! Oh, Cecilia, he looks exhausted, the poor boy!"

I watch these two, crazy old dames somewhat nervously. Obviously I was spared nothing. "I think you're mistaken. I just wanted to ask you…"

"Come now, come now," Cecilia insists, "don't make excuses. Our wishes are always granted."

"What wish did you make?"

"We asked the Lord to send us every week the most pitiable creature there is. We always welcome them on their wandering road. Isn't that right, Hortense?"

"Always, Cecilia."

"And today it's you."

I cannot help smiling. "Well, in that case, you will allow me to use your telephone for just one call."

The two faces before me turn sad. Cecilia seems more disappointed. "Oh! Of all the good things we have to offer… Hortense made apple pies for the occasion… Such a good apple pies…"

"And even a cherry pie," Hortense continues. "You're not going to refuse them, are you?"

It is because I am thinking of Valerie that I shake my and accept.

"Well then, it's agreed, but we absolutely must…"

The two old ladies drag me into the cottage and start flitting around the big common room, happy and satisfied, but I spot the telephone in the back of the room. I try to take the first opportunity to ask again because I do not care a wink about apple or cherry pies. The gravity of the situation makes me rush things a bit, but suddenly I hear a police siren start wailing.

I jump up and run to the window. A black Chrysler has just pulled into the yard in a cloud of dust. Two uniformed policemen get out, take a quick look around and head toward the house.

There is no more time to lose. I grab Cecilia and flatten her against the wall next to the door. "Don't move and I won't hurt you."

I put my hand over her mouth to keep her from screaming and then I call out to Hortense, "I'm the one they're looking for. But you haven't seen anybody, got it?"

I see the poor old lady turn pale, looking ridiculous holding the cherry pie in her hands.

"Go on, open up. Hurry!"

She obeys, awkwardly, and through the open door I see the policemen. A greeting, a voice. "My apologies, good ladies, but we're looking for a man who is hiding in the area. A tall, brown-haired fellow, dressed in a gray suit. Have you seen anyone who might fit this description?"

"Oh, no... no... I don't think so... I haven't seen anyone..."

"Very well, but watch out for him," he advised, "and call the police immediately if you see him."

"Yes, yes, of course. He's a killer, I suppose?"

"Worse than that. A dangerous madman. He got away from us this morning, but we'll end up catching him, don't worry. Goodbye."

Hortense closes the door and I let go of Cecilia. The black Chrysler drives out of the yard and disappears.

The two old ladies had stepped away, hugging each other, and are watching me now with wide eyes. I do not even think of giving them any kind of explanation. I hurry to the telephone asking, "The phone book? Where's the phone book?"

With a trembling hand Cecilia points to the small desk on my right. I find it in the drawer, look up the name Watson and hastily dial the number. Five seconds later I hear Valerie's voice. "Robert? But what happened?"

"No time to explain. They almost nabbed me a number of times, but I got away."

"Where are you?"

I tell her about the house and its location off the highway.

"Okay, don't move. I'll try to get there tonight."

"But... the gas?"

"I found another jerry can with less than a gallon but it'll be enough to get to the station."

"The leak?"

"I'll manage."

"Okay, but don't go to the Shell station... I'll explain later."

"All right. Trust me."

I hang up and take a deep breath. All I can do is hope and pray to see Valerie alive again. Now I have to wait it out. God knows if time will pass quickly. The two old ladies, still terrified, are huddled together in a corner. I am wondering if the adventure they are living through will cure them of their weekly vow.

Night finally falls as I pace the room, trying to calm my nervousness. Soon I hear the sound of an engine and throw a smile at Hortense and Cecilia. "Thanks for the pie. It was excellent."

CHAPTER VIII

I am still wondering how we can get to Washington. We have avoided four roadblocks, which forced us to take a bunch of side roads and lose precious time. I had to knock out some poor guy whom we asked for directions when we got lost in some deserted area and who recognized us in the headlights.

Pictures of us in black and white above the reward leading to our capture have been posted all over the place. The radio is continually broadcasting our descriptions, but I have the feeling that the search is focused to the north of Boston, up around the Canadian border. Why? I have no idea. Obviously a false trail. And this, no doubt, is what will help us reach Washington safe and sound. It could also be that luck is now on our side.

But Valerie and I are not talking about it. We are still not out of the woods and we are not deluding ourselves about all the obstacles we will have to face to overcome the ignorance and general stubbornness. Beginning with Captain Lewis. An old friend, certainly, but...

Unfortunately, it is a different kind of obstacle that we face when we show up at Captain Lewis' house after parking our car in the neighborhood. The old maid who greets us early in the morning looks surprised at our visit, as well as my tricky attempts to hide my bearded face behind my coat collar.

"Captain Lewis hasn't lived here for a long time," she explains. "You are friends of his, you say?"

"Yes, that's right, but I've been abroad. I didn't know."

"Well, it's already been more than a year since General Garrett moved in here."

"General Garrett?"

The woman looks at me, a little exasperated. "I don't think General Garrett can be of any help. The Pentagon has put him on extended leave since his terrible accident." She points to her eyes.

"Serious?"

"Blind."

Valerie nudges me with her elbow to make me insist and I end up convincing the good maid to let us meet briefly with General Garrett after I kept repeating the name Graham Rutherford. A name that came to me in a flash... The main point was to see Garrett and try to find out what became of Captain Lewis. He should probably know.

Garrett is a tall, bony man who we find in the small sitting room, buried in a huge, leather armchair, dressed in a navy blue bathrobe with little white dots. His dead eyes stare into empty space. Guided by our footsteps, he greets us and starts rattling off in a deep, resonant, yet subtle voice:

"Lewis, huh? You want to see Captain Lewis? I am very sorry, sir, but Lewis doesn't live here anymore, as you must know. Without the authorization to tell you all the little secrets of the Pentagon, I can, at least, say that a new arrangement was made with the FBI for Captain Lewis to modify their organization. Lewis had to move as a result, which came as no surprise, and because the house was available they gave it to me. But I imagine that this is not your concern. What interests you is to get in touch with Captain Lewis. Of course, I understand, but I'm afraid it will be very difficult for you, sir, very difficult, because the hierarchy inside the Pentagon is not a fixed, one-way path and I'll tell you why. The Pentagon is a hydra whose many, often imaginary heads are constantly changing. The Pentagon is an unsolvable enigma that can never unravel the most clever enemy agents. A section under Morgan today comes under Smith's control tomorrow. Lewis is just a pawn on the chessboard. A pawn coming and going at the whim of everyday decisions. The telephone, you might ask? No, even there you'll have no luck. Imagine, sir, that there are 318 lines at the Pentagon for 4,695 phones. Suppose you try it. You dial one of the 318 numbers. You might make your first wrong call but get either no answer or a busy signal. You'll keep calling until someone confirms your mistake, unless you end up with a recording. You might also find the circuits overloaded and have to repeat your call a hundred times before getting through to one of the 318 official lines. And remember that anyone with a sense of mischievous humor can pretend to be the Pentagon operator and with a voice of authority sent you from one department to another, making you waste all kinds of time. But let's forget about these risks and say you get through. The operator is going to have to do some searching to find what department Lewis belongs to. First there will be imaginary departments, the ones to check the authenticity of the call, then the old, cancelled departments. Remember Morgan today, Smith tomorrow. Finally after 4,695 attempts you'll get the private, top-secret number of Lewis. But then, after this undreamed of luck, there are nine chances out of ten that Lewis won't be there. Lewis is eating; Lewis is sleeping; Lewis has personal business; Lewis is away on business; Lewis is there or Lewis is not there. Of course, they'll tell you, but only if you haven't hung up in the meantime and are forced to start the whole process over again with all the same risks as before. And it will happen over again with all the 318 lines, the 4,695 phones, the imaginary departments, the checks and cancelled departments because there is no guarantee that you will get the same operator. They, too, have to eat, sleep and deal with personal issues during the 24 hours of their daily lives. Oh yes, I know, it's awful, but that's the game. Have you ever heard about the monkeys typing at random on a typewriter? Some people think that after some endless amount of time they'll end up reproducing a verse of Shakespeare. It's the law of chance and probability. Well, sir, you're in the same boat. Yes, in the same boat. You'll get through to Lewis, but when? Do you have enough patience and enough time in your life to wait for that day? And what about him? Lewis is very old. No, absolutely not, you can't start this game with an adversary whose days are numbered. Believe me, sir, it's a game that…"

General Garrett's voice trails off down the hallway where Valerie and I are headed out. The door clicking shut behind us gives us some relief. It is all far too much for us.

Garrett! Another unconscious victim of the psychic attack triggered by our enemies.

How many others are in this situation? How many?

How many have been bewitched by this infernal passion for games, to look at life, the world and the universe as pieces in a universal game? Yes, how many other Garretts are there among our fellow men now? How many doors are already open onto the demonic world of "the masters of silence"?

How many? How many?

It is raining when reach the Bentley. Valerie's hand clutching my arm brings me back to reality.

I say it is raining. I can add that a cop is walking around the car. He checks the license plate against a paper that he just pulled out of his pocket. Oh well... Anyway, it was to be expected.

"Robert, what are we going to do?"

At the end of the street is a bus station where we find temporary refuge from the rain that does not let up. We are alone.

"Robert?"

I think about it. "There's only one solution. The White House."

Valerie looks wide-eyed at me.

I manage the strength to smile and repeat, "The White House." Then, more precisely, "The President." But I dare not add, *unless*...

Valerie understands very well.

CHAPTER IX

John Dixon Maxwell wrote that they entered the White House like an open house, probably alluding to the daily visits of the public between 10 am and noon when anyone get into the famous dwelling after paying the fee to an ordinary, apathetic guard.

I had time to consider the question during the long hours I have spent stuck between two huge magnolia bushes bordering the right side of the park just a few feet from the corner of Pennsylvania Avenue and 15th Street. No one seems to have noticed my little trick. The rain is still drizzling down, unpleasantly, which maybe helped me out. What do I know?

I watched the last visitors leave the presidential house and cross the park to the exit. The guard closed the gates behind them and disappeared, also hunched under an umbrella. I did not see him again.

It is almost 2 pm and I am still here, in the rain, keeping a close eye on the long, chiffon curtains in the first-floor bay windows. It is the president's office.

Farther along is the grand reception room and farther still is the library. Yes, all this has been imprinted in my head since my childhood, since the day I learned that the greatest man of our country lived in this famous house. And it is this great man that I am going to confront in a few minutes and who will decide not only my fate but the fate of three million human beings.

If I fail, well, the whole world will fail with me and nothing will be able to avoid the disaster that is ready and waiting.

Hey! The curtains have just been opened and a silhouette appears in the window of the president's office. The President is lost in thought as he watches the rain falling. I keep a close eye on him for a minute or two. When he disappears after drawing the curtains, I make my move.

I do as I had planned, without a single wasted movement, everything calculated down to ten seconds, no more, no less. Just enough time for me to cover ground to the window and jump inside the office with all the daring and determination in my blood. The act is so sudden and brutal that the great man bent over his desk shoots up and stares at me in a daze. His hand, however, by reflex is already reaching for an alarm.

I stop him at the last moment.

"No, Mr. President, listen to me first, please... I beg you... I beseech you..."

"But what the devil..."

"There's nothing to fear. I'm not armed and I mean you no harm. I just want you to listen to me. What I have to tell you is very serious. Yes, I ask you again, Mr. President, Sir, listen to me."

He stands up, his expression waffling between curiosity and astonishment, worry and bewilderment. Curiosity mostly in his first question.

"Who are you?"

Worry after my response and then:

"The man we've been seeking for two days?"

Astonishment when I nod my head.

"And you have the audacity to show up here in front of me? You must be crazier than I thought!"

"I am as sane as you are, Mr. President. Unfortunately, I had no choice. You're the only person left who can help me."

Bewilderment, disbelief and even irony.

"Really?"

He watches me with some compassion and nods his head.

"Let's not complicate things to your disadvantage. Personally I don't have the least intention of listening to you."

"Even if I tell you that the sonic annihilator is a weapon designed by extraterrestrial creatures to expedite their invasion?"

"Extraterrestrial creatures? Come on!"

"I found out all about it when I met Valerie Watson in the world of the fifth dimension."

"Yes, I know, I was told about it. Too bad it isn't Professor Greysson's opinion."

"But of course you don't know that they're using him. You don't know that there are already thousands of victims of these creatures' subversive attack. You don't know that any minute now men like Greysson are going to blindly follow the orders of the invaders. Then it will be too late... too late. We can't fight these beings."

"That's enough."

"But damn it, what more do you want me to tell you?"

I suddenly realize that I had got carried away and had pushed too hard. Cold rage was washing over his face. His voice snapped out, dry as a whiplash:

"Your insolence can cost you dearly, Mr. Milland. Don't abuse my mercy and compassion. I order you to immediately..."

His mouth keeps moving and forming words.

I suddenly feel like I am deaf.

But what's happening? The President leaps out from behind his desk and looks around, stupefied.

Horror! The chair he knocks over crashes to the floor without the slightest sound.

I imagine the scream coming out of his mute mouth. Mute from now on in the world…

PART FOUR

CHAPTER I

…of silence!

I see him jumping on the alarm buttons, but I do not even try to interfere in this tragic environment where words are useless. And then I turn around.

Two men have just showed up in the room, seeding panic in the midst of total silence. The two huge fellows rush at me, but the President waves them off. He himself runs to the window and throws it wide open. A window opened abruptly onto the silence of the world. No sound exists outside. It is over… Finished… Nothing but a deaf city overrun by panic.

Even the falling rain is inaudible. No more pitter-patter in the puddles. Not the slightest spluttering on the gravel.

Nothing! Nothing but the weight of a dreadful silence!

If only they would trust me before it is too late! I turn to the President and with a nod I try to translate my thoughts: *So, you're convinced now?*

He runs to pick up the telephone, but quickly realizes the futility of his action and hangs up.

No, Mr. President, no more telephones, no more radios. All this has ceased to exist. In his eyes I see vast despair, the image of infinite sorrow, the spark of eternal remorse.

I grab a pad of paper and pencil from the desk and we pass it back and forth to scratch out the following dialogue:

"Destroy machine once and for all... Right away!"

"Matter for the Defense Department and Pentagon."

"Send messenger or else we're lost."

"Possible accident. Got to know first."

"Nothing more to know." I underline my words furiously.

The two bodyguards have watched this little duel of pens trying to control the nervousness that keeps growing stronger in them. But soon an outright panic explodes in the presidential office. Ten people burst in. They look like deaf-mutes striking ridiculous, pitiful poses. A few seconds later and the room is infested with pantomiming men who discover to their horror that they are all struck by the same malady.

I am catching a glimpse of the situation at the moment all across the United States. People who do not understand what is happening to them and who imagine that they have become deaf. They cannot know yet that that they are victims of the opposite problem: *that it is the sounds around them that no longer exist!*

I shiver when I think, for the first time, that humanity is lost.

Until now I was still nursing some hopes, but at present I face another obstacle: the general panic that will play into the enemy's hands in the little time we have left. Really it only takes a quick glance around to see that the panic is everywhere.

A huge crowd has just burst onto the White House lawn; soldiers and civilians are running around helter-skelter faced with only a weak resistance by a few armed policemen who are also overwhelmed by the situation. The extraordinary activity around us is all the more frightening in that it is silent. I feel like I am watching a show on a television with the sound turned off.

Then I see Valerie trying to fight her way through. I jump through the window and they do not try to stop me. Throwing myself into the mob, I grab hold of her and drag her away. We go back into the building where morbid mayhem has spread to every corner. But the policemen who saw me with the President come to my aide and help me back into the office. The President looks at me, completely lost, and motions me to follow him into the next room. He also invites certain VIPs who are standing around trembling and showing obvious signs of frenzy. Only the President has regained his calm. He recognizes Valerie. I see him sigh and when he looks back at me I understand the gravity of the situation.

He writes feverishly on a piece of paper and hands it to me. I read what he has written:

"Sonic annihilator sent into orbit this morning. Cape Kennedy 8:42. Impossible to destroy."

CHAPTER II

I found Captain Lewis.

It is true that the 318 lines connecting 4,695 phones inside the Pentagon are useless and I was astonished that a single, "deaf and mute" man, all alone with a simple message, could have accomplished such a formidable task.

Within just a few hours the messenger sent by the White House managed to reach Lewis' administrative department on the other side of the Potomac and now they were all here, Lewis heading the way, or at least almost all of them because it was a matter of the real leaders of the "sonic project." Only those from Cape Kennedy are still absent, but considering the mayhem we are all struggling with, it is to be expected that they will not arrive before tomorrow.

For the moment the debate is raging in a big, private room in the White House that has been transformed into HQ for the situation. In the middle of this extraordinary session, emotions have reached their climax.

Everyone is bustling around me in the heavy, total silence and without making any more noise than a ghost. Each of them are trying to express his opinion using the means proposed by Lewis: Morse code with lights. Flashlights were handed out and a stenographer works as interpreter to record on a typewriter the series of questions and answers expressed by the light signals for those who do not understand the Morse alphabet.

It is dreadful. I do not mean the circumstances of our debate amidst the blinking lights, but rather what I have finally learned about the consequences of the top-secret project approved and carried out by the American government.

First of all some news that froze my blood with fright. The phenomenon of sonic annihilation is not affecting the United States alone. We suspect that the entire world is buried in silence because the wave reducer set in orbit works on all the waves emitted simultaneously across the globe. This is proven to us by the little information we receive at the airports around Washington this afternoon from the statements made by travelers coming from Europe, Australia and South America. Everyone has suffered the effects of the "sound gobbler" at the same time in their different latitudes.

With the announcement of this news I sense the heavy responsibility that weighs on the American government. But this is not the problem because matters are so serious that we are now considering it a no-win situation.

The "sonic project" from the start concerned the launch of the annihilator into orbit with an electronic command post on board the satellite that could be controlled from the ground and was capable of aiming the annihilator beam at a precise point on the globe. But now the trigger seems to have gone off on its own without the control signals sent from Cape Kennedy and without anybody being able to explain the technical accident that caused the frightening disaster.

To destroy the machine would be the ideal solution, but this kind of problem makes me understand the meaning of the word impossible today. Impossible because the satellite is armed with an exceptional system of defense. It has a force field capable of disintegrating any solid object within two or three miles with a ray. Even a missile carrying an atomic bomb would have no effect in a space duel of this type.

But damn it all there has to be way to stop the antisonic generator by remote control, right? None at all.

The blinking light that Captain Lewis flashes at me is clear, concise and categorical. And that is when I rise up, I explode, encouraged by the trust and moral support of Valerie.

"Because we are all to some degree bewitched by the telehypnotic powers of our enemies, because all of this is part of a carefully thought out plan, because your thoughts are not your own—the accident was inevitable."

I am fighting against the general stubbornness, against the irony and incomprehension and the staunchest objectivity. Oh, if only they would believe me! But no… no… All my efforts to convince them end in failure, which does nothing but feed the unrest in the gathering.

And yet I have the feeling that three or four delegates from the Pentagon have tried to look at the problem from my point of view. But Lewis, in spite of our old friendship, comes back at me with the technical arguments that are hard to deny and he ends his tirade with a storm of lights that once again coldly sums up the present tragedy considered as a no-win situation.

"Let's not get buried under the weight of useless suppositions and absurd affirmations that have no serious foundation and will only give this disaster an even more tragic tone. We have to put aside these questions of an extraterrestrial threat without a second thought if we don't want to succumb to panic and psychosis that would spell our downfall. Certainly, we don't deny our responsibility to the world. Certainly, our duty is to consider the disaster with a calm mind and watchful eyes, even while we are still in its clutches with the rest of the world. Certainly, we must all unite our efforts to try to stop the effects of the anti-sonic generator and to find a way to destroy the satellite that carries it, but it is important that we not delude ourselves. It will take a long time, maybe a very long time because for the first time in the history of humanity, man is a victim of his own genius, of his own recklessness and daring. Yes, I repeat, it will take a long time because in our present state of knowledge, I don't think there is a man on earth who is capable of solving our problem."

I can feel myself turn pale. In a split second I have just realized all the dreadful consequences of Lewis' reasoning. His sincerity is equaled only by the terrible reality of things. And with a weary hand I send out my response.

"These men you talk about exist, Lewis, but the most awful thing is that *they're no longer able* to solve the problem. You are first among them!"

"Still your stupid ideas, Milland. It's irritating."

"This was all to be expected. Now it's too late."

"I said it would take a long time."

"No, on the contrary, it will take a very short time. The war is over and we have already lost."

"Nonsense."

"Well, just wait and see."

That is how the meeting ends, on the President's order, with everyone exasperated. Vigorous measures are to be taken right away to suppress the panic that keeps growing from one end of the city to the other. Then the news we receive is rather alarming.

At the Capital all the members of the government are going to meet to decree a state of emergency, so in

132

the confusion around us we evacuate the White House. It is when we arrive at the gates, swallowed up by a maddening crowd, that Valerie and I are joined by Captain Lewis. Big beads of sweat run down his hard, weathered face. His hand grabs my arm and I do not need to hear his voice to understand the meaning of his gestures, his facial expressions and his eyes. What he tells me fills me with disgust.

"Milland, it's out of our old friendship that I'm warning you. You shouldn't have gone off like that. You almost convinced some of us with your absurd and alarmist ideas. If you spread this psychosis we'll be lost... Get away quickly... Don't stay here... or else they're going to kill you like a dog..."

I figure he might very well do it himself. It would take nothing for him to pull the gun out of his holster. Maybe he has already received unconscious orders, but he is still fighting with what remains of his willpower. Our old friendship. Of course.

With one last look behind us, Valerie and I melt into the chaos and the crowd.

CHAPTER III

For two days we wander randomly through the ghost town. If only there were still words to describe all the horrors that Valerie and I have witnessed since we were cast into this new nightmare!

Madness, crime, pillaging and brutality are rampant throughout the city, everywhere there are men, men who have turned into animals with the bodies and faces of men. Corpses are piled on the ground by the hundreds, maybe thousands, and no one thinks of taking them away. Who would do this, I ask myself. All activity has come to a halt and the city is completely disorganized, turned over to total, unbearable anarchy.

While most of the corpses rot in the street, some are crushed into a bloody mess by the cars that are racing around in a panic, leaving red streaks on the pavement that end up turning black in the burning rays of the blazing sun that is insensitive to the tragedy and madness of men.

Children lost or abandoned wander haphazardly, crying, wailing and begging with their mute mouths agape for some help from the men and women who do not hear them.

Because the whole city has become a jungle. Because the law of the strongest has replaced the law of morality. It only took a few hours for the solid edifice of our virtue to collapse in a heap like a house of cards.

And all this at the hands of those who in the throes of this dying world want to become masters of the situation. Gangs have been organized to sack the city, taking advantage of the panic and chaos that reigns everywhere.

We saw armed groups attacking food warehouses, breaking the windows of jewelers and luxury shops.

Poor fools! Is their only reason for living really just to die in luxury with a full belly?

Others, on the contrary, prefer to end it all because the situation is more than they can handle. Take the guy who just splattered at my feet in silence on the sundrenched sidewalk. He had jumped out of the window of a building and we saw him twirling in the air like a ragdoll.

This morning we saw a car stuffed with a whole family that crashed into a huge wall on purpose and people just stood around and watched, then went away to see it all start over again somewhere else.

This time it is the same thing. People are leaning over the poor guy trying to recognize him, if he was a neighbor, a friend, maybe a relative and while they are dragging the corpse over to the wall, I take Valerie over to a ransacked store. I bend down to pick up a package of dried fruit that is lying amidst some torn up boxes, broken crates and pieces of cardboard. We have not eaten anything since yesterday. In fact, we have not even thought about it. We spent all our time avoiding the crowds and the constant mobs in front of the stores. I will not even mention the restaurants and bars. Not a single one is open.

No, we were just trying to escape the search parties that might be looking for us, but in truth no one seems to care what became of us. We slept in a public park that was utterly dark and when I opened my eyes this morning and saw the nightmare continuing in the city streets, I asked myself the same questions:

"But what are they waiting for? Isn't this what they wanted? Why aren't they attacking? Why don't they get it over with?"

I have been asking myself these questions for 48 hours. Yes, of course, it should not be long now, but I am curious to know how these diabolical creatures will go about launching their final assault. The one that will wipe humanity off the face of the earth forever.

Who knows? Valerie and I might be the first victims. Not the last, anyway, because the Smith and Wesson I found this morning in the park, left on the grass, will spare us...

Valerie's hand squeezing my shoulder shakes me out of my dark thoughts. She points down the long row of buildings stretching out before us along Rhode Island Avenue. I know what she is thinking. We have watched a long exodus since the morning. Whole families abandoning their homes and leaving the city to look for refuge in the neighboring suburbs, fleeing the anarchy and chaos. But to find an empty apartment in the city is not an easy thing because we are not the only ones to have the idea. Pillagers have already got to work and walked off with all the valuables left in the luxury apartments downtown.

And what's the use? For the little time remaining to us I wonder if it is really worth the trouble. But Valerie is insistent and I understand her. She cannot go on like this. She is worn out.

She begs me mutely, "Let's try. I've had enough. All these people scare me."

I lead her into a 20-story building picked at random. We find some doors closed, others open onto man's ugliness, his ferocity and onto his monumental folly. We see rooms sacked and furniture overturned. For several hours we come and go, climbing up and down, opening new doors on apartments still occupied or totally devastated.

We end up on the 12th floor of a neighboring building where we see a tall fellow breaking into a apartment with a white cross chalked on the door. The man has his back turned to us, but just when we reach the landing he suddenly collapses. His scrawny body slides down the door, hits the floor and falls backward. My instinct tells me to rush over to him, but I realize what has just happened in the silence. A bullet passed through his body and blood is spurting out of his belly.

I swing around and see a little redhead with beady eyes watching us from the top of the stairs, aiming his pistol at us. From the sign he makes I figure he is ordering us to clear out because the apartment with the cross is now his property. He comes down, wearing a cruel smile, kicks the door open and repeats his mute order, but only at me. His other hand signing to Valerie is easy enough to understand. I translate it as, "You, scram. It's the girl I want."

The swine! It takes me three seconds to react, without too much thought. I push Valerie in front of me toward the redhead, which allows me to pull out my Smith and Wesson without him seeing. Then I push Valerie to the side, throwing her against the wall and pull the trigger, counting on the element of surprise. I see the bullet drill through his neck. A ridiculous look on his face, his eyes bugging out and a torrent of blood soaks his white shirt. He takes two steps forward, his mouth gaping open like a drowning man, then he falls headfirst onto the body of his victim. Like I would for a wounded dog, I shoot him in the head to put an end to his suffering, then

I turn to Valerie who has not fully realized what is happening.

After a quick glance in the stairwell, I gesture to the two corpses. "Quick, help me... the elevator..."

I push the elevator button. Valerie helps me drag the dead bodies into the car and we send the whole package down to the first floor. I shrug my shoulders. Someone will take care of it. Then with my handkerchief, I wipe off the cross and push the door wide open.

CHAPTER IV

It is a luxurious 3-bedroom apartment with a huge living room furnished in Empire style. Whoever lived here must have had good taste, judging by the harmony of colors, curtains, furniture and rugs that we discover in our exploration. A whole family without a doubt because there are still children's clothes and toys left behind pretty much everywhere, as well as men's and women's clothes hanging up in the closets.

In the kitchen we find a few provisions that we inventory right away. At least we will not die of hunger before "the gentlemen from the fifth" arrive. I am the only one laughing at this pathetic expression as I realize that Valerie does not know Morse code. But this is not the time to teach her since there are still many things to do if we want to set up as best we can for what remains of our life.

First, to reinforce the front door so that we will not be caught by surprise. With silence all around us how can we be sure that no one is trying to break into our refuge? We can only trust our eyes; nothing else exists.

Before I share my thoughts with Valerie, I nod my head. "I have an idea."

"What is it?"

I try to make her understand by indicating the doorbell. "First of all a light signal in case one of us has to leave... Put it in every room... Will also be good if someone tries to jimmy the lock... Second connection to do here. Got it?

"And at night?"

"An electrified line… Electrocution pure and simple."

She smiles, likes my idea, but we still have to get the material. "I'll take care of it… Not too hard."

But Valerie is an angel of protection and her idea to wrap my head in bandages, although unpleasant in the stifling heat of the morning, at least has the advantage of hiding my face, which is a wise precaution if we remember Lewis' advice. But I pull it off with ease and find pretty much everything I need by the time I get back to Valerie a few hours later.

Lord! I hardly recognize her. Her shapely form is like a dream in the close-fitting, black silk dress. Her hair is gathered up in a bun, shiny and sparkling like with stardust. Then she starts turning round, slowly and silently, like a fairy on her cloud.

She takes my hand and leads me to the table in the living room. Everything is here: chandeliers, silver dishes, a few vases with still fresh flowers bunched into slim, graceful bouquets.

It is tremendous! I suddenly feel like I am in a dream and when Valerie's lips touch mine, I forget the world and its nightmare. It is like I am spinning round, hanging onto a merry-go-round.

Oh, my head… it's spinning… spinning…

"Robert!" She shakes me gently and I pull myself away from her body, her lips, everything she is offering me for this last evening. No, there will be no more… *There cannot be any more!*

Tomorrow the world will collapse. Tomorrow the die will be cast. The ball will fall into its slot and the wheel of fortune will stop on its final number… On the big chessboard a triumphant hand will move the last pawn.

CHECK AND MATE!
"Robert!"
God, how my head is spinning…

I cannot get to sleep. It is impossible. I am obsessed by the silence. It is like an acid eating away at my nerves. How much longer do we have to live in this nightmare? How many hours?

And if everything were to happen in our sleep, just like that, in a flash, in the middle of the night? No one would have time to realize anything. No one, or very few… because the streets are deserted and from the high terrace, after dinner, I saw the last lights of the sleeping city go out. It was like the stars in my dream, falling one by one in the water of the infinite lake… yes, the infinite lake where the eternal sleeper still floats on the rippling waves of my inner memories. A creature whose powerlessness knows no equal but my own and who watches the Fall… the terrible Fall of a cursed world, the collapse of a carnival Universe.

What an awful symbol! What dark foreboding!

He is, like me, the last harlequin of a grotesque masquerade. Well, gentlemen, what are you waiting for? Blow out the lanterns. The party is over. I laugh! I laugh because I have seen, at the top of a skyscraper, the words marching past on the electronic bulletin board. Fine words and fine phrases signed by our illustrious president.

"However great the disaster may be, we will survive. Nothing is over. At my side worthy men of good will are working round the clock to stop the plague. This is why I ask everyone to stay calm and confident. We must consider this catastrophe with a cool head. Committees will be formed to fight against abuses and excess. Our judgment of those who want to drag the world into anarchy and barbarism will be pitiless. From now on we ask all good men…"

From now on! Oh, the fine words… The absurd words… Promises in Time… Promises in the wind… This is why I laugh… Come on, gentlemen, quick, blow out the lanterns… the party is over!

They have thrown the last streamers and confetti. Tomorrow the street sweepers will come. The last street sweepers after the last carnival.

All of a sudden I see the dreary sweepers, or at any rate I imagine them. With their long, dark shadows almost lost in the depths of the void. But mostly it is those ghastly, gaunt hands that haunt me, that obsess me. Oh, God, those hands! And the marks… the marks.

But what is this, Lord, what is this here? These black streaks that shine and sparkle around me. They are everywhere! On the ceiling, on the carpet, on the walls…

They are attacking the bed now, soaking the sheets with their hideous ooze. I want to scream… I want to shout… but I am paralyzed by fear and horror.

NO!

A silent laugh rips through the sound of silence. NO! The walls spin, spin in a whirlwind of drool that becomes the trail of the monstrous laugh. It is like hell itself has flooded the city and invaded my room. And I dive, I fly apart in the incessant whirlwind that swallows me… that swallows me… and I spin… I spin… and…

And my head hits the soft carpet.

A cold sweat covers my body.

My head stops spinning. My heart stops beating.

I open my eyes.

"Robert!"

Valerie stands before me, looking at me in a panic. Her lips keep moving, repeating, "Robert... Robert... Robert..." Then, "Well, what then? Wake up!"

I look. I look outside at the rising sun. I look at the world coming back to life, the world waking up to a new dawn. I do not understand anything... I do not...

The sweepers! But what became of the dreadful sweepers? What are they waiting for? But I'm telling you that the party's over! Over, don't you get it? OVER!

Damn, what is happening?

CHAPTER V

A new day has come. Life has returned. Between hands of poker, Valerie and I fill up sheets of paper, a way of "babbling" and killing time.

Valerie is a great partner! This morning she beat me twice at checkers and once at canasta.

It is crazy what games we found in the toy chest in the children's room.

At poker, too, she plays pretty well, but I can count on winning at chess. Of course one has to take account of the permutations and factors of probability… but I am a very good player, I have no fear.

And then again, what does it matter if she wins today. I have all the time in the world to beat her now that we have found a solution to destroying the infernal machine that is turning and spinning round the Earth. A stupid accident, in fact!

All it takes is to hit the right number and life will return to normal. They will find it, I am sure. Life is a game. The world is a game. Everything is won or lost on a throw of the dice. That is the rule of the universe.

So, I look through the big picture window at the puzzle of skyscrapers… the sun… the clouds… even the street where idle people are racing their dogs.

I smile and enjoy it. But it is time to take a shower, so I grab a coin and flip it. Who will go first?

"Heads. It's yours, Valerie. You won!"

ANTICIPATION

FICTION

RICHARD-BESSIERE

CETTE LUEUR
QUI VENAIT DES TENEBRES

FLEUVE NOIR

THEY CAME FROM THE DARK

My name is William Ashby.
This is my private journal.

CHAPTER I

Tuesday, July 25, 1967

"There's still a place inside."

With these inviting words from the elaborately dressed doorman the doors of the Time Club open for me. A stone staircase descends into a smoky cellar. A real dive, all shadows and lights, stinking of alcohol and tobacco. Garbled mutterings... Shifting forms... and soft music coming out of some hidden stereo speakers. In other words, the usual scenery for this kind of place. And God knows how I know them!

I do not know why, but at this moment I feel an intense desire to turn around and go back upstairs, out into the vacant land and forget the whole thing, like I am being plagued by some dark foreboding. But what is it really? And why?

Truthfully, it all started this very morning after I left Dartmoor and found myself on the banks of the Thames, dazed by all the noise and activity. It is normal after five long years in a 10 by 12-foot cell. A little like after a long sickness and finding yourself in the middle of a huge fair. With the noise of the crowd comes that from the cars and the dizzying, constant switching from red to green... and green to red... intersections... Red. Green. Red. Green. And on and on... in the fog and the rain.

Because it was raining again this morning, just like five years ago. The same inescapable drizzle, always the same, only in London, that never leaves you alone, so to speak, all year long.

Saint Paul's dome disappeared in a huge, black cloud and trudging along toward High Holborn I gradually rediscovered the little shops and big departments stores on Oxford Street and Piccadilly, then Westminster Abbey and the Royal Courts of Justice... The British Museum... And then...

And then the moment came when I had to decide between three streets open before me. Which one should I have taken? Maybe I choose the bad one, who knows. But I had not taken three steps down the sidewalk when I felt like I was not alone anymore among the faceless crowd. Someone was watching me. A funny little chap only five feet tall looking grimy in his yellowish gray skin.

I thought I had seen him in front of the prison when the gates were opened to let me go free. It was his bowler hat that attracted my attention or more precisely the unusual way he wore it, reminding me of the ludicrous shenanigans of a circus dog.

He was leaning to one side and on his cold, stony face was a casual look, completely unjustified in this creature who seemed to come from another age, from another epoch, with his tight-fitting clothes and his attitude of an old lord from the Victorian era.

I had ignored him because it was giving too much importance to the first individual I saw after five years of silence and solitude. But suddenly I was seeing him in the street with a kind of dreamy amusement in those greenish eyes of his trained on me.

I passed by him and continued my random walk, trying to chase him from my mind, but the coincidence occurred a third time when he reappeared 15 minutes later near a subway station. Then a fourth time, I spotted him in front of the Parliament with his big feet standing in a puddle of water. And still that mysterious smile, that look of a grand lord and his neck bent under his hat like a curious bird. This time I knew that I could not ignore him and that something had to give between the two of us. I stood there on the sidewalk directly in front of him and watched him come up to me with his big umbrella, his ratty old coat and his muddy shoes.

He smiled at me, leaned forward slightly and said, "Mr. Ashby? William Ashby, isn't it?" His beady green eyes did not seem to pay much attention to my nodding head, which was my way of answering. "You're looking for work? That's completely natural. But you're going to run into serious problems now and that's the most troubling thing. Of course, today maybe you're not thinking about that, but tomorrow you will quickly realize the reality of the situation."

I figured I knew what he meant. "Are the police still watching me day and night? What do you think, that I'm going to wring the neck of some old lady to steal her life savings?"

A smile that was anything but natural... "I am not the police, I assure you, Mr. Ashby."

"Then who are you?"

"My name's Brown... with a B, like Brown."

"I should warn you straight off that I'm in no mood for jokes. What do you want?"

"Just to give you a chance. A once in a lifetime chance."

"Really?"

"You're 38 years old, you're an electrical engineer, studied at Oxford, but you've wasted your life. You never found anything... let's say anything right for you and that's the cause of everything." He spoke impersonally, like he was rattling off some lesson learned by heart.

"How do you know all this?"

"We always inform ourselves thoroughly on the people we intend to hire, Mr. Ashby."

"Hire for what?"

"Honest work, well paid. But we want people who are available, with no strings and who are eager to discover other horizons beyond a city as filthy as this one, especially when it harbors so many bad memories. It's your case, I know."

Now his voice was becoming forceful and bold. Holding out his hand to curb my impatience and curiosity he dug into one of his pockets, pulled out a piece of paper and unfolded it slowly. A few names were written on it: Time Club, Putney Commons, Greg Zachariah.

The little Brown anticipated my questions. "Be there at ten o'clock tonight. The Time Club is a brand new nightclub in Putney Commons, right next to some undeveloped land. Do you know it? Ask for Greg Zachariah, he's the boss. Me, I'm just a simple employee and as far as you're concerned my work ends here."

He looked up at the sky, realized that it had stopped raining and closed his umbrella. "Honest work," he added, "and a once in a lifetime opportunity! If I were you, I wouldn't think twice."

Such were his last words. A second later he was a thin, dark shadow swallowed by the crowd on the street.

I spent the rest of the afternoon wandering the streets of London, but the crazy coot's words kept haunting me. I just tried to chase them from my mind by concentrating on my immediate surroundings.

I rented a room in a small hotel at Charing Cross with my mind made up to never set foot in the Kent. The Kent was the past, with Mabel and her eternal nagging. Whatever became of her? Her last letter was two years ago... Tired of it, that is understandable, and I wanted nothing to do with her... And of course there are the pals stuck in the pub with their glasses piling up over projects that will never be finished.

No, all that is over. I do not want to see them again. They are all losers, only good for nursing their mediocrity with alcohol bought on credit and boring conversation smeared with complexes. I wasted myself in their image, one glass after another, the last one costing me five years! Five years of iron bars, bad food and whistle blasts.

Oh yes, all that is over and done with! The main thing is to be able to make the measly few pounds in my pocket last until... Oh, yes, that is the question... Last until what?

It was then, at nightfall, that Brown's propositions came rushing back. *Honest work, well paid, other horizons, a once in a lifetime opportunity...* What was really behind all these promises?

I checked the time when I left the restaurant. 9:10. I still had time to find out, but in the perpetual ticking of my watch something slipped into the sound of the se-

conds, like a voice that seemed to be saying, No… No…
No…

But I gave in. I wanted to know, to go all the way,
and it was my hand digging in my pocket that had the
final word. I was on the dirty docks of Limehouse in the
black warmth of the nocturnal fog. Sirens were wailing
and the gloomy sound spread over the invisible waters of
the Thames, sucked up by a silky void that sprawled
over the ground of the dock. Ghostly ships bore through
the white shadows, unreeling long trails of sinister lap-
ping water behind them. The clouds were low and from
time to time a quarter moon peeked out between two
banks of cloud.

9:30

I decided on a taxi. I found one at the deserted station lit by the fluttering glow of a streetlight where the
fog turned lime green. The cabbie raised an eyebrow on
hearing the address I gave him.

"There's no nightclub in Putney Commons, sir, and
certainly no Time Club."

"It must be new. I guarantee you it's the right address."

He shrugged his shoulders and the cab set off into
the velvety night and silence.

At ten minutes to ten the taxi stopped at the edge of
the plot of land and I got out and looked around. The
cabbie said, "Well, what did I tell you?"

The fog was thick. I could not see more than six
feet in front of me. "One minute, please."

"Sorry, sir, but I have to go back. Make up your
mind. Get back in or…"

Becoming annoyed I slipped some money into the driver's bony hand stretched out to me like a hand in a nightmare stabbing through the curtain of fog. The car disappeared and I was all alone.

I really was in Putney Commons on the edge of some kind of vacant lot at the exact spot where Brown's paper indicated. But in this no man's land of shifting shadows that stretched as far as the eye could see, I saw nothing. Not a trace of a sign, not the faintest glow, nothing that could lead me to believe that the Time Club was located here.

A doubt rose up in my mind, which soon turned into bitter certainty. They were playing with me. Of course, there never was a nightclub in this deserted place. Even if it were new, they would have to be total idiots to build it in this remote area... while in Piccadilly or in Soho...

However, I kept going, a little blindly but not wandering too far from the road, looking searchingly into the fog. Not a sound... Silence everywhere... the night... the fog...

After 100 yards I shrugged my shoulders and gave up. Oh well, too bad! I would walk all the way back, as if to satisfy the roving mania that had eaten up so many hours of my life. I turned around and all of a sudden a long rectangle of light appeared at my feet at the same time as a wry voice rose out of the dark.

"Over here, please."

I swung around. Dazed and stupefied I scrutinized the night. Something was suddenly appearing, as if popping out of the ground. A huge white wall with square, multi-colored windows and on top of it was a neon scrawl of bright red letters reading Time Club.

A door was wide open and in the rectangle of light a tall fellow, impeccably dressed in a long red coat with brass buttons, was leaning toward me. He took of his cap with a ceremonious sweep of his hand, baring his ridiculously round head and said, "We accept people by invitation only. I suppose you have your card?"

He followed my line of sight, staring at the sign, and his lips, like crab pincers, stretched into a smile. "Sensational, isn't it? The Time Club is the most spectacular attraction in London, the most private and the most anonymous place there is."

I tried to smile, to pretend to smile. "But, how do you do it? I..."

"A new process, sir. Based on the polarization of light. One minute we're visible and the next we're not... Funny, don't you think?"

That was far from the word I was thinking of, but his insistent eyes urged me to respond. "No, I don't have a card. I'm just here because of a guy named Brown... I'm supposed to see someone, a Zachariah..."

"Greg Zachariah?" The doorman seemed to balk and then he nodded his head several times. "Yes, yes, well then, in that case, I don't think there will be a problem. You can go in, sir. There's still a place inside."

He stepped aside to let me by and that is how the padded doors in the little entranceway opened for me onto the basement.

That was the very moment I should have turned back, as I said, but at the bottom of the stone staircase, in the confusion of shadows and play of lights, two golden eyes were staring at me with a weird, almost unreal expression. But she is real. Really alive!

She is young and beautiful, extraordinarily beautiful, with her yellow, almond-shaped eyes, her rosy, delicate lips, her slender form and long, honey-blonde hair that cascades over her rounded, graceful shoulders. She wears a green silk dress with a square, low-cut neckline revealing the tender shape of her breasts and her soft, velvety skin the color of champagne. She is sitting at a table, arms crossed, in front of a full glass. A sketchbook and pencil are within reach.

"Well, come and sit down." Her voice is dizzying, stabbing, but wrapping me in sweetness that is very hard to resist.

She stands up at my approach as my eyes unconsciously fall on the drawing paper. I see a face there in black and white, and the sudden revelation makes me even dizzier. A clear, precise, faultlessly drawn face... My face!

CHAPTER II

"I can do better, you know! Much better than this!"

The words fall like crashing waves inside a huge shell. For a minute I feel as if the noise around me has stopped, that the shadows have frozen, swallowed up in an ocean of jade, filled by the shimmering moonlight. But the creature is still in front of me, like a mermaid on the prow of a ship with an eternal smile imbued with charm and mystery. She seems to be enjoying my amazement.

"I assure you, it's worthless. The paper is not very good nor the pencil."

All of a sudden the charm is broken and I come back down to reality. Strange, insidious reality. I look back at the drawing paper.

"It is my portrait, isn't it?"

"It looks like it."

"How did you do it?"

A bartender brings two glasses and put them on a small table. I sit facing the strange woman, awaiting her answer.

"I work from memory," she murmurs while staring directly into my eyes. "A face once engraved in my mind never leaves."

"I don't know you. This is the first time I've been here."

No, you've been here before. *You've been here before!"* She starts laughing and invites me to drink, although she herself does not touch her glass.

What bad joke is being played on me? What is happening? Everything has a weird tinge, a strange feel that

I cannot pin down... and it fuels my fears as I go farther into this universe of confusion and mystery.

And then again it all seems normal and I scold myself for all these absurd fears as the big, golden eyes start staring at me again. Innocent, pure, soothing, inviting the firmest, most complete trust. One of those looks that belongs solely to Bernard Shaw's Saint Joan.

I finish my drink while she slowly tears up the portrait. "I'm sorry I can't satisfy your curiosity. I can't talk anymore about it. But it's not important, Mr. Ashby."

"And you know my name."

"Call me Marthessa, okay?" she introduces herself very tactfully.

I try to smile. "That's very beautiful. But basically, I think I understand."

"Understand what?"

"Brown told you about me?"

"Brown?"

Always that pure innocence in her eyes. Unless she has great acting skills, I believe she is sincere.

"I came here on his advice. If he's not playing a bad joke on me, I'm supposed to meet someone called Zachariah. Do you know him?"

She turns her head slightly and nods her chin at the stone staircase. A man has just entered. He is standing still on the bottom step, his hands inside the pockets of his pea coat. He is a big, fat guy, about six feet tall, the perfect picture of an old sea dog like you see in the cartoons in *Life*, with his black chin beard, his thick eyebrows, his big, round nose and his short pipe held between his teeth. He is dressed in black: pea coat, pants, turtleneck sweater and cap.

He swaggers across the dance floor, cutting through the dancers in our direction. I get up to greet him. He nods quickly at Marthessa, then turns to face me, firmly confident on his massive legs. I get a whiff of seaweed and sea foam before I hear his deep, gravelly voice.

"I'm Captain Zachariah. Brown sent you to see me, is that right?"

He nods his head as if he does not care about my answer. He grabs a chair and straddles it between Marthessa and me. Then he orders three drinks, which arrive at the table in record time. I do not like this scotch. It has a rancid, musty aftertaste. Too old or too badly preserved... something I cannot pin down. It is like Zachariah's behavior. His movements are mechanical, jerky and contradict the physical assurance that he exudes. His intense gaze also has something deeply troubled about it.

"You're looking for work. You're available and you have good knowledge of radio engineering," he says in the same neutral voice. "That's exactly what I need."

"What are you offering?"

"12 months of work on board the *Mary-Ann*. A good ship that's already cut her teeth, you can be sure."

"12 months?"

"Canada, Island, Greenland... I work for a fur and hide company. I've had a lot of desertions lately. A need a radio man, a guy who really knows what he's doing."

I sip my drink. Just to give me time to think. Marthessa has not budged. There is, however, a glimmer of encouragement in her big, golden eyes. Like an invitation to accept this strange offer.

I look at Zachariah. "Why me? There are thousands of guys in London who know radios. You don't need to graduate from Oxford for this kind of job."

"There's nothing to argue about, Mr. Ashby. I said someone who *really* knows what he's doing."

"That's what Brown said, too, this morning, but…"

"Forget Brown. You don't owe him anything for this opportunity."

"Then who?"

For a second the Captain's eyes turn to Marthessa. And I think I get what it means. No, this time I give up. It is useless to wrack my brains, I have no memory of Marthessa. *I've never seen this woman. I've never been here.*

All of this is seriously starting to get almost unbearable. I say, in all seriousness, "Listen, Captain, I get the feeling that we're not on equal footing in this game here. I also have to warn you that if you're trying to drag me into some dodgy business, I won't do it."

"It's honest, steady work for which I am offering 200 pounds a month."

"200 pounds?"

"That's my final word, except to say that we're lifting anchor the day after tomorrow."

The offer is tempting and my reaction to Zachariah's offer does not go unnoticed. I finish my drink casually, trying to disguise my involuntary weakness that questions everything.

200 pounds! More than I would ever earn in my present situation. And the pitiful coins in my pocket are a powerful reminder. And of course there is the scotch, the bad, cheap scotch that wants to join forces with my need. Every sip is a "yes" I swallow that echoes in my fevered soul.

"Well, what do you say?"

When I raise my head I have the feeling that an eternity has just passed. But scraps of hesitation still cling to my mind in spite of Marthessa's insistent gaze, which seems to weigh a ton on me. I stand up.

"Give me 24 hours to think about it. I promise you I'll be here tomorrow night."

"It doesn't matter since you've already accepted."

An inscrutable smile crosses Marthessa's face, but I still find the nerve to reply, "There might be many causes for me to refuse in 24 hours... only one will be enough."

"We don't believe in causes. Only in effects, Mr. Ashby."

"There's no effect without a cause, Marthessa."

"Are you sure of that?"

I do not have the courage to answer. My head is burning up because of the cheap booze and my tongue is turning to lead, hard to move. I leave both of them there without saying a word, without paying any attention to their ironic smiles as a way saying of goodbye.

I scurry up the stone staircase trying to recover my self-control, but I cannot do it. My head is spinning. I am drunk or too wound up, I do not know.

I push open the door in front of me, but right when I rush through I realize my mistake. I bump into a huge glass tube that blocks my way at the same time that a long, blue flame lashes my body with shocking violence. I collapse, howling in pain, looking desperately around. Damn, what have I done? In my daze I must have gone through the wrong the door.

I am in a dimly lit, small room cluttered with weird machines: columns of glass filled with greenish liquid, metal tubes, wires, coils, all of them sticking out of something that looks like a giant snail shell. There is a sharp odor like burned rubber and the electric discharge makes me think that I have stumbled into the building's generator room. At least the control room for the light polarization, if I believe what the doorman said. As I think of this, I decide I should get out of there without a second to lose. I fumble my way through the shadowy light and reach the stairs.

But where am I? The little electric lamps have disappeared from their niches, replaced by big, flaming torches that I can hear crackling. Loud voices and laughter come from the cellar. Skillful hands are plucking a guitar or a mandolin.

One voice rises above the crowd, "To the health of the Stuarts! God save the king, our beloved Charles II!"

Intrigued now I go back downstairs, urged on by the demon of curiosity and standing before that smoky room I see something so unusual, so unexpected that I have to pinch myself to make sure I am awake.

First there is the room itself, which has changed. It is no longer the same. The lighting effects are gone. Resin torches and silver candelabra have taken their place. The leather chairs have become rudely fashioned, wooden stools. No more white tablecloths and the walls are blackened by soot. But the most staggering change is the people who are bustling around in this nightmarish tavern. They are wearing 300-year old costumes. The men are in red or black velvet doublets and baggy pants with gold braiding. Some of them have leather boots with silver spurs and wear a sword at their side. The women have on long, frilly dresses showing lots of cleavage, some of them hiked up in the back revealing bright slips with silver brocade.

The scenery has changed, the costumes have changed, but the people there *are the same*.

The bartender! The couples who were just dancing in each other's arms on the dance floor! It's unbelievable! The same faces! The same voices!

But that is not all because when I look at the other end of the room, I feel an icy sweat trickle down my spine. Facing each other at the same table I recognize Marthessa and Captain Zachariah now wearing a wide-brimmed hat with a long curly feather sticking out.

As for Marthessa, *the other Marthessa with the same golden eyes*, her head now is covered in a green velvet hood with black fox trim. Behind her low-cut coat peeks out a black satin dress with a low, round neckline brocaded with pearls. She is fluttering a lacy fan and smiling angelically at the man seated to her right. I do not know him, but I see on his face the same amount of interest and astonishment that must have been on mine a few minutes earlier.

I imagine more than I hear their conversation.

"It's honest, steady work for which I'm offering ten gold crowns."

"Ten gold crowns?"

"That's my final word, except to say that we're lifting anchor the day after tomorrow."

Like a lunatic I run into the room, but what happens freezes the blood in my veins. This world here has no solidity and when I stretch out my arm to push aside the person in front of me, I touch nothing but emptiness. His body does not exist, at least to my touch… just like the others I grope at in vain. And the same goes for the chairs, tables, glasses…

Ghosts! A universe of ghosts in which I myself probably do not exist…

Overwhelmed by horror and dogged by a great fear, I get out of there and stumble up the stone stairs. I am back on the ground floor, not quite knowing how I got there, my mind a blank and a voice rings out in my ears like a gong. "There's still a place inside."

But no, this time it is not me the words are spoken to. The ghostly doorman standing at the open door is still the same, only his clothes have changed and the nondescript person entering at the moment looks to me like someone right out of a scene from *Macbeth*. Gaunt and haggard and dragging the smell of death behind him.

I refuse to pass my body through his, so I run, like a madman, to one of the windows, digging my fingers into the palms of my hands. It opens, flooding me with moonlight. A cool wind, very real, washes over my face while the knot of fear suffocates and paralyzes me. The vacant lot has disappeared. Before me stand houses with leprous, decrepit facades. Ancient!

A cobblestone path and pathetic silence troubled only by the distant sound of a bell. And then a creaking axle... Wheels rolling over the wet stones... A diabolical voice rising out of the dark: "Bring out your dead... Bring out your dead..."

A big, skeletal horse emerges in the moonlight dragging a heavy cart with a man sitting atop. Another man, on foot, is ringing a doleful bell. "Bring out your dead... Bring out your dead..."

A bunch of corpses, piled up haphazardly, overflow from the cart. A jumble of arms, legs and heads almost sweeping the ground. The worst thing is that this vision is real, solid, substantial... with the stench of rotting carcasses, the diabolical noise and all the human horror in hand's grasp.

The Great Plague!

The great bubonic plague of 1665 with its long funeral marches and its gloomy bells tolling... tolling for the dead!

Oh God, is it possible? Have I really taken a 300-year leap back in time?

"There's still a place inside."

At the sound of the voice the vision vanishes. The deserted land and the fog chase away the cursed images before me. The worthy Cerberus is still here, this time wearing the gleaming livery of the Belle Epoque. In a top hat and frock coat a dandy comes into the entrance-way and hesitates before the double doors. Then swallowed up by the stone stairs he enters the smoke-filled room, the trumpet of King Oliver and Kid Ory's trombone.

I rush in behind him, my forehead soaked in sweat, my heart beating fast... But why, really? Why? How is this possible? What is happening to me?

A "Muskrat Ramble" welcomes me into the 1910 scenery. Moustaches, monocles, top hats, ankle boots, slim waists, frills and flounces. The bartender in a white apron; soldiers in pointed caps and puttees... the "Tommies" of the Grand Epoque who are singing together the "Muskrat Ramble."

It's a long way to Tipperary.

It's a long way to go...

1914... 1915... 1916... 1918... I do not even know... The ghosts have changed costumes, but not their faces. They are still the same... in another scene. Marthessa and Captain Zachariah! Her and her eternal golden eyes... Him and his pipe that he never smokes. And the dandy in the middle of them all.

"50 pounds?"

"That's my final word, except to say that we're lifting anchor the day after tomorrow."

My mind refuses the rest. It cracks in my head like a noise from hell. The black becomes gray and the noise becomes silence in the dizzying abyss I tumble into. And in this nothingness studded with distant stars I hear voices coming from the dream clouds.

"I know you'll come back... So, sign... sign... sign!"

And another voice, defying space and time: "There's still a place inside."

CHAPTER III

Wednesday, July 26, 1967

I am victim of "something" that I do not know the nature of.

Unfortunately, the hours passing by offer no solution to the problem, which is what compels me to put these mysterious events in writing.

This morning I woke up as if coming out of a long fever, shaking and covered in sweat, but with a real world around me. Real but so unexpected!

I was on a small cot, rocked by a slow and regular rhythm as if the entire world around me was in a perpetual state of falling out of balance. But no, I understood immediately. I was on a moving ship, shaken by the strong vibration coming from the creaking wall. I catapulted out of bed to the single porthole when a low-pitched siren howled overhead.

I saw nothing... Nothing but a thick, cottony fog that imprisoned the ship like a cloak. The sea was not visible and the sky was the color of lead, strewn with icy mists. The nightmare persisted on the other side of the porthole with the disquieting silence troubled only by creaking walls and humming propellers.

I do not know how long I stood there, panting, my head pounding, then stifling the shivers of fear that ran down my spine before I decided to open the door. I had no problem doing it and found myself in a dimly lit passageway. Ten cabins on either side. But nothing... Nobody... Nothing but silence... creaking... swaying...

An iron stairway at the end of the passageway and then the steerage. This is when I start to get really disturbed. I reached the deserted upper deck but I was surrounded on all sides by bundles of fog, wrapping around the railing like long tentacles of some nightmarish monster.

Is it daytime? Is it night? I have no idea.

A pale light washes over the deckhouse and the hatchways; the bow of the ship disappears in the thick grayness, I cannot see a thing. And yet I move on, take a few steps forward in the nerve-wracking silence and emptiness. Where am I? Is there really nobody on board? I start to yell, cupping my hands around my mouth.

"Ahoy! Hello! Answer! Somebody answer!"

Creaking... always this creaking... swaying... the siren of the mists who answers me in echoes.

Come on, this is not possible! The engines are working, the propellers are chopping through the water... the water that stays invisible. There is someone here, I am sure of it.

"Ahoy! Hello! Where are you, for the heaven's sake!"

"Hey, hey, what's got into you, screaming like that?"

The voice is hard and hoarse. I hear it at the same time as I see a huge shadow emerge a few feet in front of me between two bundles of fog. I recognize it immediately. It is Captain Zachariah.

We stare at each other in silence for a moment. He has his old sea dog costume on again and the unlit pipe between his teeth. He seems surprised, upset, nervous, almost shocked by my presence on the deck.

"Finally!" he says. "You're back on your feet again. It's none too soon."

Anger wells up in me. "What's happening here? Where am I?"

"On board the *Mary-Ann*."

"How did I get here?"

"On your consent. We drew up a contract. Don't you remember?"

"I didn't sign… I didn't…"

"You signed, Mr. Ashby."

"You're lying!"

He pulls a piece of paper out of his pocket and hands it to me. There is enough light for me to verify my signature at the bottom of the contract. No doubt about it, it really is mine.

"When?"

"Last night at the Time Club."

"I never went back."

"My word, you must have been a lot drunker than I thought. The night before last you could barely stand up straight when you left us. That's pretty normal after five years without a drink in prison… You should have been more careful. Unless you were suffering some kind of partial amnesia following the shock."

"What shock?"

He keeps looking at me with that icy gaze. "We found you with the polarization generators. And in sorry shape! You're lucky you didn't burn like a furnace. But don't worry, I paid the damages."

I look at him as the past fright suddenly comes back to me. "What I saw was no hallucination, Captain."

Zachariah breaks out with a loud, almost metallic laugh. "Yes, yes. We heard all your ramblings while we were bringing you on board. I had a big feather in my hat and plague victims were walking around the land. Just for that I should have quarantined you. The danger of the plague on board the *Mary-Ann* could really make me worry. But since it was a 300-year old plague…"

He continues to laugh, but his laughter sounds fake. His gestures do not fit. Physically and morally Zachariah is just a jumble of contradictory elements.

I nod my head, preferring to drop the subject. "Okay! Since you're laughing at things I can't prove, let me at least say that I don't like this whole situation. It's illegal or…"

"Or what?"

A foghorn interrupts us. Captain Zachairah takes one step closer to me and says, "In short, if I understand you, you don't like this situation, you don't like the captain and you don't like the ship either. I'm sorry, but you are on this trip and I expect you will fulfill your duties on board, Mr. Ashby. Besides, you have wasted enough time with all this. One of my men had to take your place at the radio, so please go and relieve him without further delay."

He makes a mechanical gesture, stretching out his right arm stiffly toward me.

"First of all, however, I would appreciate it if you would change your suit. You will find all the necessary clothes in your cabin. We're on a ship here, Mr. Ashby, even if you don't like it."

I did not argue and I went back to my cabin, feeling powerless. Even though I am a balanced, strong willed man, all this is beyond me, beyond my reason and understanding. There is something going on here that I cannot put my finger on. But what?

I feel torn between what is and what is not... or at least between two kinds of reality: that which my mind accepts as logical and that which my mind refuses for lack of any reasonable explanation. The gulf between the two is too great, so I continue to get lost in a tangled forest of question marks.

The only thing that reassures me is to know that I am alive. That I am *really* alive. My brain is undamaged. My memories as well. Therefore, the problem is not in me but in this strange world surrounding me, that I am in a desperate struggle with.

So, I changed my clothes, refusing to think any more about it, and wandered around the ship in search of the radio room. I found it with the door wide open, squeaking to the rhythm of the swaying ship. Nobody was there, which again contradicted what the captain had said. I took a quick look at the set-up and what I discovered made me even more worried. Nothing but old, worm-eaten equipment! Machines that must have dated back 20 or 30 years... How would I know? Dust and rust everywhere, which stuck to my fingers whenever I touched anything. The machines looked like they had not worked in years. Of course, there was no radar or T.V.

I wondered why they had called on me. Frankly, you do not need to have graduated from Oxford to... To do what, in fact?"

I plugged in a machine, pushed some buttons, but I heard only crackling coming from the old speakers. I spent an hour or two fixing wires, checking capacitors and repairing the speaker whose vibrations shook the cabin.

In the middle of this work I felt a presence and turned my head. Indeed, a man had entered and was watching me in silence. A big guy in a striped sweater, the face of an old sea dog swelled by a roll of fat under his chin. He was carrying a plate in his big, boxer hands and put it on a table. "Your food," he told me, trying to sound friendly.

Then he looked at the equipment and shrugged his shoulders. "Just got to get it working, right? How are you coming along?"

I thought he was the man I had relieved and his question made me think that they were waiting for me in this part of the ship.

I tried to smile to hide my anxiety. "In fact, it's pretty middle ages here, but like you said, it's just got to get working."

I took time to eat, without much appetite, however, then I got back to my haphazard work. The few questions I had asked my new mate remained unanswered. He is not very talkative. All I know is that his name is Griffith and that he has been a member of the crew for a few years. According to him, we are heading for Greenland. That's all, short and sweet.

All day long he sits next to me without saying a word, lost in total indifference, his mouth shut tight.

The crackling in the speakers continued as the long, monotonous, absurd hours passed, just like this ship and this man named Griffith and this invisible sea hidden under the fog. Then, all of a sudden, while I was readjusting the screens, a series of beeps rang out of the speakers. It was an SOS repeated in quick succession. And the thought of a ship that might be in danger, probably in the vicinity, made me jump out of my chair.

With my heart racing I recorded the message. On the last word my hand trembled... The name I had just written down with a feverish hand. I turned pale, then turned to Griffith who leaned over to read what I had written. But he smiled with a touch of pity in his eyes.

"Well, what? Didn't the folks at Oxford ever tell you about the phenomenon of Hertzian remanence?"

Yes… Remanence… Residual magnetization… Waves that can travel through time by sticking in the high, ionized stratum and coming back to their point of origin. Of course I knew about it… But I still did not believe a word he said and the SOS continues to haunt me day and night.

It was from the *Titanic*, the famous English ship that sank in the Atlantic after colliding with an iceberg. *On April 15, 1912!*

CHAPTER IV

Tuesday, July 27, 1967

My watch stopped and this morning when I woke up I had lost all concept of time. Behind the porthole is the same grayness. It is like day and night do not exist in this part of the world. It is always dawn or twilight... One or the other, who knows.

One surprising detail: there are no clocks or calendars on board. Nothing that can measure time.

In desperation I had to rely on Griffith. From now on I reset my watch to whatever time he wants to tell me... That's all!

Oh, yes, there is one other, rather frightening detail (even though I still hesitate to put it on paper): No matter how often I touch my face or look at myself in the mirror I have to accept the facts—*My beard is not growing!*

CHAPTER V

Friday, July 28, 1967

The order came from Zachariah. From now on, Griffith and I will take 8-hour shifts in the radio room. Personally, I wonder why. We send and receive no messages. Nothing but lost time. In absurdity!

And this has lasted since the "phenomenon of Hertzian remanence" about the message from the *Titanic*, to use Griffith's phrase because I gave up hope of classifying the event in the realm of my positivist mind. Thus, my forest of question marks becomes a thicker and thicker jungle every day.

Once again today I got my daily ration of mystery. It started after my eight hours of duty when I got back to my cabin to eat something. I had, in fact, decided to eat alone since Griffith's presence was becoming so unbearable that I was losing my appetite. And God knows that I do not have much to spare.

I got the idea to find out whether Griffith really stayed on duty while I was gone. Very cautiously I retraced my steps and reached the radio room, ready with an excuse, but as I expected, the room was empty. The machines were turned off and only a heavy silence came out of the speakers.

At least I am certain of one thing now. The role they have me playing on the *Mary-Ann* is a farce. It is only a pretext for the real intentions of Zachariah. They are keeping me busy to keep me from being suspicious. But how far will this little game go? How many more days? And what do *they* intend to do with me?

I do not like the word "they" which flows automatically out of my pen. I am thinking of the crew of the *Mary-Ann*, which I have not had the slightest contact with so far, except for Zachariah and Griffith. But the others? Where are they? How many of them are there? It is impossible for a ship of this size to be navigated by only two people.

Needled by these thoughts I made a little search of the ship, pretty much everywhere, without meeting a single living soul. It is like I am alone now. All alone in on this ship of ill omen abandoned to silence... to creaking... to swaying...

I wound up on deck surrounded by the fog. The poop deck was half-hidden in the gray as I watched the portholes for a long time. No light shined inside them. Nothing. Everything was empty... black... deserted... like the end of the world.

A cold sweat started to bead on my forehead. I turned around and tripped over the drogues and cordage. That is when a ray of light, peaking through a hatchway, attracted my attention. I crawled over the deck to it, all my senses on alert and I heard muffled voices that led me to believe that several people were just a few feet beneath me.

Very carefully, very slowly I pushed the hatchway open and risked a glance through the crack. Icy cold air struck me in the face right away, as if someone had thrown a bottle of ether at me. The hold was kept at polar temperatures, but the people down there seemed to be strangely well adapted. I counted fifteen of them, but I was sure that there were more in the dark corner that I could not see. At least, I figured there were more.

Finally I had discovered what appeared to be the crew of the *Mary-Ann*. But why the appalling hold and the glacial temperature? What was happening?

I recognized Captain Zachariah in the middle of the group. Next to him stood Griffith, his arms crossed over his huge chest. Everyone was leaning over a map spread out on a table. Zachariah's finger was pointing to the Drake Passage, between the southernmost tip of South America and Graham Land on Antarctica. But I could not get what he was saying. They were all whispering, certainly in a language I did not understand because the few words I picked up meant nothing at all to me. Worse than Hebrew! I did not wait around, but left the hatchway with the feeling that a grave danger was threatening me... A danger I knew nothing about but that seemed, tragically, to be coming closer every minute.

A danger that was not *necessarily* on the ship but might be in the weird world around them, in the endless gray, as transparent as gelatin.

Overcoming my fear and loathing, I made my way over to the railing and stared into the fog, but the waves were still invisible, lost in the cottony void. I could not even hear the sound of the water. I did, however, hear the hum of the propellers, the relentless chopping that seemed to be coming from the stern. Unless I was wrong about the nature of the noise...

Unfortunately, that was what I had to conclude when I went to the back of the ship. There was no sound of propellers; it was just as silent. But then that sound? Where was it coming from? I found it. Not in the engine room where I went right away (nothing was working there, everything was calm, at rest, and there was nobody in front of the boilers), but in a nearby hold.

The sound is nothing, of no importance, but what I discover is beyond anything imaginable. I am standing before the same machines that cluttered that room in the Time Club where I had entered by mistake. Glass columns filled with greenish liquid, tubes, wires, coils and that giant snail shell. The polarizers again? This time I am confused... unless it is something else entirely.

And then an idea pops into my head and grows stronger when I get back to my cabin. It will not go away: I am being used as a guinea pig in some top secret experiment... Yes, that's it. A man alone, with no ties, no family, no job or home, is a perfect choice.

But who is behind all this? A foreign power?

The *Mary-Ann* is still docked somewhere, I am almost sure of it, except nobody can see it and the whole set-up is so skillfully organized just to relieve my doubts and suspicions. I see no other explanation, if I want to stay within reasonable and possible bounds. Their purpose escapes me, that's all.

I light a cigarette, trying to fight against the anger rising in me and flop down onto the cot with my head in my hands. That is when I notice the object in front of me sitting on the floor in plain sight. A gold wristwatch whose band is unfastened. I grab it and examine it closely. It seems to be in good shape and on the back I see two initials and a date engraved: J.B. 1929.

So who could have lost their watch in this cabin? And what went on here while I was gone?

But what is worse is that it was impossible for me not to see the object on the floor for the 15 minutes that I was pacing up and down the narrow space between the two cots facing each other. I could not have avoided stepping on it! There is not an inch of floor that was not tread on!

So, how did this watch get here?

O Lord, what funny ideas I have! No... no... None of this makes any sense. Either I am crazy or they are trying to make me go crazy. Totally crazy!

O God, what did I do to deserve this? And why?

CHAPTER VI

Saturday, July 29, 1967

It is four o'clock in the morning and a wailing siren wakes me up. When I open my eyes dizziness turns my stomach and the walls around me look like they are vibrating violently. It does not last. Everything goes back to normal when I jump out of bed at the sound of stomping feet in the corridor. I also hear voices, so I rush over to open the door and I run straight into Captain Zachariah.

"What's going on, Captain? What's happening?"

Zachariah makes a nervous gesture. "Get back in your cabin, it's not your job. We'll deal with it just fine without you."

"What's it all about?"

"A shipwreck. We're picking up survivors."

"A shipwreck?"

He sees the doubt in my eyes and as if reading my mind he points to the porthole in my cabin, telling me, just before disappearing, "You have an excellent lookout post there. I advise you not to leave your cabin until I tell you. Griffith is at the radio and he doesn't need you."

"But…"

"You understand?"

The door slams shut on my explosion of anger. I jump over to the porthole and find myself completely stunned by what I see.

And here all my ideas melt down! We really are at sea. The fog has vanished and in the spotlights from the

Mary-Ann I can see the waves moving, fringed with foam. Barely a few hundred yards away, fighting against the waves, a ship is listing at a dangerous angle. Lifeboats, jam-packed around the giant in the rough sea are struggling to board the *Mary-Ann*.

I see them climbing on the crests and falling back down into the troughs. One of them capsizes, dragging a group of castaways into the sea who disappear a moment later like being swallowed up by a myriad of liquid mouths.

It is awful!

But I no longer know how much reality I should allot to the scene. What is real in all this? A mirage? Hallucination? Psychosis? No, I do not think so. My suspicions and my total consciousness of things are enough to deny any hallucinatory effects as I watch the scene unfold in a cruel and tragic reality.

In the background the ship is foundering. Slowly, relentlessly. I see it sink into the swirling eddies that kick up monstrous waves. A moment later, sucked in by the deep, it disappears entirely from the spotlight beams.

Only three lifeboats board the *Mary-Ann*. In the first one that clings to the side of the cargo ship a crazed man loses his balance among the men piled in who push and shove and start falling all over each other.

A big wave comes and carries it off. The hapless boat comes back.

Hands reach out to it, but another wave takes it and throws it forward. Once again it comes back in the spray of foam. The man is heaved up along the hull and then it is the turn of the others.

The men from the first lifeboat, then the second, then the third...

Later

I did not move from my cabin. The spotlights were turned off, replaced by the moonlight. Silvery sparks flashed on the waves. The Ocean resumed its monotone dance.

Above me the ship is very busy. Voices are pretty much everywhere and sounds of footsteps in the corridors. Fifteen minutes goes by before the door flies open onto a sailor whom I do not know. He helps in a man wrapped up in a warm blanket and sits him down on the empty cot. Without a word he turns around and leaves the man who will not stop grumbling.

All of a sudden I recognize him. He is the one I saw fighting with the sea in the lifeboat that I thought was lost for sure but that hung on by a miracle. He is tall, thin and has a short, gray goatee. He looks around 35 years old and has really round eyes like a hound dog. They had given him clothes that were a little too big for him and the blanket thrown over his shoulders had seen one too many generations of moths.

He raises his eyes and stares at me with a look of deep gratitude. "Thanks... thanks to you, too." His voice is friendly with a strong Yankee accent. "Oh, Lord, what a disaster! And it all happened so fast... So fast!"

He stands up clumsily in his blanket. "My name's John Bradley. I'm a professor at Harvard."

I introduce myself in turn and shake the hand he offers me warmly. He carries himself with a lot of dignity, but he is still in shock and I have to help him sit back down. Since I still have a little coffee in the thermos I give him a cup, which he sips slowly.

I ask, "How many survivors?"

He thinks and sighs, "21 out of the 64 that were on board the *Cormorant*. That's bad, huh?"

"What happened?"

He licks the sugar off the rim of his cup, then shakes his head. "To tell you the truth, no one knows. I was sleeping when the alarm went off, but according to the coal-trimmers the hull got ripped through in one of the starboard holds."

"A collision?"

"No, there was no collision. And yet it would be… with what? I wonder."

"Well, an iceberg. You know, in the fog…"

He shakes his head. "There was no fog. It was a clear night. No, the rip can't be explained, but it caused us to take on water and no one could stop it. Fortunately you were in the area and you came at our first call. Oh Lord, we were counting the minutes!"

He blinks and watches me with interest, then asks in a different tone of voice, "Haven't I seen you somewhere before, Mr. Ashby?"

"Uh, no, I don't think so."

He continues staring at me, then shakes his head. "Ah, yes, I see. You look a lot like a poor guy we found last year lost at the South Pole. Yes, there's an uncanny resemblance. The funniest thing is the guy's name was Ashby, too."

"And what happened to that guy?"

"He died on the *Cormorant* on the way back."

"Ah, well, there you go. I'm not a ghost."

Professor Bradley smiles weakly and automatically glances at his left wrist as a mix of surprise and disappointment crosses his face. "And now I've lost my watch."

Suddenly I think of the initials engraved on the back of the watch I found in my cabin before the shipwreck. A J and a B! And isn't this guy's name John Bradley?

Gnawed by doubt I take the watch from under my pillow and hold it out to the professor with a trembling hand. I ask faintly, "This wouldn't be it?"

He does not believe his eyes as he takes it and thanks me with a big smile, while asking, "Where in the world did you find it?"

"Well... I..."

I do not know what to say. I do not have the courage to tell him the truth. No, it is not possible! I would not understand, anyway, but I still try to find an apparently logical explanation.

"Here... when you came in. But I thought it might have been dropped by the sailor with you... I just wanted..."

"It doesn't matter. Thank you, Mr. Ashby." He keeps talking, "A brand new watch... a gift from my wife..."

I am only half-listening.

"Mr. Ashby!" His voice has changed again, suddenly, and rattles me.

"Yes?"

"Have you been on this ship for a long time?"

"It's my first trip."

"An old tub, isn't it?"

"Pretty old, yes."

He continues, "Tell me, has this boat ever had any problems? Any shipwrecks?"

I look at him, astonished. "Why do you ask that?"

I noticed a little hesitation in Bradley. He shrugs his shoulders and lies down on the cot, holding the blanket tightly on his chest. Then he goes on, "After all, it's not impossible to bring it back to the surface. According to Morgan, our quartermaster, your boat went down with all hands on board ten years ago in the Bermudas. He says he recognized it from when he worked as a sailor." He clears his throat. "And then a bunch of nonsense..."

"What kind of nonsense?"

He yawns. "Bah! Sailors are superstitious, you know. He was on the poop deck with the captain at the time of the accident. Says the *Mary-Ann* appeared out of nowhere right nearby after their first call for help. He thinks we're on a ghost ship. Ohh, Lord, what do you think about that, Mr. Ashby?"

With another smile and another shrug he continues, "Okay, like I said, a bunch of nonsense. Believe me, Mr. Ashby, I don't believe in ghosts."

He drops off to sleep in the silence, the creaking, the swaying...

I walk over to the porthole and look out, look everywhere. The fog has returned, just as thick. The sea... the waves... the moon... there is nothing anymore. Nothing but the clouded nothingness that blankets the *Mary-Ann* like a shroud...

CHAPTER VI

The same day. Even later…

I see Professor Bradley again after my eight-hour shift in the radio room. When I enter the cabin I find him standing in front of the porthole, hands in his pockets and a cigarette in his mouth. His forehead is creased when he turns to me.

"Nasty weather, isn't it, Mr. Ashby? Weird, nasty weather."

If only I could make him understand… explain to him what is happening… But how? Would he even believe me? Of course he seems like a good guy and we seem to get along rather well, but is this enough for him to accept the terrible danger that now looms not only over me but also over him and the 20 survivors of the *Cormorant*?

I hesitate, but he makes it easy for me. Without meaning to. He asks, "In your opinion, how long before we'll be in Buenos Aires?"

"Buenos Aires?"

"Yes, that's where we'll have to get off. Some of us went to ask your captain this morning, but he was nowhere to be found."

"But…"

"But what?"

"I think there's been a mistake."

"How's that?"

"We're headed for Greenland. We're in the northern hemisphere."

He stares at me, wide-eyed. "Oh my, young man, what's got into you? Our shipwreck last night happened in the Drake Passage."

I have the sudden feeling that all the blood has been drained from my veins. An image springs to mind. Zachariah's finger on the map pointing to the Drake Passage! In that room two hours before the shipwreck. Oh my God, what does this mean?

In a shaky voice I respond, "Between Tierra del Fuego and Graham Land, right? In Antarctica?"

"Bingo!"

"But, well, that's impossible. The *Mary-Ann* left London only three days ago. We can't be…"

"What are trying to say?"

The fact is clear. One of us is obviously crazy. However, my mind is made up and I am not stopping here. "Listen, Professor, I promise to explain everything to you, but please answer my questions first."

"Yes, okay, but still…"

"Where did you embark?"

"Boston."

"When?"

"Around three weeks ago."

"What was your destination?"

"The South Pole. Specifically the coasts of the Ross Sea. My colleagues and I were supposed to join the Byrd expedition."

"Byrd?"

"Well, yes, of course, Admiral Byrd! You must have heard of him! All the papers are talking about nothing but him nowadays."

"Nowadays?"

"Well, yes… what's got into you, my friend."

I manage towhisper faintly, "But... but Admiral Byrd died a long time ago, Professor."

Bradley's face turns beet red. "I don't like this kind of joke, Mr. Ashby!"

"The problem is that I'm not joking about anything."

"So what's this all about then?"

I glance at his wristwatch. "Hold on! I think I remember you saying that your watch was a gift from your wife, right?"

He grumbles. I feel the professor is losing patience, but I have to continue. He narrows his eyes and raises his voice, "Listen, my boy, this is all getting a little too much for me."

"For heaven's sake, answer, I beg you."

"Yes. So?"

"How old are you?"

"Fifty-three."

"You must have been a young man in 1929."

He plops down on the cot and looks at me with cold terror in his eyes. "Are you crazy, Mr. Ashby?"

"If you don't help me, I think there's a very good chance I will become so."

"But *this is* 1929!"

And there are the words I have been fearing. 1929! The year of my birth! It is unbelievable!

So, what is happening? Is such a thing possible? I do not have the courage to deny Bradley. I know that he is not lying... and that his words only echo the horrible, frightening reality. The question I want to ask him is on the tip of my tongue. My head is going to explode, I feel it.

"What... what day is it?"

"March 4. But really, Mr. Ashby, what's got into you? Are you all right?"

This time it is too much and the sensation of the terrible danger lying in wait for us forces me to make the necessary decision.

"What I have to say to you is very serious, Professor, so please try very hard to understand."

"I'm listening."

I spurt out the whole story of getting out of prison, the Time Club, the temporal visions I experienced, my presence on board the ship, the *Titanic* and the strange machinery I found on board the *Mary-Ann*. I told him my doubts, my fears, my anxieties, all my crazy ideas. Everything!

He looks uncomfortable but not convinced. Far from it! He keeps staring at me in terror. As if I were the devil in the flesh.

Finally, he mumbles, "Mr. Ashby, none of this makes any sense."

"So, you don't want to try to understand."

"That's not what I mean. What I mean is that I don't believe you." His voice trembles as he loses his composure.

"Very well! Then you won't believe me either if I tell you that I found your watch in this cabin two hours before the shipwreck? Yes, two hours before you got here."

"Mr. Ashby…"

"As you want! Well, then, take a look at this now."

I do not give him time to think. I pull out my wallet and hand him my identification. He looks straight at my birth date. August 20, 1929! I give him my prison discharge, stamped and signed. Another date: July 25, 1967. To finish it off I pull a folded newspaper out of my pocket. A *Times* with the same date; God only knows how I kept it.

"Go on! I'm giving you news 30 years in advance. Three columns on the war in Vietnam… Two more on the space programs of Russia and America... A photo of the President…"

"Stop!"

He jumps up, completely confused. I figure he is on the verge of panic. His face is white.

"Stop! Please, be quiet!"

He stands there for a minute, staring at the porthole… at the steamy, ghostly fog dancing over the invisible sea.

Then all of a sudden he shouts, "Take me to your captain! Right now, let's go!"

He gets to the door first, but stops there. It is locked from the outside. All are efforts are in vain. We are stuck in here.

CHAPTER VIII

The dates in my journal make no sense anymore. I have decided to drop them. Time itself does not mean anything except for what is on our watches, Bradley's and mine, that ticks off its monotone in the mechanisms.

A sailor came to bring food. Two others stood behind him holding weird weapons, ready for everything, for the slightest move on our part. Then the door closed again and the locks turned. We figure that it is the same for all the survivors of the *Cormorant*. But we do not understand. What is their purpose in keeping us prisoners in our cabins?

Bradley is still hesitant about the exact nature of the events we are living through. He talks about a gap, a temporal interpenetration with reciprocity. Of course he has studied Einstein, Minkowski and all the rest, but his knowledge of relativity (alas!) offers no solution to our sorry situation.

Nor does it explain why the only stool in the cabin was suddenly displaced this morning before our stunned eyes. Good thing no one was sitting on it! It dematerialized on one side of the room and rematerialized on the other. Six feet away.

Bradley's scientific mind is back on top of things.

He is searching.

He is also searching to know why his beard is not growing anymore.

Me, I made another observation. Even more serious. I got a superficial cut on my finger while opening a can.

A small drop of blood appeared, then another... then another... After an hour it was still bleeding.

I had to use a bandage and wrap it up. And everything was all right. But whenever I take the bandage off the bleeding starts again. The cells are not regenerating... *Healing has become impossible!*

CHAPTER IX

Bradley and I are still asleep when the door of our cabin flies open with a bang. A sharp, stern voice rattles us. "Get dressed and get ready! We're drawing up in a few minutes!" The sailor takes a quick look around the cabin, then without another word slams the door shut.

Bradley and I jump up and rush to the porthole, but we see the same, incomprehensible sight outside. Fog and grayness. Nothing that can give us the least clue to where we are about to land.

"Where the hell are we?" Professor Bradley murmurs, almost to himself.

"Certainly not in Buenos Aires. Don't kid yourself."

"My God…"

That is all he can find to say in his confusion, but these two words alone are more than enough to translate the mortal fear that grips us by the throat.

Ten minutes later we reach the port and are led by two sailors armed with double tubes to Captain Zachariah standing straight and tall on the forecastle. The survivors from the *Cormorant* have already left the ship, the last of them on the gangway just now disappearing into the fog along with their jailor. We still see nothing. The shadows melt into the gray, into the pea soup surrounding the *Mary-Ann*.

Zachariah turns his hoarse voice to us. "Follow closely the instructions given to you." He coughs a little and continues, "There's no danger if you don't do anything stupid. And keep in mind that your fate depends on your behavior."

I step forward, holding in my anger and the furious desire to grab him by the throat. "What's the meaning of all this?"

He stabs his still unlit pipe toward me, saying, "Remember this well, Ashby. Right now you are a fortunate man, but don't press your luck."

"I demand an explanation, Captain."

He shrugs. "I'm not authorized to tell you anything more. As far as you're concerned, my work ends here. Goodbye, Mr. Ashby."

I recognize the same final words that ended my conversation with Brown after I left Dartmoor. The chain drags on, but what will I find at the end of it? Or *Who?*

I decide not to press it and hurry to catch up to Bradley who has reached the gangway with our guards. We walk down it slowly, following the instructions given to us, and reach dry land. A land that we cannot see through the thick fog. But the ground under our invisible feet is something soft, squishy, like we are walking on gelatin.

I grab the arm of one of our guards and let myself be guided. Bradley's brown shadow in front of me looks like it is floating in muddy water. I hear voices and guess that it must be the men from the *Cormorant* a little farther ahead.

Finally, little by little, the ground feels like it is becoming harder and the fog less dense. The light grows stronger and I think I can make out some human shapes huddled together a little farther ahead to the right. We speed up to join them.

One man will not stop swearing in a fit of anger sprinkled with expressions that seamen just do not use.

"Billions of blistering barnacles! What's going on here? Where've they brought us? This is completely unacceptable, outrageous... It's piracy!" He spits out some curses, then continues, "By Neptune's beard they won't get away with it, believe you me!"

It is the captain of the *Cormorant*, a tall fellow with a weathered face full of freckles. He spots me at Bradley's side and stares at me with surprise.

"I'm in the same boat as you," I say, cutting to the chase.

"You were on board?"

"As a passenger."

"They wouldn't by chance have told you...?"

"They didn't tell me anything, Captain"

"Say, sir, this boat really is the *Mary-Ann*, isn't it?" It is another guy who asks this question and I know right away that it is the quartermaster Morgan.

"That is indeed the name."

Mumbling all around while a voice orders us, "Move it!"

But the captain asks again, "Do you have any idea what is happening?"

"None at all."

I leave them there as Bradley drags me away. "Better to say as little as possible if you don't want to throw the good men into a panic."

I am of the same opinion as Bradley. To explain to them what we know so far would do absolutely no good.

And that is when the fog thins and we shriek in astonishment at the scene around us. We are inside a huge crater, at least that is the impression I have on seeing the long, rocky ring encircling us. But how the devil did we get here?

The fog behind us dissolves slowly to reveal hundreds and hundreds of feet of altitude rising into the gloomy, colorless sky streaked with hazy lights. *How could the Mary-Ann have landed in this place?* How could we have crossed these cliffs that seem impenetrable?

"Move it!"

We file between the guards, more and more surprised at what we discover. A crater or an arena? In any case, a huge space where sparse vegetation grows in weird shapes. There are what look like cacti covered with frost and icicles. Milky roots crisscross over the ground where flowers sprout up, glassy and sparkling, but only at the foot the cliff, as if they were planted there for some obscure purpose.

Inside the arena is nothing but land, rocky and barren, with a pinnacle in the middle standing hundreds of feet tall. But this is no whim of nature. No, it is man-made. A weirdly shaped, metal tower. Like a beer bottle with an orange sitting on top of it. In the skin of the orange are portholes pretty much everywhere.

"Move it!"

A chill wind comes down from the heights in a long, endless wail. It is the only noise that can be heard in this strange world, peopled only by shadows and mystery.

We are led by our jailors across the piles of rocks, but the guards from the *Mary-Ann* seem to me to be on the alert. I feel it in my bones. They keep looking at the sky and their hands clutch their weapons as if they are afraid some kind of danger.

And yet I see nothing... Nothing but the sky, the colorless sky, almost palpable, that surrounds the arena, fringing the summits with its weird, shimmering lights, verging on unreality.

"Move it! Hurry up!"

A gate appears at the bend in the path. The doors are open and we enter a kind of enclosure, very large. A fence, supported by steel beams, rises over our heads as far as the eye can see and in here the faces of our guards seem to become calm again. Their weapons are lowered, no longer threatening, and their eyes no longer look up. All traces of fear seem to have disappeared for good even though I cannot understand the nature of this new mystery. What is there in the sky that can worry them so?

"Look!" Bradley's hand squeezing my shoulder wrenches me back into a more objective reality.

We are led toward a wooden shack built at the foot of a pile of rocks that fences off the enclosure at this spot. A moment later we are inside: one big room cluttered with beds, straw mattresses, stools and a long, rudely fashioned table.

A real stalag!

There are plenty of provisions, more than enough… in a closet that our guards point out. The captain of the *Cormorant* tries to assert himself one last time, but his threats have no effect on our jailors, who now seem completely uninterested in us. One of them, before leaving, points to the fence outside and warns, "Whatever you do, don't touch it. It's all electrified. Get it through your heads that there's no escape."

He nods a few times and with a kind of diabolical smile adds, "You got it right! Escape is *impossible*."

CHAPTER X

Later

Hours passed. Clock hours. I could not put up with the tedious conversations inside the stalag. Always the same questions nagging my brain like a tolling bell. I left. I wandered around the maze of steel poles, alone, haphazardly, lost in solitude and in hopelessness.

Then a shape appeared in front of me and I recognized Professor Bradley. He looked worried and I could tell he had rushed out to find me, as if I were the only person worthy of his trust.

He said to me, "I've been looking for you. I can't stand it in there. How to explain it to them, eh? I don't have the strength."

"Explain what?"

He nodded, then scratched his head in confusion. "Yes, of course... but, see, I've been thinking and..." He hesitated.

"What do you want to explain to them?" I pressed him.

"Well, that we were stopped in time. Yes, stopped! That's the right word. Your time and mine no longer exist. We don't live in normal time. It's something else..."

"What are your conclusions based on?"

"Well, first of all our beards and hair and nails have stopped growing. Then that cut on your finger that won't heal. Biologically speaking that means that all cellular development has completely stopped in us. In other words, we're not getting any older—old age is an effect of time, don't forget."

"In that case, we'll be immortal?"

"Immortal? Yes, as long as we don't have any accidents that could start us bleeding."

"Nice consolation."

He shrugged his shoulders in the face of my skepticism. "Please, don't ask me for explanations that I can't give you. I'm just stating the facts. That's all. Maybe it's some kind of experiment and we're the guinea pigs. What do I know?"

The idea had already crossed my mind, but the way they treated us did not fit the bill. "No, professor, you said so yourself, it's something else and this something might very well be behind that." I pointed to the rocks encircling the arena. "If only we could get a glimpse of what's on the other side of that."

He must have guessed what I was thinking because he responded quickly, with fear in his voice, "You can't... That'd be crazy..."

I did not have time to answer because the quartermaster Morgan popped up all of a sudden, out of breath, running toward the shack. His pale face betrayed a mortal fright. He stopped in front of us, stared wildly for a moment, then before bolting off he shouted, "I knew it... I told them... The *Mary-Ann*... A ghost ship! O Lord, I saw them! I saw *them*!"

Now thrown into a panic Bradley and I looked at each other and at the same time ran off between the steel poles in the direction Morgan was running away from.

Our mad dash took us to another side of the enclosure where an electric fence blocked our way. Out of breath, we stared hard into the arid, desolate space in front of us. There were no poles of gates there. The space was empty except that here, too, were shacks. A dozen of them lined up... And also... and also creatures we could see among the rocks. Haggard and gaunt, like human skeletons sprung from some tomb or charnel house... but bearing their destiny with humble dignity.

The faces! O the faces! It was horrible!

Yellow, marbled with dark veins, expressionless, wrinkled like elephant trunks, they stared at us. Their glazed and murky eyes were barely even white slits in their bony sockets. And all the dead were stumbling blindly, aimlessly, mindlessly, dragging around their wobbling carcasses and the last breath of their lives.

A word came to mind and I mumbled it under my breath: "Zombies!"

Yes, zombies, halfway between life and death, forlorn creatures constantly rejected by both but still drawn to the cold and the grave.

Lord! What did these awful visions mean? And where did these nightmarish creatures come from?

Then I noticed the clothes draped over the bony bodies. Rags, really, but clothes from all times and all ages. Walking characters in a grotesque masquerade, a carnival from beyond the grave. Louis XV frock coats, uniforms from the Empire, medieval jerkins, Janissary cloaks, breeches, doublets, Musketeer capes. And 20th century tweed suits!

The whole chaos in a hideous procession reeking of death and the catacombs.

And then, all of a sudden, voices shouted out around me, cries of horror and panic. It was the men from the *Cormorantt* who had followed the quartermaster here.

In the midst of my confusion I could not understand what Morgan was saying, but Professor Bradley got the gist of it. He stammered, "Oh my God, Mr. Ashby!"

He was pointing at a group of zombies who were standing apart from the rest of the sinister parade. There were half a dozen creatures wearing sailor uniforms vaguely resembling my own. Their faces still had something human, something living about them, despite the decay and the deep grooves of wrinkles pretty much everywhere. They were watching us with their black-ringed eyes. They lifted their arms and shook their hands at us in silent but passionate pleas.

"Well, what? What is it? Speak up!" Bradley's stammering voice was barely audible. "Oh my God, Morgan knows these men. Ten years ago on the *Mary-Ann*... His old friends... The men lost in the shipwreck in Bermuda..."

I felt like my brain was exploding. His words were like hammer blows pounding inside my head. But panic was already breaking out around me and I had to get a hold of myself to help out the captain of the *Cormorant* whose courage and composure, which seemed absolutely extraordinary to me, had no effect on the poor men. We finally managed to drag our partners in misfortune back to the stalag, but here again their overexcited minds went wild. Like a gale of madness that we could not control.

And it was Morgan stirring them up with his alarmist talk that could snap the nerves of the bravest of them. "You saw them, right? You saw them just like me... with all those dead men... I tell you the boat that picked us up is a ghost ship and now we're surrounded by the dead... nothing but the dead."

"That's enough, Morgan! Stop or I'll smash your face in!" I run up to him in a fit of anger. "You're making everyone panic with your stupid nonsense. So shut up!"

"You're going to tell me that those aren't the sailors from the *Mary-Ann*?" Drool was dribbling out his mouth and madness was in his eyes.

"And what if they are? What gives you the right to talk like that? Those men were alive, very much alive... like you and me and all of us here. So stop babbling like an idiot."

I put a stop to his craziness. My fist to his face when he tried to pounce on me in a sudden frenzy. He was nothing but a confused animal ready for anything, even the worst. He shoved his companions aside and charged at me again, catching my throat with his big hands. We rolled on the ground in a savage, relentless battle and just as I wrestled free of him he kicked me in the chest and I crumpled to the floor of the stalag.

The rest of it happened in a flash and at the time I am writing this I still wonder what would have become of me if...

I saw the glint of a blade in Morgan's hand as he rushed at me in a blind rage. But he had not taken two steps when he started howling. A knife was stuck up to the hilt in his belly. Morgan dropped his and by reflex grabbed the handle with both hands before collapsing to the ground in a sea of blood.

Everyone ran to him except Parker. In fact, have I said yet that Parker was the name of the captain of the *Cormorant*? The expression on his face bore witness to the deed he had just done.

I broke the deadly silence between the two of us. "You killed him!"

"Had to be done, Mr. Ashby. Nothing is more contagious than madness. Besides, it was either you or him."

Someone leaning over Morgan cried out, "But can't we do anything for him?"

What could we really do in this strange world where a minor cut could bring death? And the wound Morgan got was too serious to even think about stopping the bleeding with whatever was on hand.

Then the answer came from behind, clear and categorical. "It's impossible. There's nothing we can do for him."

I swung around and found myself face to face with the most stunning creature. A young woman with sad eyes in a round face, almost child-like, with prominent cheekbones, small ears and very black, long hair pulled into a tight bun. She was not very tall, but she held herself extraordinarily well in her long, white outfit—a nurse's outfit!

She stepped into the silence, approached Morgan's body, still jerking in its last gasps, and turned to face Captain Parker.

"Don't worry about a thing. I'll take care of getting him out of here. Right now your men have to get ready for the medical exam. That's all, captain."

Her voice was cold, but some trace of emotion was there in every word she spoke. Anyway, there was nothing more to say and the lady disappeared through the door with the stone-cold indifference of a statue.

A few seconds later Morgan breathed his last. I watched him die, but I was lost in my thoughts. Then I realized that I had lost the little, gold chain that I wore around my neck and that I never took off.

I found it where we were fighting but it was missing the medallion that my mother had given me, that I safeguarded religiously.

I looked for it everywhere until Professor Bradley finally found it between two straw mattresses. But it was half crushed as if someone had trampled on it.

And that's all. Except that an hour later two stone-faced guards came to take away Morgan's body.

CHAPTER XI

I always reread my last entry before putting in writing the recent events. But when I open my journal to record this first day spent on dry land, I break out in a cold sweat.

Lord, what is happening?

Four pages that should be white are covered with my writing. *I have already written about this day that I am getting ready to relate.*

But, come on, this is not possible! I do not remember writing a single word since we stepped off the *Mary-Ann*. And yet, there is no mistake, the writing is mine and it tells exactly what happened from the moment Bradley and I were told in our cabin about the landing.

I scan through the lines feverishly, one page after another... one page after another...

Unthinkable! Everything is here: my conversation on the deck with Captain Zachariah, our walking onto dry ground in the fog, the arena with its central tower and the weird plants with glass flowers, and the enclosure, the fence, the shack and then...

Wait a minute, this is strange. From this moment on I do not understand. Things are different, changed, transformed... *I do not recognize the events that follow.* Well, now, what's going on here?

What is all this about the quartermaster Morgan popping up and running around like a lunatic... the zombie creatures... and these ghostly apparitions that Morgan recognizes as his former companions on the *Mary-Ann* who disappeared in a shipwreck ten years ago?

I must be going crazy because none of this happened.

Certainly, Bradley and I were talking outside the shack, but it was not Morgan who interrupted us. It was two guards armed to the teeth to bring us to the medical exam. It took place in a nearby shack, a real test room directed by a charming creature whose indifference and reserve, however, hid a strong passion. Brunette with big, dreamy eyes and the face of a caryatid. Exactly the same creature I described in that passage that is also completely incomprehensible. There was no fight between Morgan and myself, not the slightest argument. What happened had nothing to do with me or with Parker. The scene that occured before our eyes, without any logical explanation forthcoming, was more like magic. Morgan was talking in the middle of the stalag when all of a sudden a knife was stuck in his belly. Captain Parker's knife! But Parker never stabbed him. We were all witnesses.

A wave of panic swept through us all before the young nurse showed up and events unfolded as written on the paper. All she said was, "There's nothing we can do for him. I'll take care of getting him out of here." An hour later two stone-faced guards came to take away Morgan's body. So, it ended in the same way except that in the events I lived through there was *no cause* for Morgan's murder. No human intervention. *A murder without a murderer!*

Even though…

But how much faith should I put in the first version? What does all this mean?

That is what I am wondering with sweat running down my brow when I suddenly realize that the little gold chain that my mother gave me has disappeared. I jump up and run through the stalag looking for it every-where.

Astonishing… Incredible… Extraordinary…

I find the chain in front of the long, wooden table and the medallion between two straw mattresses. Crushed! Like it was stepped on!

Good lord, how could this have happened? Could I have forgotten all the events of the first version? *Could I have lived two different days… in only one day? At the same time?*

CHAPTER XII

I cannot get to sleep.

I meant to tell Bradley, but I finally gave up the idea. It would do nothing but increase the tension that all of us feel since the incomprehensible death of Morgan. Maybe later…

The air around me is full of grumbling and sighs, wailing and prayers, without end. Madness is creeping up on us. I figure it is inevitable a few hours from now. We cannot continue in this state of things. The calamity is gradually gaining ground as surely as the ditch is being dug between us and this phantasmal world that our minds cannot grasp.

For me there is maybe only one way to postpone the disaster and I think it lies in my habitual defense, namely: solitude. Away from the moaning and groaning that is giving me an intolerable headache. I leave the stalag and when I glance at the medical room I get an idea. The young lady is still there, busy putting some files away. I see her white shape through one of the windows. What world does she belong to? What is her role in this monstrous drama where death and madness seem to be battling for the spotlight?

What makes up my mind is that I am sure her cold indifference is hiding a secret fear. Things like that do not lie, especially in a woman, which I realize when I open the door and find myself face to face with her. Her face turns white and waxen, but I am going to make her talk one way or another.

I do not beat around the bush. "You know what I want to ask you so come on, hurry up, talk, or else…"

She steps back, scared of my audacity and especially of the grim determination she can hear in my words. "Please, you can't be here. It's forbidden."

"Don't mock me with your rules and orders. This has lasted long enough and I demand an answer."

"Get out of here for heaven's sake! I can't talk to you. If someone…"

All of a sudden her wrists are in the vice-like grip of my hands. She looks at me in astonishment, her mouth gaping open.

"Talk. Come on, talk! Can't you see I'm at my wits end?"

"Let me go. You're hurting me."

"At least you know your torturer. Not like Morgan, right? Who killed him? How did he do it? And why?"

"I don't know anything about it… I don't know anything… Oh, I beg you… that hurts… it hurts…" Something has snapped in her. Tears come streaming down her pale cheeks. "I'm in the same boat as you, Mr. Ashby," she confesses. "I've got nothing to do with it. Oh, please, have pity!"

I let her go, convinced that she is being sincere. "Then who are you?"

She nods her head but seems distracted. "I'm a nurse… or at least I was. Here all I do is medical exams… like the one you had today. Maybe that's why I'm still alive? I don't know…"

She points to the bookshelf with our files on it. "Even though I have no idea what happens to the men coming through here…"

"Where are we?"

"I don't know. I have no contact with the outside world."

"How long have you been here?"

I realize how absurd my question is, but she understands perfectly well what I mean.

"Every 24 hours I put a line on a kind of calendar I made. It's been 48 earth days now."

"Earth days?"

She examines me closely, from head to toe, then ignores my question.

"Your suit isn't familiar to me. What era do you come from?"

"Uh, well... 1967."

She squeezes her eyes shut in a weird way. "The 20th century! That's unbelievable!"

Unbelievable is the appropriate word, even more so after what she blurts out to me. 162 years separate us. In fact, she is a 26 year old French girl with the name Catherine Labois, belonging to the Napoleonic era. She left the real world on *October 28, 1805* right after the famous Battle of Trafalgar. Her date of birth: July 8, 1779!

Unbelievable, for sure. But there is more.

How did she get here? She has no idea. With her family ruined, suspected of being hostile to the imperial regime, she had been seduced by a fabulous proposition made to her by a little man calling himself the envoy of some Spanish lord who was in dire need of a French doctor.

Her description of the "little man" fits Brown to a tee and then Captain Zachariah when she tells me about her meeting in the Tavern of Time in the Bois de Boulogne. The Tavern of Time! So, different copies of the Time Club exist in the real world. Temporal traps that lure their victims across time and space? For Catherine there is no way to explain it and the rest is beyond her understanding.

She found herself on the *Mary-Ann* with a bunch of poor fellows who shared her fate until they landed. Since then this enclosure has become her sole universe with these medical visits she gradually took charge of concerning the "new arrivals."

For a minute we sit there, lost in thought, but when I tell her about London, about England, I notice she cringes a little. I smile and say, "I take it you don't like the English much? Of course I understand... but we've come a long way since Trafalgar, you know."

She smiles, too, for the first time. "Yes, I'm sure."

"We're old friends now. We've even decided to dig a tunnel across the Channel."

Her eyes open wide as she repeats, "A tunnel across the Channel?"

"Yes. At least that's what I heard in Dartmoor. You know, in prison news spreads fast."

This time her fear is out in the open.

"Oh, don't worry, I'm not a murderer. I got five years for an auto accident. I was drunk and depressed and they blamed me for this accident that I don't even remember. But the English laws are very strict about..."

She narrows her eyes. "You said an auto."

"Yes."

"What's an auto?"

I scratch my head. "Well... it's a car with four tires, a steering wheel and an engine up front. And it goes fast."

"Like Cugnot's car?"

I cannot help smiling at her innocence. But she jumps up, like she has got a sudden case of the jitters, and rushes to the window, telling me to stay quiet. Her quick glance outside is followed by a sigh of relief.

"It's all right, it's only Toppy."

I, too, take a look at this Toppy. It is a dog. A scrawny, hairy dog that looks like a cross between a husky and a setter. He is wearing a beat up leather collar with brass rings on either side and is sitting quietly in front of the door, his long tail sweeping the dust.

Catherine throws him a little food while confessing to me, "He comes here every day. I think that without me he'd die of starvation."

"I didn't think animals could live in this place."

"Oh, no, there aren't any."

"So?"

"Toppy belongs to this world."

"In that case, where did he come from?"

She stops to think for a moment before answering. "I've asked myself the same thing many times. I think he must come from beyond the rocks that surround the arena. He must have found a passage…"

I am staggered and show it. "You haven't followed him? You've never tried to find out?"

No. To be honest, I never had the courage. Besides, the environment cripples me. It's too hard for me… I can't do anything… it's like…"

I do not press her. As she shows me to the door I want to apologize, but words are useless and the look we give each other is more than enough. And then there is her smile. Her pleasant smile that is the most sincere forgiveness I have ever received.

The dog outside has disappeared and instead I bump into Professor Bradley who looks like he has been waiting for me impatiently. He asks, "Well, what were you doing? What did you tell that lady?"

After I summed up my conversation with Catherine he expressed his disappointment with his usual grumbling. "So, in short, that got us nowhere."

"No... There's Toppy..."

He looks at the paw prints that I point to in the dust, then he directs his eyes toward the cliffs. "You're not telling me..."

"But of course, professor. If Toppy got through, there's no reason we can't as well. And that's exactly what I'm going to check out... without a minute to lose."

He keeps shaking his head, undecided in the face of my determination and resolve.

"Come on, make up your mind... We can't wait forever."

In the end he is the one who drags me off. "After all, maybe you're right. When a man is drowning, he'll grab onto a piece of straw, won't he?"

CHAPTER XIII

Toppy's paw prints lead us to the edge of the camp. We walk along the electrified fence, all our sense on alert, keeping a close watch on the surrounding area but also keeping ourselves unseen. There is nothing but silence and solitude, as if we were the only living creatures on this unknown world.

We continue our stroll between the posts and after a while find the passage made by Toppy, a ditch dug under the fence between two rocks. We have no problem making it big enough for us to slip through.

I go first with Bradley telling me how to crawl (slowly and cautiously) to avoid any careless maneuvers. A hasty move could mean a fatal contact with the fence. But everything goes well. Five minutes later Bradley has joined me on the other side with a skill and dexterity that I did not think a man like him could have.

We find the trace of Toppy's prints and they lead us over a little path made between the rocks and some bushes full of tiny, crystal, bells that tinkle when we brush by them. The one Bradley picks shatters between his fingers into a myriad of phosphorescent specks; the long stalactites of frost hanging from the knotty stalks snap off at the slightest contact. As if the presence of man in this place was a sacrilege!

But this is really the least of our worries as we progress, led by the paw prints that are now disappearing on the path along the granite wall.

Much later we stop to catch our breath and exchange a confident look. So far everything has gone very well and we hope that it will continue to do so. We start walking again, as cautious as ever, until we reach the rocky fringe that overlooks the arena. All remains calm below us, and profoundly, eternally silent in the bizarre landscape.

The paw prints have stopped for good here and Bradley, who is leading the way, points to an opening in the granite. The entrance to a tunnel, totally dark, humid and with a weird smell that reminds me of gunpowder.

"It must be this way," Bradley assures me as he marches confidently forward.

We walk blindly for a moment through the dark, winding burrow, but after five minutes it has got so narrow that we are not sure whether we should keep going. But then we see a dim light coming from above. A chimney to the open sky most likely, even though we can only see a ghostly, almost unreal glow up above.

Two tunnels stretch out before us. Just by chance we choose the one on the right, the wider one. It heads straight toward an opening of pale light at the same time as the temperature drops with surprising speed. A biting, icy cold that makes us shiver. The air here is dry and every breath is like a steel rod jammed into our lungs.

What is happening? Where did this sudden, violent change come from?

And then Bradley bends down and picks up an object lying in a pile of rocks. He squints and says, "Well what do we have here?"

I go to take a look. It is a small, aluminum container with a brass hook on the side. It reminds me of Toppy's collar, which had brass rings. So, there is no doubt about it, the animal lost this can which means we are headed in the right direction.

But Bradley swears out loud and adds, "Look at this, Mr. Ashby."

He is pointing to an inscription on the can: *Amundsen Expedition. 1911.*

I feel lost in mystery and I mumble, "What does this mean?"

"Amundsen! Roald Amundsen! But that would put us in…"

He rushes forward against the glacial wind that comes from the depths of the tunnel. I catch up to him at another opening. He is standing there, motionless, pointing out.

"Mr. Ashby, look! We're in the South Pole!"

I do not believe my eyes. Before us is a huge, white desert as far as the eye can see, with a blizzard blowing over it. In the distance on the dusky horizon stand sawtoothed glaciers; ravines cleave the land pretty much everywhere. But I also see a small, white ball running around stubbornly in the swirls. Toppy!

"That dog," Bradley stammers at me, "belongs to the Amundsen Expedition… In 1911… His master must be buried in the snow… That's who he's looking for…"

"1911! So, we're back in touch with the real world of 1911?"

"The real world perhaps… As for the date…" He turns his frost-bitten face toward me. "I told you so. Behind us time means nothing. It's neutral time. Maybe this tunnel is a kind of natural bridge between the two worlds… A time portal! But opening onto what time? Yours? Mine? Amundsen's? Or that of Catherine Labois? Look, Mr. Ashby, there can be only one portal opening onto all the ages since the beginning of the world and what we see here might be a South Pole thousands years ago but Toppy doesn't know it… every time he comes and goes the time changes… and he keeps looking for his master in the stream of centuries."

I nod my head like a boxer knocked senseless. "Now I understand why our guards aren't so vigilant. What do they have to fear from us? We couldn't go three feet in this frost-bitten desert."

The temperature is unbearable and our limbs are already starting to feel numb and paralyzed. I drag Bradley into the tunnel and we are soon back in a cavern where the temperature is more normal. But we have lost our way in the maze of forking tunnels and run into a wall of rock. A dead end!

CHAPTER XIV

We retrace our steps, but at the entrance to the cavern we hesitate. There are three, dark, silent tunnels for us to choose. And yet we have to choose. Once again we decide to take our chances on the right.

We hardly start walking when I grab Bradley's arm. He looks at me and murmurs, "What is it?"

"Listen…. That noise… Don't you hear it?"

He listens carefully, but the silence has returned, as thick and heavy as ever.

"I don't hear anything," he whispers.

"It was… uh, yeah… like a buzzing…"

He shrugs his shoulders and says, "The wind from outside. It must be that. If we can get back to where we started from…"

We walk on, but soon have to stop at another branching. The tunnel splits into two more. We start to get scared at the same time as a kind of warning signal goes off in our heads: We are lost (no doubt about it) and we look at each other without saying a word.

But all of a sudden the buzzing I talked about starts up again and this time loud enough for Bradley to be utterly dumbfounded. "By God," he mumbles, "what in the world can that be?"

It sounds like thousands of wasps. "Well, it's not the wind!"

The noise continues monotonously at the same volume, echoing drearily through the tunnels.

Suddenly tempted to find the source, Bradley points down a passageway. "It's coming from there. Come on!"

We head down the tunnel, with all senses on alert, as cautiously as we can, but just when we enter a huge space dimly lit by a phosphorescent glow, the weird noise stops as if by magic. What we see paralyzes us with horror and disgust. The floor is a boneyard. We are standing on human remains that crack and crumble under our feet. Dried out skulls stare at us through their hollow sockets like nightmarish masks; shriveled up corpses are lying everywhere in gruesome positions; leg bones and arm bones, gnawed away, stick out of the foul, white dust.

But there is something more frightening than this!

Morgan's body is in the middle of all this. We recognize it in spite of the mutilations that have torn it half to shreds. It looks like a colony of starved rats attacked and ate most of it.

Bradley and I feel a dreadful desire to run, fear hot on our heels, but all of a sudden the buzzing breaks out louder than ever. It is coming from the back, from the countless little holes dug into the rock. Inside of them are monstrous creatures. We see them wallowing in their filthy feast, their gaping mouths stuffed with pieces of bone that they grind and crush greedily.

Necrophages!

The entire wall seems to writhe with slimy, hairy, little legs and with bugged-out eyes that stare weirdly.

"Watch out!" Bradley warns as he jumps to the side.

A monster has sprung out of a niche and jumped onto a pile a refuse. Its big, membranous wings beat the air with a dull thud, kicking up clouds of white dust. It is the size of a golden eagle with a long, ringed body that throbs. Its legs end in crab-like pincers and click wildly the closer it gets to us. It watches us, studies us with a kind of demonic intelligence, then suddenly lunges at Bradley.

I act out of instinct more than reason. I grab a big rock and throw it at the monster, hitting it on the head. It swings around toward me, rockets into the air, then swoops down in my direction. I barely avoid it by diving into the boneyard, just out of reach of its snapping claw. The monster flies over me with a loud buzz.

"Over here!" Bradley shouts.

I see him waving around a leg bone like a club. There is something ridiculous and unreal in his gesture, but he, too, is acting on instinct. And it looks like the monster knows it too because it is thinking twice now about how to attack us.

I exploit its hesitation to run over to the professor. Just in time. The foul scavenger is back on the attack, trying to get us from the rear, but Bradley saw it coming. His improvised club comes down hard on the monster's head and one of its eyes bursts out. We watch it bouncing off one wall after another with raging anger mixed with roaring howls. It drops to the ground in a heap after slamming into a sharp rock and with its last surge of energy tries to drag itself toward us, still snapping its claws.

Bradley is completely worn out and the bone he is holding is split down the middle. I take it from him while a ferocious growl echoes behind us. I turn around and see Toppy in the entrance. His jaws are shaking and his fur standing on end. In a flash I see our way out as the monster keeps dragging itself slowly toward us.

I take off my coat and sweater and tell Bradley, "Quick, do the same thing. Pile this in the entrance and start a fire."

He understands my plan as I jump around to the other side of the monster. It is surprised by my unexpected move and tries to turn around, but it is too late. Like a spear the split bone pierces the one good eye, which pops and explodes. The monster twists around, exposing its white abdomen and I stab it three times. This time it is fatal.

Bradley is already striking a match in the entrance, but what I feared most is already happening with the other necrophages in their nooks. The one I just killed is probably the leader of their pack and now the signal has been given. An endless, quivering wave of white bodies flows out of the holes as if guided by some mysterious control and in an instant the space is resounding with an angry buzzing and a furious beating of wings.

I reach Bradley after jumping through the flames that are starting to leap out of the burning pyre built from our clothes and papers. I turn around one last time and am stunned to see not one single creature in the cavern. As if seized by panic they all flew back to their niches and I think that over the crackling of the flames I can hear their plaintive cries and sorrowful moans.

"Let's not lose this chance! Let's go, quickly!"

Since Toppy is now leading our small group down the long, dark tunnel, I say, "Toppy knows the way. Don't worry, trust him!"

Indeed, the good dog leads us out into the open and we find ourselves on top of the rocky ring around the arena. We scramble down the slope in record time, but as soon as we reach the bottom of the cliff someone is standing in front of us. A guard! He is blocking the path with his double-barrel gun pointing at us.

"Well, that certainly got you far, didn't it?" he scowls at us. "Didn't he tell you that escape was impossible?"

But there is fear in his eyes, which keep wandering back to the cave entrance above us.

"Come on, let's go! Hurry up!"

Then he notices Toppy who starts growling.

"Ah, there you are," he utters.

What happens next is too fast for us to do anything. He moves his gun, aims at Toppy and shoots him point blank. The dog is thrown by the blast and lands at my feet.

"You little…" Without thinking, in a fit of rage, Bradley jumps at the guard.

In the split second that follows I realize what is happening. He is no match for the huge guard who steps aside and is already aiming his gun at the professor as he rolls on the ground, tripped up by his own burst of energy. I leap at him in turn, grabbing him around the ankles and we roll around, wrestling savagely. I manage to push him off and take his weapon away. We jump up at the same time. He is just about to run at me but hardly gets one foot forward before he drops to the ground, his skull smashed by the blow from the butt of the gun that I swing at him. I feel like I hit a wall of steel. But no, his head is split open and a kind of white slime leaks out of the gaping wound.

"Drop that rifle and don't make a move!"

The order is blunt and firm and the barrel of the gun poking my back makes up my mind. Four other guards have just shown up and two of them are already dragging Bradley back toward the fence.

"Don't you get it—the camp is your only salvation," another voice says. "Look! Look up there, Mr. Ashby!"

I look up at the cliff. A swarm of monstrous wings is pouring out of the opening, circling above us like vultures. Gunfire cracks and a few necrophages plop down onto the rocks and frost bushes.

We hustle back to the camp and shout to the guard to open the gate. I see a group of monsters swoop down on Toppy's corpse. The strong claws tear it to pieces and each creature takes a piece back up the cliff.

Something strange is that no necrophage bothers with the guard's body. He is still lying in the dust, his arms spread out, spared by the voracious monsters who are presently giving up the attack and retreating into their dark sanctuary.

"Get moving!"

We reach the shack soon afterward and are shoved inside. Another strange thing! We are alone. The room is empty and the mattresses are piled on top of one another. All our partners in misfortune have disappeared.

CHAPTER XV

Two hours have passed. Left to ourselves Bradley and I have come up with countless speculations about the events we lived through. But none of them offer a valid solution.

First of all this weird country has a temperate climate. How can it be in the South Pole where the average temperature is 40 to 50 degrees below zero? Is it a freak of nature or the product of a science that we know nothing about? But then who knows this science? Who does it belong to? These beings whose mysterious, ruthless will controls us? Who are they? Where do they come from? From what age?

And those monstrous winged creatures, what role do they play in this absurd world? And why did they attack us so violently? What connection is there between them and our guards?

And the time? Yes, the time, how can it stop so that, as Bradley says, the notions of past, present and future are mixed together in only one coordinate?

Our soul is already a battlefield that we have to clear up if we do not want to go crazy, which I fear is the worst of all catastrophes. And yet I decided to confess to my companion what I found in my journal, meaning the baffling version of events that tend to prove Parker's involvement in Morgan's inexplicable murder.

Bradley's scientific mind was back on track and after a long reflection he repeated, "A neutral time... Zero time... That's just one more proof. We're living through several events at the same time, but in reality everything happens in the same fraction of time. Every solution has to be seen in terms of relativity. So if we take the Lorentz equation as a reference frame…"

I raised an eyebrow at his reasoning. "That's possible, but that still leaves us in a paradox. For us the events continue to come one after another and they are bound to the idea of duration. There can't be any chronological series in a neuter time."

"Unless this duration is negative or just psychological. In short, we've created this duration by the mental processes inherent to our nature. Our mind can't tell the difference between real time and neuter time. It keeps classifying events in a logical sequence by relegating them to a past that doesn't exist. Look, don't you remember—the famous S.O.S. Titanic, the shipwreck of the Cormorant and then us, I mean you, me, Catherine Labois, Toppy… We all belong to different time frames but we're together here in this zero time. I'll tell you again, we have to start with the Lorentz equation and if we consider…"

His train of thought stopped there. Two armed guards burst into the stalag and took us away.

At present I am marching in step between the steel poles toward the inside of the arena. Where are they taking me? Why did they separate me from Bradley? I am thinking of him when we reach the edge of the enclosure. Will I ever see him again?

At the thought of this a awful doubt runs through me, like a feeling of anguish and confusion that I cannot fight against.

So, I walk and watch… I watch the new landscape around me. As always it is rocky and dusty but the piles of rocks we weave through bear no trace of vegetation. I see other armed guards patrolling the around the curious structure that I can well imagine being the seat of authority. It stands so high in the air that the top of it is lost in the pale light that washes over the arena from one wall to another.

We walk around it and all of a sudden the scenery changes. The ground beneath my feet is soft, doughy, and the humidity rises until we reach a wooden walkway that leads through what looks like a huge swamp.

Black, stagnant water appears between the pointed rocks and the stench is almost unbearable. Phosphorescent mists hang over the cesspool, stretched between the rocks in long, floating tentacles. The temperature has lowered, but the atmosphere is suffused with a fetid moisture, like on the beaches of Cornwall at the approach of winter.

But worse is to come… That thing we are heading toward that looks like a gigantic mortar shell lying on the ground. A really weird construction! All in metal with rows of portholes on four levels. What in the world can it be?

Then I notice that the front has a huge gash in the shiny metal. Twisted sheets of metal stick out of the opening in a chaotic mess. It is like a shipwreck. The shipwreck of a giant spaceship 500 yards long! Lord, what is going on?

I stop, dazed and confused, in front of the strange find, but the firm, unfriendly grip of my guards forces me to keep moving. Thus we enter the shipwreck through a wide entrance of greenish light that seems to come out of the walls. Then we are walking down a corridor decorated with bizarre, unrecognizable designs. I have the strange feeling of walking into another universe, into "something" beyond human understanding and earthly logic.

In total silence we reach the end of the corridor where two other armed guards hurry to work the steel panel that slides open in front of me. A single room, big and spacious, decorated with geometric designs and low, shimmering furniture. In the middle of all this is an extraordinarily beautiful creature who seems to be floating in the greenish light like a mermaid in an ocean of jade.

Beautiful and monstrous at the same time!

A mermaid with big, golden eyes that should belong to a cat or a dream.

Marthessa!

CHAPTER XVI

For a long moment we just stand there, facing each other, in a private, silent battle in which only our eyes clash like sharpened daggers. Finally, she is the one who walks forward, with her swaying gait and a cruel smile on her red lips.

"You are bold and brave, Mr. Ashby. Especially bold, very bold. But I'm afraid you're just wasting your noble sentiments. There's no escape from here. Didn't they tell you that?"

"I realize that, madam."

"I wish you'd heeded our warnings. But so be it! It doesn't matter. The main thing is that you know it now."

"What can I say? But who are you? And where do you come from?"

She takes another step in my direction. "I think this conversation should clear up certain questions that are bothering you. Indeed, the time has come."

Marthessa points to the steel walls around the room. "You've already guessed that this is the wreck of a spaceship and we're not from this world. In fact, we come from another universe, a distant universe, totally different from yours and that doesn't exist on any of your star charts. The purpose of our voyage is unimportant; you wouldn't find it interesting. You just have to know that it was completely by accident that we came out into your space-time continuum and crashed on your planet after an unexpected accident."

She sees the bewilderment in my eyes, along with the fear and suspicion. "Oh, no," she tells me, "don't worry, we have no intention of conquering your world, not even the least desire to interfere in the evolution of your miserable humanity. We just want to hold onto this portion of the Antarctic continent where we've managed to set up the natural conditions that are agreeable to our species."

"Purely artificial time values, right?"

She avoids my question, preferring to get straight to the point. "And of course you want to know what role you play in all this. Well, I'll tell you. But first of all, I would like you to take a little peek over here."

She leads me to the back of the room where I find, to my horror and disgust, the lifeless body of a creature lying on a long table. I recognize it immediately with its skull split open from the parietal to the occiput. It is the creature I had to kill to help Bradley.

Coldly, without any wasted movements, Marthessa grabs a steel rod and uses it like pliers to widen the opening in the skull. There is a horrible crack followed by a little white foam that hardens quickly on contact with the air. I feel sick to my stomach when she orders me, "Look, Mr. Ashby, look closely!"

It takes a great deal of will power for me to see what is there. Or rather what isn't. *There is no brain*. No human organ is sitting in the skull that she is cracking open. I see nothing but... Yes, it looks like wires, coils and electronic circuits like the inside of a television set. At least that is the image that comes to mind at the moment. Although... My doubt lies in the strange, slimy stuff marbled with dark veins that I cannot identify, that I cannot name, that makes no sense to me.

I look at Marthessa and ask, "A... a robot?"

There is irony and a kind of contrived amusement in her eyes. "No, Mr. Ashby. This creature who died by your hand was as alive as you are. His physical appearance shocks you because in earth terms you have to relate him to a cybernetic being, a robot, as you say, but he's not. Nature defies the familiar analogies that you might try to make. Its laws are not a one-way street. It can create life from carbon just as easily as from silica, choose between blood and chlorophyll, or put iron or magnesium in the nucleus of the cell. In the diversity of means, all that matters to nature is the final outcome."

She pauses for a second, then continues, "Consider your own organism, Mr. Ashby. It's just a machine. A highly precise machine whose electro-chemical coordination is controlled by the brain with its ten billion neurons which work as both batteries and transistors. Let's add a few other phenomena to this electronic network: sight, voice and DNA[5], whose physiological characteristics are called your computers and your analog machines. I'm saying all this to make you understand that to build the machine that you are, nature in your world used organs of flesh whereas for this creature in front of you it called upon other elements. In other words, we might call it living metal."

Living metal! Machines built of living pieces! And who reproduce through a process that must involve parental union! Unbelievable is once again the word that comes to my human mind as I stare at Marthessa, still proud, still dignified.

"Let's get down to brass tacks, why don't we?"

"But of course, Mr. Ashby."

With her steel rod she points to the cadaver. "You just said the word robot. Well, it's to help us build robots that you're here. Robots built on this model, but with materials from earth, of course."

---

[5] Deoxyribonucleic acid.

"What? But I have no…"

"You're an electrical engineer. We know about your degrees and your skills. We never choose at random, Mr. Ashby."

"This is crazy. There's no robot like this on Earth. I have no idea how to build one."

Marthessa turns toward a porthole through which can be seen the giant central tower. "All the facts and figures will be given to you."

"But I'd need equipment and personnel and…"

"We'll provide everything you need."

"But, look, what reasons could you have…"

"There's only one, Mr. Ashby, but it's vital. Let me repeat, we have no intention of conquering your planet, but we want to live. Just to live!"

I shake my head. "What proof do I have of that?"

"Just the fact that we can't integrate into your continuum. Two mortal enemies await us outside the arena: first *our time*, which passes differently than yours, will decay us quickly. Then your temperatures that are subject to fast and frequent changes. We can only live in a single temperature, around five degrees centigrade on earth. But to survive we have to get all kinds of materials that we obviously find on your planet and this requires us to leave here often, which unfortunately damages our bodies. So far we've already lost two thirds of our people."

"How many?"

"There are only 312 of us left out of a thousand at the start."

"Does that include those horrible creatures that my friend and I fought against?"

An icy glare flashes in her golden eyes. It is obvious that she does not want to talk about this subject.

"Please, Mr. Ashby," she replies curtly, "let's skip this subject. Besides, you wouldn't understand. I think it'd be wiser to discuss our bargain, don't you?"

"Our bargain?"

"You heard me correctly."

"And if I refuse?"

"Then you will die. And we'll start all over again with someone else. It will not change our project."

In spite of the gravity of her response, I still find the ability to smile. "In short, I have no choice."

Marthessa takes a short walk around the room, as if to give me time to reflect. She is soon back in front of me, still appearing very sure of herself.

"Let's be clear, Mr. Ashby. In any case, you can't leave this zone. You're condemned to live here with us. But on the other hand, you will benefit from exceptional favors. We will give you everything you need. Nothing will be refused. On a more personal note, in order to satisfy your natural needs, the presence of this human of the opposite sex is indispensable. And by the way, I believe Catherine Labois is a perfect fit for you."

"Don't you think you're going a bit far with all this?"

"If you don't like her, we can find another. Ask and you will receive."

"Are we bargaining like slave traders here?" She does not seem to get my meaning. She looks at me somewhat confused. Finally I say, "Okay! So be it! If that's the way it is, promise me that all my other companions will be spared. The crew of the *Cormorant* and Professor Bradley."

"I'm sorry, but certain measures have already been taken for the crew of the *Cormorant*. As for Professor Bradley…"

She stops talking and presses a button on the metal wall. A guard shows up right away. After a short conversation in an strange language, Marthessa turns to me. "Okay for Professor Bradley. Nothing has been decided about him yet. Is that all, Mr. Ashby?"

I guess the discussion is over. Two guards pop up and signal to me to follow them. Before walking through the door I have enough nerve left to say to Marthessa, "No, that's not all. Some whiskey. William Lawson's preferably."

CHAPTER XVII

Whoever desires the end, desires the means, says a proverb. And in fact the means, the ones offered to me in another sector of the enclosure were more than could be hoped for.

They took me directly to a big building divided into a countless number of rooms, laboratories and workshops where a bunch of creatures wearing protector gear were busy working. A real beehive of activity.

I was assigned to a research office where I found all kinds of electronic equipment which was familiar to me. I made a quick check and saw that it was all well made and came from all over the planet.

From now on this is where I am going to be, but my living quarters have been reduced to a bare minimum, including this office and a comfortable apartment attached to it. There are three rooms: a living room, kitchen and bathroom.

As I soon find out, they waste no time. Two other guards brought to the laboratory the corpse of my victim whose skull is completely cracked open. I am supposed to be inspired by his anatomy to build some super-robots, so I can do whatever I want with this dreadful "thing" that I cannot even touch with my fingertips.

I finally got a little courage back when Professor Bradley arrived with Catherine. Marthessa kept her promise and no harm came to them during my absence. But it took a lot of patience and calmness to explain to them the bargain I struck with these space creatures. Especially for Catherine whose knowledge of astronomy and robotics is rather limited.

As for Bradley, he exploded right away. "By Jove! Do you realize that we're in a death camp here, my friend?" When I did not answer, he continued, "Did you even ask them about the zombies? All those poor fellows who…"

"The question would never have been answered, Bradley."

"But…"

"Just like for the necrophages."

He shook his head, sighed and murmured, "How many other men have already died here in this cursed zone, eh?"

"Probably thousands. Obviously I have no idea. But unfortunately that's not all. I also know that they didn't tell me everything, that there's something going on here, and it's got to be a whole lot worse."

"So why did you become an accomplice to such a monstrosity? Why?"

I calmed him down with a wave of my hand. "Please, try to understand. I was only trying to gain a little time and get you two out of the viper's nest. Temporarily, of course, because sooner or later we'll be stuck and have to do something."

I pointed to the extraterrestrial body. "I have no intention of creating one single robot, but I'm a stubborn man, Bradley. I will find out what I want to know. That's all. Except… Expect I also keep telling myself that if there's one chance in a million of us getting out of this alive, we can't ignore it. Do you have any objections to this?"

Bradley's anger dissipated in a resonant groan. He handed me one of his cigarettes, which accepted gladly accepted. I took a long drag, savored it with pleasure, then said, "Very well then! Now let's try to get organized. You take care of the rooms in the back and I'll set up the front, next to the office, so it'll be perfect. Bradley, try to help me out. The most important thing is to fool them. Everything has to look normal if we want to last as long as possible. As for Catherine, well, I think you have to make yourself useful."

I looked at her and said, "Do your best."

I had the feeling she misunderstood what I said. "I don't mean you have to play the lover."

She blushed like a college girl. "It's only that... that I'm engaged to be married, Mr. Ashby."

Under any other circumstances I think I would have burst out laughing, but all I did was smile. It was too much for me.

"You know... after 1805..." Since she did not raise an eyebrow, I just asked, "Who is he? A grenadier for the Empire?"

She shot back, "Bertrand is an infantry lieutenant under Marshal Ney. He was at Ulm when I... when I left that time..."

"Well, let's hope he survives until Waterloo."

"Waterloo?"

At her dumbstruck look I continued, "June 18, 1815. Oh yes, dear, another blow from the English. But as I said, that's ancient history." And then I shrugged, "A very little Waterloo compared to what we need here, unfortunately." There was no response to my remark.

When we decide to eat our first meal of the "day", we realize that our watches indicate "midnight." Bradley and I also realize that we have not had any sleep or food since we disembarked from the *Mary-Ann*. That means 36 hours.

235

But what does material time have to do with this neuter time that Bradley still talks about? Will we slowly begin to feel the biological effects of the negative time? Will our organic functions gradually slow down? But then wouldn't this slow down also affect our watches?

I feel like we are getting seriously out of whack and that we had better pull ourselves together if we want to keep control of our actions, even if the action takes place in an illusory time. That is the decision we make at the end of the meal, but just as we get back to the laboratory the door swings open and three creatures pop in like jack-in-the-boxes. They carry weapons and point them at us at the same time while the third one quickly locks the door. Him I recognize immediately. To my great astonishment, it is Griffith, the radioman from the *Mary-Ann*, as big and fat as ever.

One of the guards steps toward me. He looks tense, his face hard, and in a flash he sees the corpse lying on the dissection table. He barks out, "Mr. Ashby, we have to talk very seriously."

I answer calmly, "What's going on? What do you want?"

He turns to Griffith whose goggling eyes appear to be shaking in their sockets. "This is our comrade you already know with the earth name Griffith."

"And?"

It is Griffith now who lumbers toward me. "We know all about your talk on board our spaceship, Mr. Ashby. You were asked to build special robots to take our place in the missions on the surface of your planet, isn't that right?"

"That's exactly right."

"In no way are you to help them complete this project. In no way at all, I'm telling you."

I did not see this coming! I catch Bradley glancing at me. He is just as surprised as I am. During the brief pause I regain a little composure.

"And... by what authority are you giving me these orders, Griffith?"

"As head of the opposition movement."

"The opposition?"

"Yes."

"Opposition to whom? To what?"

"You're smart enough to know what that means."

I furrow my brow. "Hmm... hmm... yes... I see... You're the head of the uprising, huh? And here I was thinking that was a human thing!"

He scowls at me. "Don't joke about this, please."

"I have no desire or intention to do so, believe me."

"In that case, we'll try to make you understand. That would be better."

CHAPTER XVIII

He hesitates before continuing, as if looking for the right words, as if afraid of saying too much about a touchy and very awkward subject. Finally he makes up his mind.

"The project given to you is nothing but a criminal action aiming to completely eliminate our race. You were told that we can't tolerate your time and especially your climate. In fact, our organisms are poikilotherm[6] and deteriorate every time we venture out onto your planet. Since our arrival here, several hundred of us have already died and all us survivors are physiologically affected to one extent or another."

He pauses a moment before continuing.

"At the start the idea of replacing us with mechanical beings obviously got a lot of support among us and a large number of our comrades are still convinced of their good intentions. But it's not true and the opposition committee that I'm head of has seen the cruel truth. We will be killed one by one when we're too much trouble or of no use to them. That, you can be sure, is the goal of the real masters of this zone."

Professor Bradley stepped forward. "What do you mean by that? Who are you talking about?"

"I'm sorry, I can't answer that question. Be satisfied with what you have been told."

---

[6] Organisms whose temperature varies with the environment. Like reptiles.

With a nervous gesture I interrupt him. "Okay, Griffith, we're sorry too. Your internal politics don't interest us."

"Don't believe any of it, but we'll get back to it later. What matters is for you to know that no mercy will be shown if you fail. The same rule applies to us. We're destroyed when we can't perform our functions. There's no place here for the incompetent or the useless. That's why I'm here, Mr. Ashby. My body is badly affected. I'll soon be of no use."

As I look at him with obvious surprise, he adds, "I need to recover my equilibrium to continue the fight. Without you, I'm lost, Mr. Ashby!"

"You must be mistaken, my friend… I'm no doctor, especially not for you and your kind."

Griffith's fat lips form a little smile. "On the contrary, you're the best doctor I can imagine. Your knowledge of cybernetics is perfect for me. Plus, our organisms are really not much different from your modern electronic machines."

I jump back. "What? You want me to operate on you?"

"It's not just a simple operation. It's my entire body that is suffering, so a little surgery would be useless. It's too late. No, what I want from you is totally different."

He shuffles over to the corpse, examines it closely, then tells me, "It's this body that I want. Just the body. We're pretty much the same height and weight. I knew him. He was in good health. But me, only my head is in good shape. You can graft it onto his body and no one will know the difference after the operation."

"You want me to…"

He cuts me off. "Wait a second, Mr. Ashby, look at this first."

One of the guards with Griffith hands me some designs drawn on several bound pages. All the connections are illustrated as well as a bunch of information about the extraordinary operation. They have included everything down to the last detail. And what is even more amazing is the nature of these organisms that breaks all the laws of terrestrial biology.

In the first place, these beings die differently. When the mind is free of matter, it goes on without deteriorating in the least and survives in a kind of vegetative life for a time that is apparently impossible to estimate in earth time. The organic decomposition does not progress in the same way as with us and in this negative time it is not necessary for an organ to be transplanted immediately after the death of the donor. A rather long period of time, therefore, is allowed to achieve the same results.

As for the immune system, it does not exist. The organs and the limbs are interchangeable between individuals, exactly like spare parts used to repair machines. The skeleton itself is a combination of elements of the same size fitted together in such a way that they can be easily pulled apart. So, Mendelian inheritance has no role among them. They obey other laws and other rules.

"Everything will be just fine," Griffith says, "if you follow very precisely the instructions given to you by my comrades."

"But I'll have to kill you!"

"No, Mr. Ashby, you will operate on me while living, simply lowering the power voltage. At such a level we can stand the pain."

Stunned, I lean back against the wall, cross my arms and stare at Griffith. "Fair enough. But, if I accepted… what would you offer me in exchange?"

The same enigmatic smile appears on Griffith's face. "*You've already accepted*, Mr. Ashby. We know it! The operation will be performed. Nothing will get in its way."

"So you can see the future?"

"A little."

His curt response does not encourage me to pursue the subject, especially since Griffith seems anxious to finish the conversation.

With irresistible assurance he tells me, "Here now is what will make up your mind. By helping us fight against the leaders of this zone, you are also giving yourself the possibility of repairing your own spaceship. It's possible, Mr. Ashby, but there are reasons to stop it, reasons that I can't tell you. I also want you to know that our most ardent wish is to return to your planet. If we succeed, I guarantee you your life and liberty. All three of you will be brought back to your respective times, wherever you want. That's my solemn promise to you, Mr. Ashby."

I turn to Bradley and Catherine. What I see in their eyes is more than enough for me. One chance in a million, I had said… Now maybe one chance in a thousand. Why not?

I say in earnest, "Okay, Griffith, I can try. When do you want to begin?"

"Right away! There's not a moment to lose."

"But the materials? The instruments?"

Everything has been prepared for this also. The equipment needed for the operation is at the end of the corridor in a room nearby that belongs to Griffith. On his order one of the guards takes us there quickly so I can finish studying the detailed illustrations and instructions for the different phases of the operation.

The first thing, obviously, is to sever the head of the corpse with a sonic saw right at the trunk of the body so as not to damage the skin that needs to be used for the splicing and has to be rolled back, like a stocking on a leg. The same procedure goes for Griffith's head. The rest depends on my skill, courage and all the knowledge I will use to splice together the electronic connections whose terrifying complexity reminds me of the inside of an IBM computer.

But I am also, above all, counting on the help of the two creatures with Griffith. And last but not least... a whole lot of luck!

My first decapitation takes place under excellent conditions with Griffith and his men looking on apathetically. It is weird. I have the feeling that they *already know* that the operation will be a success.

"Your turn, Griffith!"

He lies down on the operating table while one of his men hooks up the machine that will lower the power voltage of his organism. The other one takes care of the antiseptic injections that he measures out with expert precision. Finally, the electrodes are applied and the current is turned on, but what happens then freezes the blood in my veins. I can barely even hear Catherine screaming behind me.

It is horrible... Horrible and impossible to describe. Griffith's skin has turned the color of ash and little nodes, like calluses, pop up all over. His face is monstrous, hideous, cracked and swollen and darkening. It is like a great cancer is invading him with incredible speed. His ears grow long, his nose deforms, bulbs out above a mouth that is stretched too thin, almost disappearing. His thin blonde hair turns into a milky white mop. Only his eyes remain the same, bright, almost human.

I realize then that a nervous hand is gripping my arm. "We understand what you're feeling, Mr. Ashby, but this physiological reaction couldn't be avoided. You are seeing our true physical appearance. The change only effects the outside that has the power to mimic. These transformations are the result of underlying glandular stress that will stop when the power voltage is affected."

He points to the corpse that is lying next to Griffith. "This one kept his human form because his death was fast and violent. The organism didn't have time to react. But don't worry about the graft. Everything will go back to normal afterward. For now, Mr. Ashby, can we continue?"

He hands me the sonic saw as I look deeply into Griffith's eyes.

"Let's go." I can barely hear Griffith whispering.

With a determined hand I start in on the flesh.

CHAPTER XIX

Everything went well. According to the tests the operation was a success and it only takes 48 hours (on our clocks) for this race to heal. We carried Griffith to a room in the back and under the effect of the electronic stimulators his human face has gradually returned.

The body we grafted onto him is starting to react. The extraordinary resurrection is taking place before our very eyes, like Frankenstein's monster dug up from the grave piece by piece. The internal circuits are working again with the whole network of glands, relays, conduits and bioelectric organs.

I wanted to offer Griffith a little food, some warm soup or something to drink, but he just smiled. There is no food, solid or liquid, for these creatures; they feed in the same way as photosynthesis works in plants on earth. They capture energy from space and these energy particles undergo chemical conversions before being spread throughout the body as needed in the form of white jelly under the skin. Now I understand why the glasses at the Time Club in front of Marthessa and Captain Zachariah were never drunk and also why Griffith never ate with me on board the *Mary-Ann*.

Sleep, too, is unnecessary for them. They stay awake from the moment of birth until the day they die. Unfortunately, for us it is not the same and overcome by fatigue we had to take turns getting a little rest.

The day was interrupted only by a visit from two messengers sent by Marthessa. Plans and formulas for building the super-robots were handed over with the usual indifference that characterizes this strange and mysterious race of beings. They appear to have no suspicion of us and to our great relief they left without the slightest clue that Griffith was in the room next door. On that score, everything went perfectly.

Today Griffith's condition has improved and Catherine was able to remove the bandage, although her emotions got the better of her. And rightly so because the wound is almost completely healed. A thin white line around the neck is the only mark left by the stitches sewn onto the trunk.

Nevertheless, I make a joke, trying to lighten up the poor girl. "I guess you never could have pulled off your Revolution of '89 with a thing like that, huh?"

"You think that enough heads didn't roll?"

"That's not what I mean. Just think for a minute what would have happened if they stuck the head of Louis XVI onto Robespierre's body."

A miracle! I succeeded in making her laugh out loud and my God, it's not at all unpleasant, far from it! All the more so since Catherine has a lot of charm in spite of the statuesque frigidity that she tries to assume all day long. I am sure that we will become fast friends if we don't run into a Joan of Arc, Trafalgar or Waterloo. But then there is Bertrand, the lieutenant grenadier, 1805 and all the rest... everything that separates us in this hopeless situation.

No, there is some hope, but it is pretty slim. As slim as the trust I put in Griffith. Maybe that is what compelled me to visit his private room. I wanted to find out, to know the forbidden truth that he is hiding from us in every way he can.

I had seen one of his guards open the magnetic lock, so after a long and patient effort I managed to open it.

It is a single room, very big, with a long workbench piled high with thick files, pressurized seats and a bunch of equipment of different shapes and sizes. It looks like a repair shop. Glass tubes and steel rods are lying all over the place in the dusty clutter of wires and coils. It is a total mess, where even a cat could not find her kittens, and it reeks of ozone.

But I found nothing in the files, which were full of weird symbols, and I wasted my time fumbling around among the inscrutable machines abandoned in the dust and silence. Until, by chance, I pressed some buttons, pulled a lever and stared attentively at a box that looked like a television with a rectangular, concave screen protected by a double layer of glass.

Crackling... Hissing... A long whistling... Then all of a sudden green lights appeared on the screen, swirling around and interspersed with bright flashes. When the image stabilized, it showed a 3-D picture of the inside of the arena with the shacks and the huge central tower. Other images followed thanks to a kind of selector that I was still pressing at random: the inside of a laboratory, a view of the spaceship wreck, the fences and steel poles, and then some people marching between the poles under the watch of armed guards.

A voice shouts, "Move it!"

I recognize the poor devils who look forlorn and devastated by fear and worry: the survivors of the *Cormorant*. And there was Bradley... And there was me in the middle of the group. In exactly the same position as we had when we arrived. But that is not the strangest thing. It is what I see afterward, thanks again to the selector: Morgan's meeting outside the shack, our encounter with the zombies, the ghosts of the *Mary-Ann* and their hopeless signals… and then our return to the stalag, my fight with Morgan and Parker's knife stuck in the quartermaster's belly. I mean the whole series of events that I described in my journal and that belongs to a different temporal plane, still impossible to locate in my memory.

But what do the next images have to say? This time the screen shows the inside of the room and I see myself wandering around, puffing nervously on the butt of a cigarette. I stub it out and put it in my pocket, obviously a precaution so as not to leave any trace of my presence.

What then? Isn't this the future? Isn't the screen showing what is going to happen in the next few minutes? Isn't the cigarette the same as the one I just stuck in my mouth? My hand is already searching for matches in my pockets…

And then I get the idea. I will not do it. I keep it unlit between my lips and cut the contact. Silence… Wandering around… Maybe five minutes, no more… The time to… And then suddenly…

Lord, the cigarette has just vanished from my mouth and in my pocket I find nothing but the nicotine-stained butt…

CHAPTER XX

It takes me 15 minutes to decide to call Bradley. He is as doubtful as always and stubborn in his idea of negative time. When I tell him about the machine, he is only half convinced. He asks me in a skeptical tone, "A machine that looks into time, huh? And what does that prove?"

"First of all the flaw in our reasoning. Time does exist here in this zone, but in a different form, still with a past, present and future. Of course I'm a little hesitant to discuss such a complex problem with such a learned man as you, but I think I've got it."

"Got what?"

I turn the machine back on to where it was before. "Look!"

The screen is immediately filled up by the only window in the room. A new tuning. Two minutes pass, then suddenly the window is blown open by a gust of wind. A piece of paper on Griffith's workbench sails into the air before drifting to the floor.

We verify that the window is not completely closed and know that what we just saw is bound to happen within two minutes. But what will happen if I intervene and keep the window from opening? And that is exactly what I do as Bradley watches all my movements with a worried eye.

And what happens at that very moment provokes one of his usual grunts. The window stays closed against the wind, but the piece of paper has disappeared as if by magic and rematerialized on the floor in front of us.

I say, "So, what do you think now? In this time, the effect doesn't change, whatever you might do to change the cause."

He is pensive and mumbles, "Dang, an effect that could be independent of the cause?"

"Kind of like that, but…"

He cuts me off, "Wait a second. Let's say the paper falling is an effect. But opening the window is also an effect. It's because of the wind that it opens. And we removed that effect."

"Not the window, it's only a secondary effect. But it is a cause, just like the wind. What interests me is the principal effect, the last effect in the series of events. That, I repeat, is absolute. So in reality I can't remove the cause, I can only change it."

"I don't really follow you."

"Let's take some examples. In our own time the cause brings about the effect. That's because we can call upon a whole combination of factors that says we are destined to be hit by a car when crossing the street. But secondary events might occur that prevent us from crossing the street. The cause is removed, so the foreseen effect doesn't happen. Even better, let's suppose we use a machine like this one. We witness an accident that will happen to us in ten minutes. To change the program we don't leave the room and the effect is removed. Except here it's different. *Nothing can prevent the accident from happening*, even if we decide to stay in our room."

He asks, "You mean that events are already written in time?"

I answer with a shrug. "It's only a hypothesis, Bradley, but in my opinion, it has to be like that. I'm convinced that whatever we are about to do, *we've already done*. We've already done it because we're not in touch with real present time and this real present time for us belongs to the future. We're out-of-sync."

He thinks about it, nods and says, "If I understand correctly, this present time that we're living in is purely subjective. Like we're living in the past?"

"Exactly. What counts in this time we're living in is the effect, but since the effect can't happen without a causal link, the time, in creating the effect in the real present, automatically unleashes a determining cause in the past and it's this cause that we're living in. It's as if we were in a film being projected through two superimposed lenses. When the present effect passes through the upper lens, we don't see it. We're only in touch with the lower one that is delayed and shows us the cause first and then the effect. In other words, we're living in a causality that is imposed on us by the effects."

Bradley starts pulling at his goatee. "In your theory all events would be preset along a temporal chain. But what difference does it make to us?"

I point to the machine. "Without this, none. And we wouldn't even realize it. But this changes everything. We can know our future, which is inevitable even if we change the causes. Like I did with the cigarette and the piece of paper."

"What's amazing is that these effects have no cause."

I sense his concern. "But no, I told you, I didn't remove anything, at least on the general timeline, which is what counts. It's like we wanted to go somewhere but instead of taking the main road directly there we took the side streets. We only make a detour in space, whereas here, we're making detours in time. In the end, the effect remains the same. And the proof is that this time machine doesn't record the detours we make. It keeps to the verifiable version of things. Look at the cigarette and the paper!"

"Hold on a second!" I narrow my eyes as he says, "You told me that the machine worked in both directions, the past and the future. I suppose your argument is also good in both directions?"

"Yes."

"Well then, that's what'll explain the entry in your journal that we still can't remember but that you saw on the screen a little while ago. Yes, yes, I see… That would be the real version. The one you remember was just a voluntarily produced detour in time."

"They were only worried about us knowing the real cause of Morgan's death. But it happened just like the cigarette butt I found in my pocket. The result didn't change and that's why the entry in my journal appeared exactly when it should have. It was another effect that couldn't escape the rule like for the chain and the medal that I lost in the first version and found again in the second in exactly the same place."

"I guess there also must have been some changes made in our meeting on board the *Mary-Ann*."

I cannot help smiling. "Your watch… and the roving stool… yes, for sure…"

Bradley stares at me long and hard, but I already know what he wants to ask.

"So, what do you think we can do with this discovery, Ashby?"

I do not have time to answer because a voice calling out behind us makes us swing around.

"Bravo! Congratulations, Mr. Ashby. There might be a few gaps in your reasoning, but all in all it holds water."

And Griffith cracks an enigmatic smile.

The creature walks up to us while looking at the time machine. His voice is steady. "Very interesting, isn't it? I love your idea about taking side streets. That's pretty much what happens when we turn on the Chronorama. Well, now you know how we can see into the future, gentlemen. Isn't that right?"

He does not look very comfortable inside his new body; his reflexes are still a little slow.

He resumes in the same tone, "I should, however, tell you that your recklessness might cost you dearly. But fortunately for you this is the only machine of its kind, which explains why no one caught you in here."

"An experimental model?"

Griffith turns to me slowly. "It is a recent invention and it belongs to me. This prototype has so far just been in the testing phase. I was supposed to make some modifications. Its range into the past is practically unlimited, but for the future it's pretty restricted."

"How far can you go?"

He does give me a precise answer. "You remember the example you gave of two superimposed lens?"

"Of course I do."

"We haven't gone past the effects of the upper lens, which belongs to the present reality."

"Which means?"

"Around three hours on your clocks. Now, gentlemen, I believe it would be better…"

Bradley jumps in, "One more question if you please, Griffith. What's the connection between our time and yours?"

The extraterrestrial is hesitant to give an answer, as if our curiosity scares him. Finally, however, he responds. "There is only a purely relative connection. For us as neutral observers, we see the Earthlings moving at frightening speeds. But the truth is that we are the ones moving hopelessly slow. Therefore, if we take your world as a reference point, we might say that our time is contracted with respect to yours."

Since he does not give any more information on the subject, I ask him for more precision. He answers, "Here, for example, in this zone, minutes correspond to earthly years."

Bradley speaks up again. "That's what made me think of a negative time." He nods his head, considers and asks, "And this contraction gives you the possibility to travel in our time from one century to another?"

Griffith corrects right away. "No, not exactly. The reciprocity of our times is incompatible. In their absolute values our two times can't coexist except inside the same continuum. To balance the forces we had to use an *oscillator* that kept us from ever being in contact with even a split second of exterior time. That's how we could freely travel between different epochs on your temporal chain."

He points out the window at the central tower. "This, of course, requires an extraordinary tension that is walled in by the rocks encircling this zone. The oscillator is at the top of the tower."

There are, of course, more questions I want to ask, but to be on the safe side I decide not to press him further. As we are preparing to leave the room, we hear a noise. At first we hear a strange rumbling getting louder and louder, then the windows start shaking. It sounds like a jet engine. I run to the window, followed by the other two who know no more than I do. Above us a tapered shape is emerging from the grayness. Delta wings and turbo engines leaving a long trail in the atmosphere.

It only lasts a second. As if swept up in a giant maelstrom the thing starts spinning round and then explodes in a geyser of fire and flames. Some debris crashes and shatters near the swamp in a chaos that is impossible to describe.

We look at each other, unable to understand, and Bradley asks, "What is that all about?"

Silence.

I ask, "Where the devil did that come from?"

But I have the feeling that we are not going to get anything out of Griffith. He looks as stunned as we are.

CHAPTER XXI

We did not see Griffith again. He has not shown up even once today either. We think he must have gone back to his usual work alongside his secret activities in the opposition movement.

Now Bradley is convinced that we trust him. In any case, his success is the only hope we have to escape certain death. It is obvious that they will get rid of us once we have satisfied Marthessa's needs.

This morning they brought us a bunch of stuff that we had to sort out and choose for the construction of the super-robots. There was tungsten alloy, Teflon connections, polyethylene fiber and even a kind of synthetic tissue that looked like human skin. Where the hell did they get all this stuff?

I think our main concern is to gain as much time as possible. Our principal aim is to convince our jailors of our "good intentions." They have to believe that we are truly working hard on it because they seem to be relaxing their guard. We can even go for daily, one-hour walks inside the arena. Certain areas are still off limits, of course, so we have to stick to the paths they indicate.

Catherine and I happened to wander to the other side of the swamp where there was a deserted space scattered with fallen rocks. As I expected Catherine took the opportunity to ask me a bunch of questions about my epoch and I had a hard time getting her to understand certain things. The trip to the moon, for example, or the equality of sexes and the right for women to vote. Speaking about the last subject her face brightened with a magnificent smile.

"And how are the young ladies in 1967? What are they like?"

I, too, smiled. "Well, they put a lot of black around their eyes, they change their hair every day, they wear miniskirts and dance the Jerk. But basically they're always the same, except, of course, they're not as pretty as you."

"What is so special about me?"

I said softly, "Well, you're simple, naïve, and when you smile you have this little romantic side that's missing in my time."

"You're mocking me, aren't you?"

I protested, "Not at all! Just the opposite! And I can tell you that you'd be a hit in 1967."

She turned her head and started walking again, completely lost in her thoughts. After a dozen or so steps, out of the blue, she asked me, "Bill, what's going to happen if one of these days we can be free again?"

"Griffith told you. Each of us will be sent back to our time."

Since she looked pensive, I added, "But you know, nothing is keeping you from escaping your emperor and choosing 1967."

She said nothing.

Appearing to speak casually and without a hint of innuendo, I said, "That's right, I forgot your grenadier... I guess you could never imagine having to make a choice like that?"

She did not respond, but I'll be damned if I didn't see her blush a little

We continue our stroll in silence, letting our eyes wander over the chaos of rocks we had entered. Here the scenery is sinister and the silence weighs a ton.

We are about to turn back when Catherine's hand grips my arm. I understand because I saw it before she did. In front of us on the rocks is lying the wreckage and I recognize the form of a wing half buried in the ground. Without a doubt this is what is left of the mysterious machine that we glimpsed before it exploded in mid-air.

With our curiosity peaked we continue our way and soon spot the debris of the fuselage stuck between two rocks. On the blackened metal a symbol is still visible: a T and a U interlaced inside a circle made up of small stars and five branches. No matter how hard I try I cannot remember seeing it before. The symbol is totally unknown.

My companion murmurs timidly, "Bill, I think we'd better go back."

I am about to follow her advice when all of a sudden I realize that the decision is no longer ours.

A human form has just appeared in a hole in the rock and the long pistol aimed at us needs no additional comment. The guy is tall and well built, young, with a expression of both anguish and anxiety. He is dressed in a close-fitting outfit full of pockets and he is wearing leather boots.

I hold my hands up and walk boldly towards him. "Lower your weapon. We mean you no harm."

He seems to hesitate, then the barrel of his gun orders us to join him at the edge of the cave. There is also a lot of anger in his gestures and in his eyes. "Who are you? What's happening? And where am I?"

"Don't talk so loud, you're going to…"

"Answer!"

"Okay, okay. You're at the South Pole."

He says, "I know that. But the rest of this here… What's this all about?"

I cut to the quick. "It'll mean your life and ours if you keep shouting like that. Got it?"

I did not think twice about speaking bluntly in order to convince him. He calms down right away, as if I had just given him a kind of tongue-lashing.

"Okay, I'm all ears."

I look up and say, "Unfortunately I think this is going to be a little hard to explain. I also think that you should go first. Where do you come from?"

With the pistol still clenched in his hand the stranger flops down on a big rock. That is when I see that he is injured. His face is covered with bruises, fortunately minor, but the makeshift bandage I glimpse through the tear in his left sleeve looks much more serious. He has made a tourniquet around his elbow, but blood is still seeping from the wound.

He ends up speaking in a weary voice. "My name's Vladimir Stoyevski. I'm coming from base 126 in Buenos Aires. I was making a reconnaissance flight over the pole before going on to Melbourne where all our aerospace units are housed when I felt like I flew into a wall. My rocket exploded in mid-air, but luckily I had time to activate the ejector seat. I wasn't too banged up, so I managed to drag myself over here." He breathes deeply. "That's it."

I ask, "And your rocket? Well, what country are you from?"

He looks surprised. "Country? You mean sector? I'm originally from the Russian sector, third district. What does that matter?"

"And you're stationed at the South American base?"

His surprise turns to astonishment. "What do you mean by South American base? It's a base of the Union."

It's my turn to look confused. "The Union?"

"Well, yeah, of course. The Terrestrial Union. Say, where'd you two come out of?"

The Terrestrial Union! The T and the U. The symbol on the fuselage. That explains it. And my horizons expand.

"One last question, Mr. Stoyevski, please. In your opinion, what year is this?"

He shrugs. "Are you joking or what?"

"Please answer."

Anyway, I have already guessed it. This man comes from the future. *From our future!* And it is only out of curiosity that I asked the question.

He finally answers, "November 18, 2115. And I think that does it. Now it's my turn to ask some questions. Who does this secret base belong to? You're a commando team from the Federate, aren't you?"

"I have no idea what this Federate is, but I think it would certainly be a lot easier if I were."

"Okay, then, what's going on?"

I rattle off a short version of our situation, pretty much the gist of it, and by the time I am finished I have the feeling that he is half-convinced.

He combs his hand through his disheveled hair and looks long and hard at Catherine and me. "So if I'm to believe you, you're from the 20th century and she's from the 19th?"

"Exactly."

"And you're saying that this zone is controlled by extraterrestrials? So where do they come from?"

"That, my friend, I do not know. You can believe me or not, but your wound should make you think twice. It's still bleeding, isn't it?"

He looks at his arm and nods at the bandage. "I made a tourniquet, but yes, you're right... I've used up almost all the bandages in my medical kit."

I look him straight in the eye and say, "Your tissue isn't regenerating. Look. It's already been several days for me."

I show him my finger. When I take off the bandage, the cut I got on board the *Mary-Ann* is still fresh. A drop of blood wells up out of the tiny slice.

Stoyevski nods and furrows his brow. "So I'm screwed, huh?"

Catherine is looking at his arm, examining the wound very carefully. "Try to hold out until tomorrow. One of us will bring you what you need. We can't do anything right now. We only get one hour a day for our walk. Do you have any food?"

He smiles sadly. "All gone, sweetie. I ate up my last tablets."

I glance at my watch. Damn, we only have ten minutes left.

"Don't worry, Stoyevski, we'll take care of you. But one last piece of advice. Stay in your little cave and don't come out. If anyone finds you, you're a dead man."

I do not have the time or the guts to say anything else.

CHAPTER XXII

Today I went with Bradley to find poor Stoyevski in his cave. It is impossible to describe how troubled we have been during the last 24 hours because we know that barring a miracle nothing can stop his bleeding. The wound is too serious.

Nevertheless, we bundled up some bandages and antibiotics, as well as some food, whatever could help him hold out as long as possible. It is pretty much all we can do for him. But something incredible happened. And it twisted everything we worked so hard to figure out up to this point.

The Russian welcomed us with a little smile on his face and a little taunting in his eyes when he showed us his arm. There was no more tourniquet. No more bandage. Not a break in the skin. Nothing. No scab or scar. The bruises on his face had also vanished. He had got back his normal color.

He spoke sarcastically, "So wounds don't heal here, huh? Wouldn't you say that's it's just the opposite?"

"What did you do?"

"Me? Absolutely nothing. This morning I felt like the bleeding had stopped, so I took a look and there was nothing there. Absolutely nothing. I think it must be the air. Yes, the fresh air of the South Pole. Unless there's miracle water…"

"What do you mean?"

As a response he pointed to the swamp across from us and we stared at its dark fringe of fog.

"But I told you not to leave your hiding place."

"I didn't have a drop of water left, Mr. Ashby. But don't worry, no one saw me. The water's certainly not very good, but I can tell you I drank worse on Venus."

Then he went off on a lecture that we did not have the courage to interrupt. The colonization of the planet Venus around the year 2000, with Mars and two satellites of Jupiter whose names I forget... the terrestrial emigration to these distant worlds and the Federate, meaning the dissident population that started fighting against the hegemony of Earth in 2115. And he kept coming back to the Federate, accusing us of hiding the truth behind some ludicrous tale of which he did not believe a word.

"All right," he wrapped up, "maybe you have your reasons for this, but you're still okay in my book. Proof is that you haven't turned me in. So I'll stay here, but how long is this going to last?"

At that moment he was seized by a sudden, shooting pain and he clutched his chest.

"What's wrong with you?" Bradley asked.

Stoyevski found his smile again. "It's nothing. Just some burning under the skin. But it passes quickly. Nothing serious."

We also noticed that there were rings around his eyes. *Weird rings!*

CHAPTER XXIII

I would rather bring the last three days we lived through together into one chapter. They are all about Stoyevski because except for him everything else went off without a hitch. But there was Stoyevski and his drama played out at nightmarish speed.

Something bad was in him. Something bad and mysterious that we were totally powerless against. I saw him again the next day, alone. His pains were more frequent and he was in the middle of a fit when I met him twisted on the ground and moaning like a fatally wounded animal. He looked older. His face was thin and waxen. I had brought him some sedatives, but they were no help. He barely heard the encouraging words I tried desperately to offer him.

Yesterday was different. He was no longer in pain, but he was already a wreck. It took an extraordinary effort for him just to stand up. He was growing thinner and thinner at a frightening pace. Without his outfit he was almost a skeleton. His bones stuck out from his pale skin, which was stretched to the breaking point.

I touched him. His forehead was burning up with fever. His hair was falling out by the handfuls and I saw his loosened teeth sticking out of brown gums. Like the teeth of a corpse!

Today he was worse again and in spite of the decision I had made, I could not bring myself to pull the trigger. But it was too much for me. What I saw was too horrible... too monstrous...

There is nothing but skin and bones, a cadaver standing before me when I get there. And there was so much fear and hatred in his hollow eyes that I panicked... Yes, I snapped.

Somewhere between life and death, Stoyevski looked to me like one of those dreadful creatures... *A zombie!*

CHAPTER XXIV

Words fail me. I cannot describe the shocking events that marked this new day. My hand trembles as I recall them... as if all the horror of the world were summed up in these few lines. My God, how is it possible?

Everything came from our decision and it was Bradley once again who resolved the problem with his usual firmness.

We cannot continue in this situation. Stoyevski is lost and out duty is to put an end to his agony, an agony that we figure is eternal since it is the same as all the poor devils we saw in the nearby enclosure. Yes, whatever the cost we have to do it and with this grave decision we get on the road for the last time to head for the hiding place.

After a quarter of an hour we reach the mass of fallen rocks, but we pause before the cave opening. Total silence. Nothing moves. It looks deserted. And the glance that Bradley and I exchange only increases our nervousness.

Finally he takes the initiative. "Let's go!"

We scramble into the cave mouth, but we are barely inside when our fears become reality. The cave is empty. Stoyevski has disappeared. And a foul stench exhales from the cavity, like the inside of a sick man's mouth. All of a sudden the air turns heavy, thick, almost unbreathable. Two more steps...

The suit with pockets is lying on the ground; the pistol and its leather holster; the boots; the helmet... then all of a sudden Catherine's scream throws Bradley and me backward. The thing, the dreadful thing is there amidst the paper, the empty cans and the blood-stained bandages… Stoyevski's remains! Or at least some unnameable thing that looks like his skin. Yes, his skin. An empty skin, wet and limp, whose arms and legs are recognizable, but the insides are gone. Everything has disappeared, the organs, bones, everything! All that is left is the slimy hide in front of which we stand paralyzed for a ghastly minute. Plus there is the head! The face! Like a cloth mask thrown to the ground. With eyeholes and hollow cheeks and the yawning pit of a black mouth in the pale skin.

Then everything suddenly starts moving. Like a long snake disturbed in its sleep, the skin quivers and contracts, then starts crawling worm-like towards the opening. I run over to Catherine and we both fall against the wall.

"Bradley, watch out!"

The professor barely avoids contact with the wretched "skin." When it gets to the threshold I jump for the pistol. Controlling the overwhelming disgust in me, I fire off two shots. Two fiery jets flash out of the barrel and the monstrous thing explodes in the open air. The smoking ruins splatter on the rocks.

We all run out at the same time, but Catherine is exhausted by the effort and I have to help her. "Oh, Bill. Bill." she mumbles.

"Come on, buck up, it's all over."

Bradley is ruffled, too. He is livid. "Quick," he whispers, "let's get out of here or I think I'll…"

He does not finish and he does not have to. We leave the refuge, stepping around the charred remains that are still fluttering on the loose stones, and we run straight ahead.

After a hundred yards or so at a mad gallop we see guards heading in our direction. We panic for a moment before I react and point to the swamp down below. "Over there!"

Of course we are entering a forbidden zone, but our only chance of avoiding the guards is to sneak around them to get back to our sector. We run through the rocks, slipping and tripping at every step until we find ourselves at the edge of the swamp on spongy ground soaked with that black, oily water that laps perversely at our feet. The fog is still thick over the water. It floats in bunches and a few of them drift slowly in our direction, as if pushed deliberately by the wind. But what wind? I suddenly realize that the air is perfectly still.

"Mr. Ashby," Bradley begs, "let's not just stand here, please, I don't like this at all."

We hurry forward, senses on alert, but in making the wide circle I keep an eye on the swamp. When I turn around the bundles of fog have changed shape. They are more compact, more dense, full of misty tentacles. They look like ghostly squid walking on the water. Some of them have slipped in behind us, wandering over the winding bank. Frozen in terror we see them drifting directly toward us, with a weird, phosphorescent glow that grows stronger at every movement.

There is something corporeal to the fog. Every bundle is like a compact gathering of fine particles. *Like spores!* And the worst part is that these things seem alive. Really alive, yes! A kind of monstrous, unimaginable life. Something hideous, unthinkable, but with a kind of intelligence.

I point to a path between two puddles of water. "Let's try over there."

We run as fast as we can, splashing through the mud, drunk on fear and fatigue, until we reach a little dry space, protected from the water, but facing a wall of huge rocks rising up almost out of sight. Nevertheless, we have to find a way out to escape the monsters that now look like they are trembling nervously all over the swamp. They are coming from all directions, some even jumping onto the bank to block our way.

"A gap! There's a gap here," Bradley shows us. "Hurry!"

We are right behind him, but Catherine is exhausted, slips in the mud and sprawls on the ground. I react by reflex. A monster rushes forward and shoots out a tentacle, but I do not give it time to strike. I fire, without thinking maybe, but the gunshot has its effect. The fog creature writhes around, straightens up, then scatters over the surface of the water. The others behind it come no closer, but it is still a miracle that we reach the narrow pass just when Griffith pops up in front of us, blocking the way. He looks grim, stifling anger.

"I warned you. This zone is off limits…" He sees the pistol in my hand. "Where'd you get that?"

"Doesn't matter. You're going to talk now, Griffith. What's going on?"

"This is not the time or place. They're looking for you. There's a patrol up there tracking you right now." He balks at the steel barrel aimed at his chest, then points to a mass of rocks on the right. "Very well. We're safe here. We can speak freely."

CHAPTER XXV

We trust and follow him. But we can see how he has to struggle to tell us.

"Okay," he finally decides, taking time to think about it. "Okay, but first of all, you have to know that there are two very different races in this zone with absolutely no physiological traits in common. There's mine, whose secrets I told you about, and then…" He turns to the swamp. "The other! The one that controls, decides and dictates what we do."

"What? These fog monsters…"

"That's just for starters. The first stage of a genetic process passing through several, very different phases. In reality, it's a trimorphism."

What he tells us fills us with horror and disgust. These misty beings are indeed made up of spores that act like living cells. They can die without the whole being dying off and their ability to regenerate is of the highest degree imaginable. They reproduce by a cellular division in which each part contains the "essentials" of the other. In short, it is a balanced entity, self-sufficient and abundantly alive. With cosmic radiation acting as a catalyzer these creatures produce a kind of protoplasmic jelly that is builds up in the swamp until it matures and escapes the liquid element to venture onto dry land. When solid food is needed to survive the real drama begins. These creatures in the second stage attack flesh and blood because that, too, exists in their weird universe. They sneak up when someone is sleeping, cling to the epidermis and seep in fast through every pore. With their mimetic ability they take on the appearance of the skin they invaded becoming fatal parasites that will sooner or later, depending on their needs, suck dry and empty the effected organism. Literally devouring them! After that the "skin" detaches itself and goes in search of other prey. In the meantime, it can still look like the being it fed on, but it is only an empty shell, molded from the original. Like Marthessa... like the others!

I said that words fail me. At this point in his story I think of Stoyevski. My God, Stoyevski being used as food for these monsters! And all the others we saw in the enclosure... turned into rotting zombies... My God! The atrocity!

But alas, it is far from over. Once gorged with food a mysterious cellular chemical starts working inside the "skin" to finish up the process. The third stage comes with the production of tiny eggs that quickly spawn a multitude of other monsters, just as frightful: Giant, sexless insects whose hunger only grows with age. Real exterminators whose only purpose in life is to kill and devour. Kill, kill, kill. Devour, devour, devour.

No, "necrophage" is not the right word. They, too, feed on living beings, fighting over them with their progenitors in merciless combat.

"Merciless and absurd," Griffith says, "if you consider the connection between the two last forms of the creature's life. The "skins" beget the insects who become their worst enemies. Always hungry, these insects devour them, too, whenever they can. And yet these two races depend on each other. *Neither would survive without the other.*"

"Besides killing and eating, what else do the insects do?" Bradley asks, wiping the sweat off his forehead.

"They attract all the toxic germs in the atmosphere, but they are immune, which is not the case with the skins who are extremely vulnerable. That's why they're staying inside the rocky arena. Their weapons have scared them off so they make fewer and fewer raids in the open air. As for my race, we're safe. We're inedible to these creatures."

"And that's why you've found nothing better than to offer them the same food that the skins eat, human beings picked up throughout time from all over the earth! With the help of your Time Club, right?"

Griffith looked at the ground and nodded. "We have to obey. If we don't accept their deal, we'll be wiped out."

"What deal?"

"We made it when we stepped foot in your universe. Sure, we were part of an exploration mission, but when we entered your galaxy, our spaceship was seriously damaged and we had to land on an unknown planet where these creatures lived, as well as others like you of flesh and blood. The "spores" had spread all over space after making long voyages."

"Spread?"

"Yes. These spores can travel through empty space. They go in groups that look like phosphorescent lights glowing in the darkness. But the lights coming from the darkness are just a kind of cancer on a cosmic scale... You get it? So, on this unknown planet that had fallen prey to the monsters, there wasn't enough food for their voracity. Foreseeing a quick extermination they jumped at the only chance open to them, namely our spaceship. To save our own lives we agreed to save some of them by taking them to where there was animal life. And also in exchange for their immense knowledge. Our ship was repaired, the voyage undertaken and that's how we came here to your world. Unfortunately, another accident forced us to become the slaves of these monsters under penalty of death."

"How's that? Your thermal weapons couldn't beat them?"

"At the start, maybe. But the central tower with its time oscillator belongs to them and we know the grave danger we risk in your universe without its support, stabilizing us in normal conditions. We want to survive, too. So, now you can see why we're acting the way we do. There you go, gentlemen, that's all… that's all I have to tell you."

He respects our silence for a moment, then, since I had holstered my gun, points to the narrow pass between the rocks. "I think we'd better get back now," he tells us. "This path will avoid the patrols. I'm familiar with it. Follow me!"

Paying no attention to what he says, we stay right behind him. Our thoughts are spinning round in a dizzying dance.

CHAPTER XXVI

We were asked no questions. Not a single word about what we had discovered. Nothing. Except for Marthessa's decision passed on to us by her faithful guards: no more strolls in the fresh air until further notice. What does it matter now?

We went back to work, picking away at another day of reprieve. But for how long? How much longer? Still, something had changed, which we realized after eating.

It started with the continual rounds of armed guards. We saw them through the window heading for the other buildings. Farther away more guards were spread out around the high central tower. And then all of a sudden they fired their weapons. Bodies dropped to the ground and the carnage continued with more of them coming from the workshops, whom they pushed into the courtyard with unusual brutality. More shots, more massacres and bodies fell in the brown dust.

A few minutes later Griffith burst into our room. He locked the door and turned his panicked face toward us. He explained everything in no time at all. The opposition movement had been discovered and his collaborators, most of them anyway, were unmasked. The "skins" in human shape were cleaning house on orders from Marthessa.

Yes, it is finished and Griffith's news sounds the death toll of our hopes. Our last glimmer of hope! He wants us to hide him in the walls. He says it is his only chance. There is a small, sealed off closet in the back of the apartment, so maybe…

"They'll never look for me there," he begs us. "I can still help you. I don't know how, but I swear to you…"

I look at him with some suspicion. "You haven't looked into your magic mirror?"

"The Chronorama is out of order. I destroyed it before coming here. No one can see the future anymore."

"So how do you…"

"I can build another. It's possible."

"With what?"

"With the material they gave you to build the robots. I assure you it's possible."

The fact of having accepted his proposition puzzles me. Is it really me who made the decision? *Haven't the events already been written in time?*

Of course… the lens above… the lens below…

But where is all this taking us?

CHAPTER XXVII

Eight days have passed without incident. Griffith is still here, stuck in his closet. He only comes out "at night," in other words when we sleep and are left alone by our guards.

In the camp everything is calm with the usual routine and so far no one seems to suspect that Griffith is with us. Maybe they have given up the search. Who knows?

In any case, Griffith was not bluffing. His Chronorama Version 2 is finished. The initial tests were conclusive: this one can look 24 hours into the future. We saw a series of events so devastating that we did not think we had to change a thing. Anyway, for the moment, we are the only ones concerned.

It starts with Bradley interrupting Griffith and I in the middle of a conversation. He looks worried. "I think we're at the end of our rope," he says, referring to the final notice given to us today about the robots. "We have to make a decision."

He raises an eyebrow, surprised at our silence. "Well, what's wrong with you? Why don't you answer?"

I light a cigarette without taking my eyes off him. "That's exactly what we were discussing, Bradley. Don't worry, the decision's been made. We'll build our first robot starting tomorrow."

"Are you crazy?"

Listen, Bradley, any way you look at it we're done for. The effect exists in time, it's undeniable. We only know 24 hours in advance, but nothing can be changed. However, if we let ourselves go along with the train of events, the idea/cause that Griffith and I just had let us glimpse the possibility of destroying this zone. The effect, too, *might already be decided.*"

"I don't understand."

"If the effect exists, the laws of causality have appointed us to be responsible for it."

"Which means?"

Griffith jumps in, "When we build the robot, we'll put a magnetic bomb inside its body. I know how it works and can make one easily. Since they'll have to let us test the robot and give it a certain amount of freedom in the arena, the machine will do what we can't. The bomb will explode by remote control and the destruction of the time oscillator will certainly cause a total disaster."

A heavy silence falls upon us. Catherine makes no comment, only a little regret showing in her eyes. I know what she is thinking. Unfortunately, on this score, it is a failure. Projects of this kind are certainly not written in time.

"Well, okay, if that's the way it has to be. To work, then, gentlemen! And let's get this over with fast!"

Bradley's words fall like stones.

Eight days more. On the ninth, everything is finished. "Caesar" is ready.

That is what we named our new robot. They brought us more equipment so we could finish the assembly, piece by piece. Of course, it is far from being a success, but basically, in spite of its flaws (because our first robot would look a lot like a "hideous Jojo the Rabbit" crippled by arthritis), it is not such an incredible creature if you think that there is nothing alive in this machine built on a human model.

It talks (very little), walks, smiles and answers a few questions. It is a model of docility. A little awkward, a little jerky. But really it is not so bad. I demanded 24 hours more for a few revisions and they allowed it willingly. So, everything is going off without a hitch.

Once alone, we joined Griffith in his closet. The bomb is ready. All that is left is to put it in the android. When it is disconnected, we stick it in the belly, sew up the synthetic skin and check the radio controls. No problem. The bomb will explode whenever we press the button.

Now all we have to do is consult the Chromorama because if all goes well, it is exactly 24 hours from now that we will perform our first official tests of Caesar. And what we do will decide the success or failure of our undertaking. So, we have a kind of countdown when the screen lights up and mesmerizes us with its images.

There is no sound and scenes of no interest show up first, but after tuning the selectors Griffith finally gets what he wants: Carting Caesar out to the central tower. No particular instructions are given to us for the trial. The machine's orders are only to walk around at its convenience. Its reactions are noted by a group of technicians who accompany Caesar on the stroll.

After a few hundred yards the exact moment we were waiting arrives. The remote control we are using guides Caesar toward the metal tower. The foul creatures are there, forming a circle around the base and we can also see Marthessa, radiant and beaming in her empty skin, modeled on God knows what human being. In any case, she must have been a marvelous woman of rare beauty and her big, golden eyes contained something fascinating. Cat eyes… Dream eyes…

"Watch out!"

Griffith's voice snaps me back into reality. In a split second. An unbelievable second. A second at the end of the world! A second of the Apocalypse!

The screen, still silent, seems to explode in a whirlwind of fire, dust and rocks that fly out from the foot of the tower. Body parts fly across the screen while the huge metal structure bursts like a grenade. Separated from its foundation, the top of the tower topples over and smashes into a row of shacks. Everything else is drown in torrents of smoke and flames and brown earth.

Five minutes later the images clear up and we can see the total devastation. Everything is destroyed, broken, smashed. Nothing but ruins, rubble and chaos... And the dead... the dead... Nothing but the dead! We are among them, poor, mangled puppets lying in the dust. There is Griffith... There is Bradley... There is Catherine... There is me... Catherine and I embracing in death and our red mouths kissing in blood.

"Stop, Griffith! Turn it off!"

The rest is of no importance. We know now what we wanted to know, meaning what will happen in 24 hours. And it is Bradley once again who voices what we are all thinking.

"In 24 hours everything will be over for us, too. Too bad, but I'd rather die like this, believe me."

"Nothing is absolute."

I turn to Griffith. "What do you mean, nothing is absolute? We can't change the outcome. Our deaths are certain."

"Maybe not." He gives me a pale, enigmatic, little smile. "In our time, yes, the effect is absolute... but only by staying here. Don't you remember? From this moment on when you have the possibility to change the cause, without effecting the outcome, you just have to create a detour in time and use it to change the events so that you can go back to your own time. Then you will be free of the effect, since you won't be in our continuum. You just have to be out of the arena before it explodes."

Griffith paces around, lost in thought. "Hold on," he murmurs as if to himself. "We oscillate all along your temporal chain following a regular, constant rhythm in both the past and the future. I know how. So, I refer to the base chart…"

He grabs a pencil and paper and starts scribbling some symbols we cannot decipher, then he nods his head.

"First of all, we can only do it two hours before the explosion, no more. That's pretty much how long it will take us to reach the edge of the arena. Too long a delay would compromise everything if they notice you're missing after a few minutes. Therefore, calculating two hours… you should return to your continuum in…" He corrects one of his equations. "Yes, that should do it. In March 1970. So, around three years after you left, Mr. Ashby. Of course, it doesn't matter to you, but for Catherine and Professor Bradley it's a different story. Unfortunately I see no other way."

Bradley steps forward, obviously troubled. "Let's say it's so. What's going to happen to us on this frozen land in the middle of the South Pole?"

"The Byrd Station in 1970 is barely four days walk from here. I'll give you the coordinates."

"We'll die before we get there."

Griffith turns to me. "No, because this is what you're going to do."

CHAPTER XXVIII

The time is nigh. It is only a matter of minutes.

As a precaution I had asked for another 24 hours before trying out Caesar. Still no objection. They trust us. Our experimental robot, therefore, will not leave the laboratory at the prescribed time. In fact, it will never leave.

Its participation in the causal connection imposed by the effect is of no importance. Nothing will prevent the bomb from exploding or the disaster from happening. The *mektoub* will be fulfilled. What was written will be accomplished. And as incredible as it might seem the prescribed effect will be *an effect without a cause*.

However, we still have to escape the effect and it's not only our lives that are at stake in this dramatic decision. Griffith revealed to us the location of all the tiny universes with their own time-generators that make up the Time Clubs on the surface of the Earth. We have to help our fellow men to destroy them so that nothing of this horror threatening our world remains.

We are ready. Griffith, with dignity marked by emotion, stands up and bids us farewell. Through the window we see him show up in the central courtyard in the middle of all the bustling armed guards. After a moment there is shouting and other "skins" in human shape come running out of the nearby buildings. Then Griffith pulls out his weapon and starts sweeping the area around him, firing round after round.

We take advantage of the diversion and evacuate our rooms to hide in Griffith's private workshop. The hallway is empty. The doors are unlocked. We cross the workshop and go through another door at the back, which opens onto a huge warehouse. The space contains the supplies for the human prisoners. As we had planned we find everything we need, namely food and clothing. We get some gear together quickly without saying a word; any useless gesture is a waste of time and we do not have a minute to lose.

Finally, we are out in the open, at the end of another sector that looks deserted. We just have to get over to the wall of rock by spotting the fence of the enclosure we were in when we first arrived. Then we will have to find a passage in the rock that leads to the outside...

There are those insects here, of course, but unfortunately they are not the only danger. There are also swamps in this zone and we need to walk along them for hundreds of yards. Before starting there, we stop to catch our breath and take a look behind us. No one in sight. If the alarm was sounded, the search parties must still be in our sector, probably.

"Let's get moving!"

All senses on alert we enter the swamps, staring at the fumy mists spread out on the surface of the water. At first, nothing happens and we get halfway through without a single incident. Then, all of a sudden, they attack when we are skirting a lagoon to reach dry ground. Stoyevski's pistol saves us from any fatal contact as two volleys of gunfire get rid of the monstrous creatures.

We run straight ahead, then I realize that Bradley is out of breath. His strength is flagging and he is falling behind.

"Bradley! Just a little longer! Please!"

I turn back to help him, but the poor man collapses in the mud, totally exhausted.

"Get out of here…" he waves us off in desperation. "Go on without me… I can't do it…"

"Bill, watch out!"

Catherine's cry comes just a second before a horrible tragedy unfolds in front of us. A bundle of fog surges out of the lagoon and enshrouds Bradley's body. I push Catherine back and lunge forward, wading through the water up to my ankles, trying to reach Bradley, but it is too late. His screams are the cry of death and I barely have time to stumble back over the bank and drag Catherine out of there in a mad dash, running blind, deranged…

I have no idea how we reached the fence, the wall of rock, the passage, the tunnel leading outside… I have no idea how we escaped those insects dwelling in the caves… I don't know… I don't know…

The footsteps that Bradley and I left behind during our first escape attempt guided us through the weird maze and just as we reached the end of the life-saving passage I looked at my watch. We were 20 minutes ahead of schedule. I took a deep breath and grabbed Catherine's arm.

In a burst of spontaneous emotion she threw herself against me. "Oh, Bill! Bill!"

I hugged her tightly. "Come now, Cathy, we're almost there."

"Bill, whatever happens, I want you to know…"

"I know, my dear, but…"

She wiped a tear off her rosy cheek. "There never was a grenadier... No Bertrand… It was just to…"

Our lips and tears touched.

I said, "Thank you God. Thank you for everything." I said something else, too, but what's the use… Nothing remains of all that… Nothing but that dreadful minute that ruined everything. Destroyed everything.

Alas, yes. And it happened just as we passed through the "time portal." No one had thought of this. Not even Griffith. Unless…

We were barely out in the open, our feet plodding in snow, when Catherine suddenly slumped to the ground. I knelt and saw it… the change in her face. In an instant she had become unrecognizable. Her skin had wrinkled at incredible speed. It was like well-worn, age-old parchment. The hair sticking our of her fur hat had turned completely white… her eyes were clouded over… Her cheeks hollowed out. It look like she was 100 years old. Or maybe more.

"Cathy!"

Now I understand. Her biological time caught up with her. Freed from the temporal slowdown that protected the arena, her organism jumped back into the march of time. The time that had marched on since 1805!

Oh God, the hideous sight! The skin crumbled and revealed a ghastly skull like some crab shell. The fur gloves fell off the skeletal fingers. And then… And then everything vanished. All that was left was a fine, gray dust on the frozen ground.

CHAPTER XXIX

I walked and walked and walked... in the blizzard, the cold, the great white desert. I guess the explosion went off behind me. I did not hear a thing. Earth time knows nothing about it. Life goes on as if nothing happened.

How did I get onto this ship that is heading for Boston? Again I have no idea...

I only have vague memories... very vague. I was sprawled in the snow, half dead from the cold and exhaustion when voices hummed in my ears like the buzzing of bees. Hands grabbed me, lifted me up, rum ran down my throat, then some men dressed in furs put me onto a sled. They took me to a shelter made of ice where it was warm and where friendly faces leaned over me, giving me back some confidence.

But I hurt... my arms, legs, chest and belly. My body was on fire and I was thirsty. Terribly thirsty.

A man with the goatee held out a flask and tried to smile. "Easy, friend! You pulled through, but just barely. Where'd you come from? What mission do you belong to?"

I almost screamed when I recognized him. I sat up, staring at him, but there was no doubt about it. *It was Bradley. Professor John Bradley!*

"But that's impossible... You're not..."

"Calm down or else your fever might get nasty again. We sent a message. You'll be taken back on board the *Cormorant*."

"The *Cormorant*?"

"Yes. It's the ship assigned to our team. We're here on the Byrd mission. The admiral is close by at the main station.

I got dizzy. "I... please, what year is this? 1929?"

Bradley cleared his throat. "My boy, I have no idea what I'll be doing next year and you neither. Be happy with the present in 1928." He said this jokingly, then he patted my cheek.

The *Cormorant*... Bradley... But there was more. There was Captain Parker, too, on board the ship and the quartermaster Morgan. 1928! The first voyage of the Byrd mission to the South Pole. But then Griffith was wrong in his calculations. Off by 42 years!

Oh, my head... my body... my fever... the pains... But all this is nothing. How can I explain it them? Make them understand? It's impossible. I tried, but the doctor on board is strict: total, absolute rest. It was useless to argue. They would not even listen to me.

And the *Cormorant* lifted anchor, sailed through the frozen waters, headed back to Boston... and I am alone in my cabin, swamped by pain and gnawed by fever. I hurt... hurt... oh, how it hurts! Something that is gnawing at me. Inside. Like a huge cancer... like hungry mouths feeding on my flesh and guts... I can already taste death!

I do not even have the strength to write... to think... Oh, if only... one last jolt... one last flash...

I tear the bandage off the end of my finger. There is nothing there. No wound, no blood, everything is healed.

But no, it cannot be. When did it happen? How? I drag myself over to the mirror... I look. I look at my haggard face, the pale skin stretched over my bones... my eyes with black circles around them...

Oh, no… no… not like Stoyevski! No, not like him… *Not this "skin"… not on me…* NO!

And yet, our escape, the swamp… When I went back to help Bradley… I was in the water up to my ankles… I felt something soft and warm… yes, yes… I remember… Oh, Lord…

It is over. I am going to die. What does it matter? It doesn't matter at all to me. In any case, I cannot make it past August 20, 1929, my birth date. And my whole life will start over again: my childhood, my studies at Oxford, my wasted life, my car accident and my five years at Dartmoor. It is inevitable. Everything will start over again for me…

But then? Afterward? After Dartmoor? When I get out of prison? Oh tell me, Lord, tell me!

What is going to happen… afterward? Afterward?

SF & FANTASY

Adolphe Alhaiza. *Cybele*

Alphonse Allais. *The Adventures of Captain Cap*

Henri Allorge. *The Great Cataclysm*

Guy d'Armen. *Doc Ardan: The City of Gold and Lepers*

G.-J. Arnaud. *The Ice Company*

Charles Asselineau. *The Double Life*

Henri Austruy. *The Eupantophone; The Olotelepan; The Petitpaon Era*

Cyprien Bérard. *The Vampire Lord Ruthwen*

S. Henry Berthoud. *Martyrs of Science*

Aloysius Bertrand. *Gaspard de la Nuit*

Richard Bessière. *The Gardens of the Apocalypse*

Albert Bleunard. *Ever Smaller*

Félix Bodin. *The Novel of the Future*

Louis Boussenard. *Monsieur Synthesis*

Alphonse Brown. *City of Glass; The Conquest of the Air*

Emile Calvet. *In a Thousand Years*

André Caroff. *The Terror of Madame Atomos; Miss Atomos; The Return of Madame Atomos; The Mistake of Madame Atomos; The Monsters of Madame Atomos; The Revenge of Madame Atomos; The Resurrection of Madame Atomos; The Mark of Madame Atomos; The Spheres of Madame Atomos*

Félicien Champsaur. *The Human Arrow; Ouha, King of the Apes; Pharaoh's Wife*

Didier de Chousy. *Ignis*

Jules Clarétie. *Obsession*

Michel Corday. *The Eternal Flame*

André Couvreur. *The Necessary Evil; Caresco, Superman; The Exploits of Professor Tornada* (3 vols.)

Captain Danrit. *Undersea Odyssey*

C. I. Defontenay. *Star (Psi Cassiopeia)*

Charles Derennes. *The People of the Pole*

Georges Dodds (anthologist). *The Missing Link*

Harry Dickson. *The Heir of Dracula*

Jules Dornay. *Lord Ruthven Begins*

Alfred Driou. *The Adventures of a Parisian Aeronaut*

Sâr Dubnotal *vs. Jack the Ripper*

Alexandre Dumas. *The Return of Lord Ruthven*

Renée Dunan. *Baal*

J.-C. Dunyach. *The Night Orchid; The Thieves of Silence*

Henri Duvernois. *The Man Who Found Himself*

Achille Eyraud. *Voyage to Venus*

Henri Falk. *The Age of Lead*

Paul Féval. *Anne of the Isles; Knightshade; Revenants; Vampire City; The Vampire Countess; The Wandering Jew's Daughter*

Paul Féval, *fils. Felifax, the Tiger-Man*

Charles de Fieux. *Lamékis*

Louis Forest, *Someone is Stealing Children in Paris*

Arnould Galopin. *Doctor Omega*; *Doctor Omega and the Shadowmen* (anthology)

Judith Gautier. *Isoline and the Serpent-Flower*

H. Gayar. *The Marvelous Adventures of Serge Myrandhal on Mars*

Léon Gozlan. *The Vampire of the Val-de-Grâce*

G.L. Gick. *Harry Dickson and the Werewolf of Rutherford Grange*

Edmond Haraucourt. *Illusions of Immortality*

Nathalie Henneberg. *The Green Gods*

V. Hugo, P. Foucher & P. Meurice. *The Hunchback of Notre-Dame*

Romain d'Huissier. *Hexagon: Dark Matter*

Jules Janin. *The Magnetized Corpse*

Michel Jeury. *Chronolysis*

Gustave Kahn. *The Tale of Gold and Silence*

Gérard Klein. *The Mote in Time's Eye*

Fernand Kolney. *Love in 5000 Years*

Paul Lacroix. *Danse Macabre*

Louis-Guillaume de La Follie. *The Unpretentious Philosopher*

Jean de La Hire. *Enter the Nyctalope; The Nyctalope on Mars; The Nyctalope vs. Lucifer; The Nyctalope Steps In; Night of the Nyctalope; Return of the Nyctalope; The Fiery Wheel*

Etienne-Léon de Lamothe-Langon. *The Virgin Vampire*

André Laurie. *Spiridon*

Gabriel de Lautrec. *The Vengeance of the Oval Portrait*

Alain le Drimeur. *The Future City*

Georges Le Faure & Henri de Graffigny. *The Extraordinary Adventures of a Russian Scientist Across the Solar System* (2 vols.)

Gustave Le Rouge. *The Mysterious Doctor Cornelius* (3 vols.); *The Vampires of Mars; The Dominion of the World* (w/Gustave Guitton) (4 vols.)

Jules Lermina. *Mysteryville; Panic in Paris; To-Ho and the Gold Destroyers; The Secret of Zippelius*

André Lichtenberger. *The Centaurs; The Children of the Crab*
Jean-Marc & Randy Lofficier. *Edgar Allan Poe on Mars; The Katrina Protocol; Pacifica; Robonocchio; Return of the Nyctalope;* (anthologists) *Tales of the Shadowmen 1-10*
Xavier Mauméjean. *The League of Heroes*
Joseph Méry. *The Tower of Destiny*
Hippolyte Mettais. *The Year 5865*
Louise Michel. *The Human Microbes; The New World*
Tony Moilin. *Paris in the Year 2000*
José Moselli. *Illa's End*
John-Antoine Nau. *Enemy Force*
Marie Nizet. *Captain Vampire*
C. Nodier, A. Beraud & Toussaint-Merle. *Frankenstein*
Henri de Parville. *An Inhabitant of the Planet Mars*
Gaston de Pawlowski. *Journey to the Land of the 4th Dimension*
Georges Pellerin. *The World in 2000 Years*
Ernest Pérochon. *The Frenetic People*
Pierre Pelot. *The Child Who Walked on the Sky*
J. Polidori, C. Nodier, E. Scribe. *Lord Ruthven the Vampire*
P.-A. Ponson du Terrail. *The Vampire and the Devil's Son; The Immortal Woman*
Edgar Quinet. *Ahasuerus*
Henri de Régnier. *A Surfeit of Mirrors*
Maurice Renard. *The Blue Peril; Doctor Lerne; The Doctored Man; A Man Among the Microbes; The Master of Light*
Jean Richepin. *The Wing; The Crazy Corner*
Albert Robida. *The Adventures of Saturnin Farandoul; The Clock of the Centuries; Chalet in the Sky; The Electric Life*
J.-H. Rosny Aîné. *Helgvor of the Blue River; The Givreuse Enigma; The Mysterious Force; The Navigators of Space; Vamireh; The World of the Variants; The Young Vampire*
Marcel Rouff. *Journey to the Inverted World*
Han Ryner. *The Superhumans*
Angelo de Sorr. *The Vampires of London*
Brian Stableford. *The New Faust at the Tragicomique;The Empire of the Necromancers (The Shadow of Frankenstein; Frankenstein and the Vampire Countess; Frankenstein in London); Sherlock Holmes & The Vampires of Eternity; The Stones of Camelot; The Wayward Muse.* (anthologist) *News from the Moon; The Germans on Venus; The Supreme Progress; The World Above the World; Nemoville; Investigations of the Future; The Conqueror of Death*

Jacques Spitz. *The Eye of Purgatory*
Kurt Steiner. *Ortog*
Eugène Thébault. *Radio-Terror*
C.-F. Tiphaigne de La Roche. *Amilec*
Louis Ulbach. *Prince Bonifacio*
Théo Varlet. *The Golden Rock. The Xenobiotic Invasion; The Casta-ways of Eros; Timeslip Troopers* (w/André Blandin); *The Martian Epic* (w/Octave Joncquel)
Paul Vibert. *The Mysterious Fluid*
Villiers de l'Isle-Adam. *The Scaffold; The Vampire Soul*
Philippe Ward. *Artahe*
Philippe Ward & Sylvie Miller. *The Song of Montségur*

MYSTERIES & THRILLERS

M. Allain & P. Souvestre. *The Daughter of Fantômas*
A. Anicet-Bourgeois, Lucien Dabril. *Rocambole*
A. Bernède. *Belphegor*; *Judex* (w/Louis Feuillade); *The Return of Judex* (w/Louis Feuillade); *The Shadow of Judex*
A. Bisson & G. Livet. *Nick Carter vs. Fantômas*
V. Darlay & H. de Gorsse. *Arsène Lupin vs. Sherlock Holmes: The Stage Play*
Séamas Duffy. *Sherlock Holmes in Paris*
Paul Féval. *Gentlemen of the Night; John Devil; The Black Coats ('Salem Street; The Invisible Weapon; The Parisian Jungle; The Companions of the Treasure; Heart of Steel; The Cadet Gang; The Sword-Swallower)*
Emile Gaboriau. *Monsieur Lecoq*
Goron & Emile Gautier. *Spawn of the Penitentiary*
Rick Lai. *Shadows of the Opera: Retribution in Blood; Sisters of the Shadows: The Curse of Cagliostro*
Steve Leadley. *Sherlock Holmes: The Circle of Blood*
Maurice Leblanc. *Arsène Lupin vs. Countess Cagliostro; Arsène Lupin vs. Sherlock Holmes (The Blonde Phantom; The Hollow Nee-dle); The Many Faces of Arsène Lupin*
Gaston Leroux. *Chéri-Bibi; The Phantom of the Opera; Rouletabille & the Mystery of the Yellow Room; Rouletabille at Krupp's*
Richard Marsh. *The Complete Adventures of Judith Lee*
William Patrick Maynard. *The Terror of Fu Manchu; The Destiny of Fu Manchu*

Frank J. Morlock. *Sherlock Holmes: The Grand Horizontals; Sherlock Holmes vs Jack the Ripper*
Jean Petithuguenin. *The Adventures of Ethel King*
Antonin Reschal. *The Adventures of Miss Boston*
P. de Wattyne & Y. Walter. *Sherlock Holmes vs. Fantômas*
David White. *Fantômas in America*
Pierre Yrondy. *The Adventures of Thérèse Arnaud*

SCREENPLAYS

Mike Baron. *The Iron Triangle*
Emma Bull & Will Shetterly. *Nightspeeder; War for the Oaks*
Gerry Conway & Roy Thomas. *Doc Dynamo*
Steve Englehart. *Majorca*
James Hudnall. *The Devastator*
Jean-Marc & Randy Lofficier. *Royal Flush*
J.-M. & R. Lofficier & Marc Agapit. *Despair*
J.-M. & R. Lofficier & Joël Houssin. *City*
Andrew Paquette. *Peripheral Vision*
Robert L. Robinson, Jr. *Judex*
R. Thomas, J. Hendler & L. Sprague de Camp. *Rivers of Time*

NON-FICTION

Stephen R. Bissette. *Blur 1-5. Green Mountain Cinema 1; Teen Angels*
Win Scott Eckert. *Crossovers* (2 vols.)
Jean-Marc & Randy Lofficier. *Shadowmen* (2 vols.)
Randy Lofficier. *Over Here*

ART BOOKS

J.-M. Lofficier & D. Taylor. *Tongue Lash*
Jean-Pierre Normand. *Science Fiction Illustrations*
Raven Okeefe. *Raven's L'il Critters; Rave's Faves*
Randy Lofficier & Raven Okeefe. *If Your Possum Go Daylight...*
Daniele Serra. *Illusions*